About the author

Naila Moloo is a teenage girl who plays competitive badminton and enjoys learning about everything entrepreneurship and sustainability. Naila resides in Ottawa, Canada, with her parents, sister, cat and dog. You can check out her articles on Medium. You can also find a short story of hers in an anthology called *Speaking Up for Each Other*, which you can buy from most online bookstores.

CHRONICLES OF ILLUSIONS:
THE BLUE WILD

Naila Moloo

CHRONICLES OF ILLUSIONS:
THE BLUE WILD

Vanguard Press

VANGUARD PAPERBACK

© Copyright 2021

Naila Moloo

A CIP catalogue record for this title is
available from the British Library.

ISBN 978 1 784659 44 8

*Vanguard Press is an imprint of
Pegasus Elliot MacKenzie Publishers Ltd.*
www.pegasuspublishers.com

First Published in 2021

**Vanguard Press
Sheraton House Castle Park
Cambridge England**

Printed & Bound in Great Britain

To Sophia, my best friend

Acknowledgements

The first person I have to thank is my dad, who is my rock and has supported me through everything I've ever done. I have learned everything from you and I appreciate all you do; I have no idea what I would do without you. Words honestly cannot express how grateful I am for you.

Of course, Sophia, who I've dedicated this book to — you are my role model and you always have my back, even when I'm an annoying little sister! Love you!

To my grandparents, who are so inspirational; you guys manage to balance everything perfectly and somehow still be the nicest people to ever exist. Thank you for being two of my biggest supporters — you are amazing!

To Kuts and Fahad, who are such awesome people and whom I have spent so many incredible moments with. I love playing Halo until three a.m., going to cottages riddled with spiders, and honestly just hanging out with you guys all the time. Some of my best memories have been made with you, and the amount of book ideas I've had in your house are uncountable.

To Kyam, Lyla and Emre, you guys are quite possibly the cutest human beings to ever exist. I can't wait for you to be old enough to one day read this book! I love you so much, and many more *Avengers* and *Frozen* short stories coming your way.

To Debra, my editor. Thank you for helping to pave the way through this journey and for being so encouraging. I have learned so much from you!

To my best friends, the BCs (the meaning of that will have to go untold — it's a pretty weird group name), I have made too many strange memories with you and you have sparked so many ideas for my writing. You are all crazy supportive and amazing people and I appreciate you so much! We have been through so much together and you have always stuck by my side. I love you guys loads and thank you for making me laugh every day!

To all my supportive family: Mom, Fahra, Zahra, Grandpa Amin, Zul, Almas, Emily, Rahim, Iliyan, Kyam, Auntie Zabine, Shaffique, and Nimet, U Al — I love you all and thank you for being you!

Lastly, I'd like to thank Pegasus Publishing for having faith in this book and taking a chance on me; I couldn't have done this without you!

PROLOGUE

ATIKUS MOVED SWIFTLY THROUGH THE CROWDS OF PEOPLE.

"Silence!" a voice boomed through the arena.

Everyone froze at the sharp tone of the master's voice. Atikus forced his body to still. His heart hammered in his chest as Diablos stepped through the curtains from the backstage, bowing regally as he entered the central spectacle. His sly lips were curled into a mischievous smile, hungry for action. His hands shot out abruptly, and two giant gates appeared on the cream wall beside him.

Atikus and Harlow had watched this ceremony once before, and they had found it both horrifying and outraging. Atikus couldn't believe that Harlow would be the fighter, or, as Diablos would call him, the man-slaughterer. No one had ever survived this, and as strong as Harlow was, Atikus wasn't sure his friend would be an exception.

"Who's ready for another game of the Executionists?" roared Diablos thunderously, clasping his palms together.

The excited spectators burst into applause, whistling and whooping. Atikus, on the other hand, was having trouble breathing. He couldn't let this happen to Harlow. Harlow was an important man in the real world. People needed him. How could Atikus sit back and watch him be slaughtered? In frustration, he thumped his fists against the wooden seat in front of him. He knew how powerful Diablos and his monsters were. They wouldn't hesitate to shred Atikus as well. At this moment, no one could save Harlow except Harlow himself.

Atikus felt the hair on his arms rise as the first gate opened and Harlow was pushed into the arena. He held a sword at his side and, unsurprisingly, he didn't look the tiniest bit afraid. His eyes were brave and round, craving battle.

Don't you realise you're going to die? Atikus wanted to scream at his bold partner in crime with whom he had worked for so long.

"Harlow, our man-slaughterer for today!" announced Diablos.

Everyone screamed with pleasure. They never thought they would see Harlow Blackstone in this fighting arena, Atikus bet.

"And… a special monster you're all familiar with… my FangWing! This one took *years* to train, I tell you," said Diablos.

The audience was enlivened further, their loud shrieks ringing through the field. Atikus wanted to cover his ears and tell them to all shut up.

The second gate slid open and a scaly, apricot-orange dragon stepped through the gap. A tongue flew out of her mouth, and a vicious hiss erupted from her throat.

"Fight, fight, fight!" chanted the crowd.

"No…" Atikus could feel the scratchy neediness in his voice, but he didn't care. He needed a miracle, or this would all be for nothing.

"Fight, fight, fight!"

Amidst all of the racket, wheels were swiftly turning in Atikus' head.

"Fight, fight, fight!"

He gritted his teeth together as Harlow pulled his sword and started off the battle by slicing at the FangWing's chest. A scratch appeared, but no blood fell. The FangWing, now fully alert, growled with anger. She turned to the man in front of her and knifed her claws through the air wildly. Harlow dodged the first hit, but he wasn't so lucky the second time, a slit opening on his forehead. He lunged at the fearless dragon, blinded by blood, but she was quick to avoid the easy hit. She bared her poison fangs at Harlow, sidling underneath him and slashing at his back. A giant gash formed there, red and raw. Blood poured from his body, and his shouts of agony and anger echoed through the arena.

The dragon used his weakness and continued going mad in the stadium, clawing anywhere at any chance she got.

"That's what I'm talking about!" Diablos barked with satisfaction.

His voice seemed to spark something inside Harlow because his eyes narrowed to slits in concentration.

The audience pumped their fists in the air.

Atikus watched with terror as his friend's nails grew out of his fingers. Was Harlow really considering doing magic here? So many things could go wrong.

Everything could be exposed.

Secrets.

Atikus suddenly felt something sloshing around in his pocket. A horrible realisation flooded through him as he picked up his hourglass. He had seconds left. Atikus had to leave before he was stuck here forever.

But what about Harlow?

"Argh!" A yell slipped from Harlow's lips as he grew to a bigger size, his body starting to glow with a blue illumination.

The audience howled with excitement, and Atikus glanced at his hourglass. A knot of guilt formed in the pit of his stomach as he gathered his glass crystal in his fingers. He took one last look at his partner, whose body was being torn into ribbons of light.

Goodbye, Atikus thought to Harlow. *One day, you'll be discovered. Survive for that day.*

With that, Atikus squeezed his teleporter and disappeared from Harlow's world of magic forever.

1
Ora

I EDGE ACROSS THE MARBLE TILES, MY FEET PRICKLING UNDER THEIR COLD TOUCH.

Darkness blinds me as I move slowly, and I feel for the familiar bump on the dull lavender walls. My dexterous fingers sidle across the peeling paint until they reach the shallow bulge. I press down, and the dying chandelier flickers on, flooding a dim light through the room. I realise just how much I hate this room as I look around. It has imprisoned me far too long, giving me false hope of escape. I've memorised its ugliness — the drab, lifeless colours; the glaring sculptures that terrified me when I was a young child.

For punishment, I would get put in here, but someone would always watch me. Today, no one looms over me, scrutinising my every move. Today, I will bolt from the awful life that awaits me. No one would expect this from me, not the night before my supposed "big day". Everyone presumes that I'll be in bed, dreaming of the paradise that I will soon be living in.

Yet all I want to do is escape Portsmouth and hide out somewhere far, far away so I can enjoy my own life, abiding by only my rules. Before that, though, I have to complete the first step and get myself out of this lock-up home. I determinedly make my way to the door, moving my feet gracefully and being sure to stay light on my toes.

The door is so close. All I have to do is creep up the spooky wooden staircase, and there it is. As I gently step onto the first step, the wood creaks and wobbles.

The second step is worse. As soon as I move onto it, the wood gives way and cracks under the pressure.

Curse Headmistress Gertrude for never renovating this dead place,

I think bitterly.

Quickly, I hop onto the third step, chanting prayers under my breath. I freeze when I hear feeble voices. Headmistress Gertrude and Vice Grimaldi, accompanied by some other teachers who act like guards. My breath catches in my throat. I took such care and precision sneaking into the head's office, twisting open her secret shelf that barely anyone knows about, and stealing the golden key of escape. It can't all have been for nothing. All I need to do is fling myself into the night's crisp air and run away. I've never truly been outside this door, but I'll manage somehow.

Fourth step. Fifth step, and I'm on the platform. My hands trembling, I position the key into the keyhole and turn. The steel door flies open, but an alarm sounds.

"In there!" shouts a closer voice, and the door to the room is pushed open.

I swallow a mouthful of curses and pull myself through the opening, shutting it firmly behind me. I glance backward, only to see I'm on a balcony overlooking the meadow.

No.

This can't be happening. I'm supposed to find myself *on* the meadow, so I can make an easy escape. The jump is too far. There's no way to flee the balcony. There's no secret passage or tunnel that I can slide down to bring me to the grass below. The only way to do this is to leap, but that would be suicide. I frantically look for anything that could help, but it's only me and the balcony.

Suddenly, the door flies open. I spin around to see Gertrude, Grimaldi and the guards standing behind me, their arms crossed, faces beet red. Gertrude's angry eyes drill into me.

"What do you think you're doing, young lady?" Gertrude hisses, her voice cutting through the air like a knife.

I don't know what to say. I'm not sure I want to speak at all. This plan completely blew up in my face, and now I'll endure a good beating in punishment. But after that, I'll be forced to carry on with my nightmare of a life. How can I do that? How can I continue living like this? I have nothing to lose.

I jump.

My legs flail, and I hear piercing screams from above me.

"*Orabelle!*" shrieks Gertrude, her furious voice ringing in my ears. "*Orabelle, you foolish child!*"

Gertrude yells at me, as if I can fly back to the balcony and stop falling, but she's right. This is foolish. *I* am foolish. I should've taken a beating instead of bounding to my death. Launching myself over that balcony railing is the most foolish thing I could have done.

I fall fast, and my arms dangle helplessly as I plunge closer and closer to the ground. Everything melds together, and soon the world is a canvas of watercolours, swirling around me. My hair is tossed in all directions, my head spinning uncontrollably. The meadow grass flickers closer and closer to me the longer I fall. Gertrude's screams grow distant. There's no time to think; the ground is here.

I close my eyes and feel my feet hit the grass with such an impact that it gives me a headache. Bruises form all over the soles of my feet. My toes curl over, and some of my nails crack.

I open my eyes, petrified. I realise I'm alive and barely injured. How did this happen? How was I lucky enough not to fall on my back, my stomach; my head? It's nearly impossible, but a stroke of luck I'll gladly accept. I realise suddenly that I must continue with my plan. I can't just stand here. I have to run.

I move my almost-paralysed bare feet as quickly as I can, watching the sun melt against the dark sky in strokes of crimson, orange and petal pink. Stars dapple the sky, so wherever I look, there are specks of magic and light streaming through the shadows.

The beauty comforts me, but not for long. I'm stuck in my head until the sound of *pat-pat-pat* behind me rocks me back to reality. Footsteps.

Go.

I pant heavily as I run, my bruised feet tiring quickly.

Go.

The word thrums through my head over and over again. I can't get caught. Not after everything I did. More footsteps edge towards me, faster and louder now. I don't dare look back. I need to get out of here, but the truth dawns on me. If I do get away from these people, where will I go? I've saved up money to get a train to Boston, but then what? I won't have enough coins in my pockets to spend on a house, or even an apartment. Where will I work? Where will I get educated? I'm only fourteen. Before the thoughts can overwhelm me any further, clammy hands seize my wrists, my arms, my legs.

"I don't know how you survived the jump, but I will make sure you suffer until your very last moment in this orphanage," Gertrude breathes down my neck. "You leave tomorrow, and you never come back."

I try to fight against the hands tugging at me, but they're too strong. I scream out in resistance, but no one takes any notice.

"Don't destroy your big day for yourself," Grimaldi says into my ear. "It's what everyone wants. Take advantage of it." He's kinder than the headmistress, but I still despise him for letting this happen.

"Let me go!" I shout, kicking and pushing whoever I can.

"Someone wants you," continues Grimaldi, jabbing a beefy finger in my face. "*You.*"

"I don't want them to want me!" I cry.

I strike Grimaldi's shin, the nearest thing to me, and he howls in pain.

"Stop moving — or else," Gertrude threatens me, and her fist makes sturdy contact with my back. If it weren't my "big day" tomorrow, she'd make contact with my face. Now she'll beat me in more concealed places.

Tears of frustration well in my eyes, but I don't move. A steady, familiar creak rings in my ears, and I feel hardwood under my feet. I open my eyelids, and I want to scream when I realise, I'm back inside the horrid orphanage.

"Leave us," Gertrude snarls maliciously.

Grimaldi and the guards scurry away fearfully, and soon it's just me and Gertrude.

"They're afraid of you," I whisper, willing my voice not to shake. "They're afraid of the person you are."

"Fear is a type of respect," agrees Gertrude. "You, Orabelle, are a wretched, slimy creature. I'll be glad to have you out of here. I never want to see you again."

Back at you, I want to say, but my throat is dry. I shudder when

Gertrude takes a rough hold of my arm and drags me up the stairs. If I were going to sleep, she would have brought me to the dormitory. Instead, we're in a dull, beige-painted room. I've been here many times before.

I don't bother resisting as Gertrude lays me on the bed.

I squeeze my eyes shut as the iron-handled whip comes down.

2
Anya

THE ONLY PLACE I CAN GO IS THE FOREST.

I let my legs carry me through the winding trees, through the twigs that encumber the dirt to the rock sitting before the jewel-blue stream that snakes through the whole woodland. I perch upon the large boulder, breathing in the familiar aroma of damp earth merged with crisp autumn leaves, the constant scent of London. I sigh a breath of relief to be in my comforting hideaway spot. I watch the glittering water slither across the ground, trying to calm myself down and rid myself of thoughts.

Inhale.

Exhale.

Inhale.

Exhale.

I feel my watch for comfort. It has a golden strap studded in diamonds. It's one of the few reminders I have of Father; an heirloom of his. Sorrow consumes me but I refrain from crying. Soon after, Esme finds me. I love Esme fiercely — she is like a second mother to me — but right now, all I want to be is alone. Hot tears pool in my eyes as Esme embraces me in a doting hug. I usually feel so safe in her arms, but after the news I've just received, I don't know how to feel safe.

"Anya, I know this is… horrible," Esme says, trying to find her words. "Dax is strong, though. Don't forget that." But she's shaking. Esme, the strongest person I know, is afraid.

I grit my teeth. "Esme, he may be strong, but he's eight years old. He's a mere child, and he can only handle so much. What a riveting start to summer."

"He's okay," she tells me, kissing my forehead gently. "We'll get to the bottom of this, I promise you."

"How do you know?" I whisper, making space for her to sit beside me on the rock.

She just shakes her head. She's trying to soothe me, even though she's shaken herself.

I've already lost my father. Now my brother, too? How could this have happened? How could I have not noticed my brother's absence in the house?

Dax and I have a connection that I can't explain. We feel each other, somehow But I hadn't felt him being stolen away. I'd just continued sleeping. Now, he's gone. Kidnapped, even. Maybe worse. I will myself not to think about it, but I can't help shuddering at the idea of the outcomes that may have already taken place. More droplets of salt glaze over my eyes.

"We'll find him," Esme tells me, but it sounds like she's trying to convince herself instead of me.

"I don't understand," I cry into her shoulder. "Who would steal someone like Dax? An innocent boy. An *eight-year-old*." I feel anger rising in my chest. I want to scream. I have no idea who took Dax or where he is. He has no phone, so it's not like we can track him. For all we know, Dax could be anywhere in the world.

Something washes over Esme's face, and I'm not quite sure what it is. Guilt? Frustration? A bit of both? That's what I feel, but the look on her face seems different… more intricate and confusing. I can't put my finger on it.

I don't have time to dwell on it, because Mother suddenly appears in the trees. Her cheeks are red, but just like Esme, she has some kind of concealed emotion playing out in her eyes. "Darling, come inside with me," she says gently, taking my hand in hers and nodding at Esme to follow.

I want to ask Mother where Dax is, but I know she hasn't a clue; she's just as helpless as I am. Mother usually knows the answers to all the questions I load her with, but in this case, she's completely oblivious as to what has happened to her baby boy, Dax.

"Tomorrow's your birthday," she tells me as we reach the house, and she guides me inside to the family room. Balloons have been blown up and are now sadly drifting along the floors. "I have the most amazing gift for you. One I'm quite sure none of your friends have received for their birthdays. It's going to change our lives. You'll see." I look at Esme to see if she'll give anything away. She seems a bit sceptical, but covers it up quickly when she sees me staring. "It's very unique, I'll give you that," she chimes in with Mother cheerily.

"I truly don't need a gift," I tell them dolefully. "I would feel wrong celebrating the day after my brother's disappearance. We should be holding search parties instead of a *birthday* party."

Mother freezes for a moment, and she exchanges a mysterious look with Esme. Then she turns back to me. "Tomorrow is a day to celebrate *you*. Dax is being searched for." Some kind of uneasiness comes over her as she speaks these words, but she waves it away as quickly as it came. "And the gift has been arranged for quite some time. It's more than a pair of running shoes or anything you've gotten in the past. I can't give away anything more. You'll grow to love it. That's all I'll say." Mother looks as though she's trying to be excited, but her eyes are strained and drooping, and she doesn't look like her normal self.

I try to look happy, too, but my lips refuse to turn upward.

Esme must pick up on how I feel, because she adds, "Anya, I know this is a hard time, but we'll figure this out together, all right?"

How? What if it's too late by the time we "figure this out"? Instead of asking these unanswerable questions, I try again to force a smile. My heart feels cold and hollowed out, my body gone numb. Dax may have annoyed me at times, but now, all I want is to hear his whiny voice. Tomorrow will be the worst birthday of my life, because it will be the first birthday without my brother.

Father died when I was only five years old. I remember him reading me fairy tales from thick novels, lulling me to sleep; kissing me goodnight. I still remember bits and pieces of him—his round, handsome face, his curly brown hair, his laugh. I remember his laugh very well. When he disappeared into thin air one day, I was devastated. He was gone, and no one knew where.

Esme has been with me since I was a baby. She and Father were close, so everyone in the household was in mourning. Mother was pregnant with Dax when Father died, and she was so worried she wouldn't be able to raise him. Esme, who had been my nanny, promised Mother that they would do it together. And then Esme just sort of melded into the family. But when Dax was born, he brought a light to the Blackstone family. Now he's gone, and the gloom seems to have returned in his place.

"I don't want to turn fourteen," I mutter.

Mother's eyes turn sadder. "Anya, we're going to get your brother."

"You keep telling me that, yes," I say bitterly.

"I have a plan."

"What kind of plan?" I'm intrigued.

But, much to my dismay, Mother tells me, "Nothing that concerns you. I'll handle it. Don't you worry."

"I want to help," I plead desperately. "Let me help, Mother. Please."

"I'll handle it. I promise," Mother says in her pacifying voice.

"This is for your own good," Esme promises.

"All I want to do is help find him, but I've been banned from that, too," I snap, not being able to help myself.

I angrily turn away from them and flounce up the stairs in frustration. Why won't anyone allow me to do a thing? I'm not a child any more.

My hands skim across the knobs of all the doors, and I stop at the door that has been locked since the day Father died. I don't remember what's in here from nine years ago. I ache to recall what I saw in the room all those years before, but my mind is always blocked when it comes to this door. Whenever I ask Esme or Mother about it, they shake their heads and merely say that some things must be kept secret for the safety of others. This couldn't annoy me any further at this moment. I've never been more curious to open this door and unsheathe all its mysteries. I try twisting the knob, and as I suspect, it doesn't budge. I wobble it more in exasperation.

Why are there so many secrets in the Blackstone household?

If Dax were here, I'd be able to pour out all my emotions on him, and he'd give me some dumb response that would make me laugh. But there's no Dax. I'm not sure there will ever be a Dax again.

The thought brings more tears to my eyes.

Esme and Mother are at my side before I know it, and Mother is cradling me in her arms. I feel like my five-year-old self all over again, crying like this; facing another loss. Is this a loss? I'm not quite sure yet.

"Oh, Anya…" soothes Mother, petting my hair, which is now completely soaked through with sweat.

"Everything will fall into place." Esme sounds so mousy. So unsure.

I want to be angry at someone, but Esme and Mother are innocents. They can't do anything. I just wish they would include me in their plans. I wish they wouldn't keep so many things from me when I know I can be of use.

"Mother, what's in this room?" I demand, my voice dry and wheezy. I try to look confident, but there is a gaping void inside me, growing larger by the second, stretching through me like an elastic band, waiting to break.

"Anya—"

"I know, I know, some things must be kept secret for the safety of others. But I'm a teenager now, and I'd like to know." I don't know what other way to put it. How can I make them take me seriously?

Esme interjects into the conversation. "Anya, we wish we could tell you. But amid those walls, in that room, lies danger. Danger far too grave for us to let you walk into. In that room is falsehood. It will drive you mad. Even your mother and I don't go in there."

"But you *know* what's in there," I breathe angrily. "Is there anything that could save Dax behind this door?"

"Don't you think we would have done it already?" Mother knits her eyebrows together as if trying to hold in her frustration. "You're not the only one who wants to find Dax."

I swallow. She's right. I'm exhausted, and I'm acting up. I mutter an apology, and Mother nods and wraps her arms around me, strands of brown hair slipping out of the loose bun that sits atop her head. She has to crouch. She's always been tall.

"I understand where this is coming from," she whispers to me. "I know how scared you are. But my plan will pull through. Take my word for it. Now, I'm going to bed, and I suggest you do the same. Goodnight, An. In the morning, everything will be a little less foggy." Mother pads off to bed at that, shimmery nightgown trailing behind.

I wonder if she's right. Will it be less foggy tomorrow, or will I still be dazed, afraid and confused? If I get no answers, how will my questions be able to just fade away? I don't want to think about it any further.

I say goodnight to Esme and head to my room. It's large, with two beds. But now, one is empty because Dax is gone, and it makes the whole area feel vacant. I nestle under my blankets, drawing in sharp breaths and praying for my darling brother who's out in the world, somewhere, feeling lost and alone.

My birthday is tomorrow.

If Mother's gift is as good as she describes, I hope it will be something that changes my life forever.

3
Ora

A RINGING SOUND SPLITS THROUGH THE AIR.

I force my heavy eyelids open to the sound of the bell alarm that goes off each day in my dormitory at 6am. The chandelier is abruptly switched on, which is followed by a series of groans. I blink rapidly, taking in every ray of light and all the grunting from my indolent classmates. I flex my legs and arms, feeling sharp pangs in my toes and legs and back. Everything feels sore. I moan, but as the realisation of what day it is washes over me, I suddenly feel a lot more enlivened.

Today is the day I have been dreading for a long time. But, if I could never escape this orphanage, I wouldn't want to stay here for the rest of my life. I suppose getting adopted is better than the other option. I just wish that I had thought out my plan better. I should have prepared for the balcony. I should have brought a rope. Then I would have been able to slide down and run away. It's too late for that now.

Gertrude storms into the room. "Why are none of you getting out of bed? All of you lazy pigs, up, up, up!"

I pull myself off my lumpy mattress, now fully cognisant of everything going on. I know the protocol of the day ahead of me. Everyone at the Corkwood Orphanage is aware of what goes on the day someone gets adopted. I'm just surprised that person is me this time.

I change into my best lace dress, the most expensive thing I own, and pin a part of my hair into a waterfall braid. I used to have a friend, Colton, who'd bought me a hair braiding book for my tenth birthday because he was the only one who knew how much I enjoyed it. Then Colton got adopted and left Corkwood, leaving me alone with my braid book and no other friends.

Everyone leaves the dormitory. Some utter a meaningless goodbye to me, and some completely ignore me. I'll never see these people again, and I doubt I'll remember them. I have no close friends here. Gertrude stands at the front of the dormitory with a coral-coloured suitcase standing beside her.

"Pack up," she orders me, and I sense something smug in her voice.

I glare at her coolly. Last night was the last night she would ever hurt me. At least when I leave this wretched orphanage, hopefully I'll never get touched like that again. I grab the suitcase, set it on my ugly bed frame, and start folding the little amount of clothes I have. I don't want to keep any of these pathetic pieces of apparel. Perhaps I'll be able to throw them out when I get to my new home.

New home.

That sounds so funny in my mind. So different. I'm going to have a mother, a sister and a brother. I'm going to have a nanny. I've been told all this. I can't help the excitement and nervousness building up inside my body. Having siblings… I've never had a sibling. Even Gertrude's malicious eyes boring into me can't ruin my mood. I zip up my suitcase and turn to the headmistress. "I'm ready."

She smiles a crooked, toothy smile. She can be happy that I'm leaving — so am I. "Follow me down the stairs," she snarls.

We go down a twisting staircase that leads to Gertrude's office. It's stuffy and hot in her cramped work area, but goosebumps prickle my arms. I can't believe this is happening. Soon, my new mother and my siblings will walk through the doors of Corkwood and sweep me into another life. I'm not sure how it will be living among such new people. What if we don't get along? I've never been loved by anyone. Will my new family learn to love me? Will I learn to love them? If I hate it, will I be able to pull together a plan to attempt a runaway? So many questions flood through my mind.

I'm not entirely sure if I'm ready for this. Being adopted is such a big thing. Colton and I stayed in touch for a short time after his adoption. He had moved to Boston, which he said was gorgeous, and he told me he adored his new family and was making lots of friends. After that, we fell out with each other, never exchanging any more words. I hope I fit into my new life as well as Colton.

I sink into the velvety mint armchair that I have sat in many times when I've gotten into trouble. Now I sit here waiting for my parent to pick me up. I can't help but shudder. Will she be like the evil stepmother from *Cinderella*? Will she whip me like Gertrude when I upset her?

Part of me wants to run and try to escape again — sprint through the meadow, to the train station; to a life where no one will have to care for me and pretend to love me. I realise I'm gripping my suitcase handle so tightly that blisters are beginning to mould themselves into my skin. I release my clasped hands quickly. There is a knock on the heavy wooden door of the office. Maybe it's Vice Grimaldi, coming to tell me that my supposed-to-be adoptive mother has decided that she no longer wants me. I twist a lock of hair between my fingers nervously.

Gertrude ruffles her skirts and stands on her spool heels nimbly. She makes her way to the door slowly. Far too slowly. She pulls open the door, revealing a beautiful woman with a mop of luscious, jet-black kinks that fall past her shoulders. Her skirt is petal pink with strewn-in flowers. A smile plays out on her lips when she sees me. No one has ever been so happy to see *me*.

"Hello," she says calmly.

"Mrs Blackstone," says Gertrude coldly. "Always a pleasure."

Have they met before? I wonder, as Gertrude steadily glares at my mother-to-be.

"Please, sit down. This is Orabelle." Gertrude goes back to her seat, patting her clammy hand on my knee on her way, as if trying to look comforting.

"Ora," I correct, but my voice comes out dry.

"Ora." Mrs Blackstone smiles warmly. "I'm Veronica. So pleased to meet you."

A lump, forms in my throat. I'm not sure what to say. I'm frozen, and my lips refuse to move. Instead, I just nod.

"Ora has been such a delight over the past twelve years," says Gertrude with a lying smirk.

Twelve years.

All those years ago, when my parents abandoned me here, they didn't care. No one has ever cared. I've been stuck at Corkwood for my whole dejected life. My mother and father simply left a one-year-old baby to fend for herself.

Veronica regards me with a sort of fondness I've never been treated with before. "It must have been tough," she whispers. "I was you once."

"What do you mean?" I ask, surprised.

Before Veronica can reply, Gertrude cuts into the conversation. "Mrs Blackstone, I'll need you to sign this paper quickly, and then you can be off."

"Gladly," Veronica replies, the tenderness gone. She pulls out a beautiful silver pen with a blue butterfly carved into it. She signs the paper Gertrude gives her and turns to me. She must see me admiring her pen because she asks, "Would you like it?"

"Oh." I clear my throat sheepishly. "No, it's all right. It's yours."

"Well, what's yours is mine, right?" Veronica says, her eyes smiling. She places the dainty pen in my palm. "Ready to go home, Ora?"

I nod, trying not to be overwhelmed by the word *home* again.

"Goodbye, Gertrude," says Veronica, taking my fingers in her own. "We'll be leaving now."

"Orabelle, you'll be missed," lies Gertrude. And with that, we leave.

As soon as we walk into the crisp air, I feel a rush of excitement pump through my body. I can't remember the last time I went outside without Gertrude snaking after me. Now it's just Veronica and me. I realise with a pang that my sister and brother aren't here. Are they not interested in me?

"Where are my adoptive siblings?" I ask tightly.

Veronica's face falls. She doesn't answer for a while, and I fear I've said something wrong. But then she says meekly, "My son is lost."

"Lost?" I repeat with curiosity, but right away I wish I hadn't asked, because her face turns even sadder.

Veronica turns to me and stops walking. "My son was kidnapped," she explains to me.

My jaw drops. "I'm sorry."

"It's not your fault," Veronica says quickly, and she puts a strained smile on her face. "This is your big day, Ora. I have no doubt we're going to find Dax soon. And in the meanwhile, it's my other daughter's birthday. You're going to be the best surprise."

"I'm a birthday gift?" I ask, arching my eyebrows. "My adoptive sister doesn't even… know about me?"

Veronica shakes her head. "I think you'll be the best thing that's ever happened to her. She lost her father long ago, and just so recently, her brother. She feels lost. I want another daughter, and she is in need of a sister. You'll bring such light. You're going to be a fitting member to the Blackstone family."

I can't help beaming at her kind words.

We continue walking hand in hand, past the Corkwood Orphanage waterfall I've seen so many times. We stop at a limousine.

"Are we… riding in this?" I breathe.

Veronica nods. "It's a remarkable day for you. It's got to be special."

A tall man opens the limo door for me. Surprisingly, a giggle erupts from my mouth. I clasp a hand to my lips with embarrassment, but Veronica looks happier now, though there's still sorrow there. She climbs inside the vehicle with me as someone loads my suitcase into the boot. The limo is beautiful. There are long sofas, glowing aquamarine floors, and shelves crammed with delicious foods. It's everything I would imagine from all the books I've read. I never really thought I would *be* in a limo!

"Where do you live?" I ask. It sounds strange rolling off my tongue, but Veronica doesn't seem to mind.

"A couple of hours from here," she informs me. "We'll be going to London."

"I've always wanted to go to London," I think aloud. "And Boston, like my friend. I've always wanted to visit there as well."

Veronica smiles at me. "We'll go there this summer, then."

"Truly?"

"If you'd like."

Happiness bubbles through me. Living in Portsmouth has been interesting, but this is no longer my home. It's time to get out of here. This way, I can leave the orphanage and my whole past behind me. I can start afresh. The limo starts up, and I suddenly realise how tired I am. I lie on Veronica's shoulder, and exhaustion overcomes me quickly. This is the first peaceful sleep I've had in a long time, and I'm going to enjoy it.

I wake up to the refreshing sounds of birds chirping. When I open my eyes, I turn to the window by my side, the one that sunshine is streaming through. I soak up the heat, bathing in the light. I feel relaxed, which is a foreign feeling to an orphan like me. Veronica is humming a tune beside me, whistling here and there. Like a pretty lullaby.

"How was your nap?" she asks when she sees me.

"Better than you'd guess," I reply.

"We're only minutes away from home," says Veronica. "Anything you want to know before we arrive? You can ask me questions whenever."

"What did you mean when you said you were me once?" I interrupt eagerly.

She pauses. Then, she says, "Well, I was an orphan, too. I got adopted when I was eleven, but those years were the darkest times of my life. I went to Corkwood Orphanage as well. Gertrude was still the headmistress back then. Can you imagine how old she is?" Veronica jokes, laughing.

"Did you ever find your birth parents?" I press.

Veronica draws in a breath. "Not before it was too late."

"Oh. I'm sorry."

"Yeah. It was no one's fault but mine. I got their address, but I didn't go for two whole years, and then… well."

At that, I hurriedly change the subject to her daughter. I find out that she's fourteen today and that she is like a mini-detective, because she's always looking into mysteries and trying to unveil their secrets. We may be similar in that way. I hope we get along.

Soon after, the limo pulls into a smooth driveway that leads to a breath-taking mansion. I step out of the car, gaping at the glittering black stone house. The stained-glass windows are patterned with swirling colours, and they reflect into the house's lake, making the water look like a whirling vortex of magic.

"This place is beautiful." I gape, nervously fiddling with my pen, which is wonderfully cool against my palms.

Veronica places a comforting hand on my shoulder. "This is *your* place now."

I can hardly believe my ears or my eyes. This morning, I was living in a dull orphanage, sharing a room with twenty-nine other students, and now look at me. I can't wait to see where I'll be sleeping tonight.

Veronica unloads my suitcase and rolls it to the large wooden door leading into the house. There are twisting designs etched around the entrance that I have to stop and admire for a few moments.

"Are you ready to meet the rest of your family?" Veronica asks me, bouncing me back to reality.

I force my head to give a firm nod. My fingers skitter to the wood and clench into a fist. I finally muster up all my courage and knock on the door.

My heart leaps when it swings open with a creak.

4
Anya

I HAVE BEEN TOLD TO WAIT.

I've been waiting for over an hour now, sprawled across my bed, listening to the steady ticking of my clock. It's been a bore, to say the least. All I have is a photo of Dax to comfort me. My fingers trace the edges of his oval-shaped face, and I pray that one day I will be able to see that face again. I urge myself not to cry. The tears do me no good. Mourning him isn't nearly as effective as plotting to find him. My bedroom door opens a crack, and Esme pops through, closing it behind her.

"Can I come downstairs now?" I beg. "Sitting here gets extremely dull."

Esme chuckles, though her face saddens when she catches a glimpse of Dax's picture. When she sees me looking at her, she livens up again. "Anya, we want you to meet someone."

Esme opens the door, revealing Mother standing next to a beautiful girl with a waterfall braid running through her locks of hair. The girl is slightly shorter than me, and she looks extremely nervous.

"Happy birthday," she croaks.

"Do I know you?" I ask her, more rudely than intended.

"This is Ora," explains Mother, and I sense a protective, loving energy coming from her.

"And Ora is…?" I say impatiently.

Mother gushes with excitement. Finally, she blurts out, "Your adopted sister."

At first, I think I hear wrong, or Mother is kidding. But the realisation hits me when I see Mother's serious face, her hand intertwined with Ora's. A rush of emotions flood over me. Finally, I find my words.

"So… we lost Dax, and you decided that he's gone for good, and you want to replace him with someone else?"

Mother looks surprised. She stumbles over her words. "Well… no, of course not. I just thought it would be a nice…"

"You thought it would be a nice distraction," I shout angrily. "How could you bring someone into this house when we just lost Dax? How could you not talk this over with me?"

Mother's mouth is tilted open in shock. "Treat her with some respect, please. Ora's spent her whole life in an orphanage, and this is her big day."

"I thought it was supposed to be *my* big day, too," I mutter selfishly.

"It's okay," says Ora, pulling away from Mother's grasp. "I understand. I'll go to the family room and… give myself a mini-tour." She disappears downstairs.

"Why are you being like this?" Mother demands, her eyes filled with hurt. "This was planned long before Dax got lost. We were going to pick her up on your birthday. You've always wanted a sister."

I swallow, hating myself for making Mother feel like this. She did this for *me*. "I'm not sure I want one right now," I grumble. "I miss my brother."

"I know you do." Mother nods, sitting beside me on the bed. "But it's not like we're going to return Ora. She's a part of the family. She's legally adopted."

"Okay." I breathe in. "I have a sister. Ora Blackstone."

The joy that crosses over Mother's face lights me up. "Yes." She grins with a sniff. "Ora Blackstone."

Esme joins us on the bed. "And your sister is waiting. Afraid, lonely, and confused. Feeling unwanted."

I created that feeling of unwantedness, I realise with a pang. I feel horrible, but Ora probably feels worse. "I'm going to go introduce myself properly," I decide. "Can I do it privately?"

"Of course," Esme says, and watches me guiltily slink away.

Ora is on the sofa, looking around awkwardly. She doesn't feel like she belongs, and that's clear. She doesn't feel like this is her home, and why would she?

"Hi," I say shyly, joining her on the couch.

"You know, it's okay," Ora replies quickly. "I don't want you to hang out with me because your mother forces you to. You can tell her we're friends, and you don't ever have to talk to me if you want."

"No, of course that's not what I want," I assure her, guilt goring my insides. "I *do* want to get to know you. I do want a sister. It's just a big surprise. And at such a tragic moment in my life. Although, I guess I shouldn't complain."

Ora laughs. "I know that's what it seems like as an orphan, but my parents left me when I was a year old. I don't remember them, so I can't truly miss them. I miss the *idea* of them, certainly. Or, at least, I have been. But now I have all the Blackstones, and Veronica is the parent I've always wanted."

"Well," I stutter. "I'm here for you."

Ora smiles. "That's sweet. But I think you probably need some comfort as well. Losing Dax, that's hard. That's traumatic. This is tough for you. I know I may be a complete stranger to you, Anya, but if you ever do want to talk, I'm good at it. At the orphanage, little kids poured out their emotions on me all the time."

I nod. "Thanks."

We sit in silence, and then I speak in a whisper, "There are so many secrets in this house. Finally, I have a partner in crime to help me understand them."

Ora grins mischievously. "What kind of secrets are we talking about here?"

"Come with me." I take her upstairs to the locked door. "Esme and Mother always act so strange when I bring this up. It's been locked ever since the day of Father's death. I wonder if somehow it relates to that day. Is there anything that can save Dax? It's apparently 'dangerous', but I don't know how."

"Well, I don't want to make any trouble. I'm new to this house," says Ora. She still adds with a glint in her eyes, "Have you tried picking the lock?"

"Countless times," I reply with a sigh. "I've also considered breaking down the door, but I'm not sure how to do that without anyone noticing."

"No, I don't think that would be the smartest idea," agrees Ora. "However, an eyeglass screwdriver always works for me when picking a lock. See, I tried running away from the orphanage multiple times. I picked the headmistress's office lock and grabbed the key that led to the escape door. I used the key to open the door. All the other doors were always guarded, but not that one."

"And? Sidetrack — what happened?" I ask, impressed by the daredevil inside her.

"It led me to a balcony," she says bitterly. "I was forced to jump a great height to the meadow below me."

"You jumped?" I gasp. "So it wasn't very far down, then?"

"No, it was," she guarantees me. "I didn't want to face the headmistress's beating, though, so I did it. Honestly, I thought I'd die. But I was lucky. I only hurt my toes, which are healing abnormally fast."

"Do you ever think it could be more than luck?" I wonder aloud.

Ora looks confused. Then she says, "No, of course not. What else could it be?"

"Many things. Maybe…"

"Maybe what?"

"I don't know. I have strange thoughts sometimes." I apologise quickly, changing the subject back to her. "When exactly did you jump?"

Her cheeks flush red. "Yesterday," she mutters.

"Yesterday?" I can't help being surprised. "You were running away from… us? From your adoption?"

"Yes," she admits, squirming. "Don't be angry. I just thought it would be worse. No one's ever treated me with kindness. I didn't know what it felt like until I met your mother. I'm glad Gertrude caught me. I love it here already."

My heart softens for her. She's scared of the world because of how the wretched orphanage handled her. "I understand," I tell her kindly. "Hey, that eyeglass screwdriver idea sounds pretty cool. I think we have one of those in the basement, in a junk drawer, or something of the sorts. How about we sneak there tonight when Esme and Mother are asleep?"

Ora looks tempted, but she says sadly, "I really can't afford to get into such trouble on my first night. Your mother may kick me out of the house. Then where would I go? It's clear Gertrude would never accept me back into her orphanage, although I'm very sure I wouldn't want to live there again."

"Ora, you can't believe that could happen."

"It's true for people like me. Orphans have been adopted and sent back the next day. It's tough to see, but even tougher to bear."

"Don't worry about those things. My mother would never do that. Trust me, she loves you already. You would never get kicked out of here. And she's your mother now, too. Remember that."

Ora grins again. "How much trouble would I get into if I did go along with this lock-picking plan?"

"I'll take the blame for the whole thing." I perk up. "I'll tell them I dragged you into it, and you'll look innocent, and they'll briefly be angry. But after that, I doubt they'll care."

"But what if they *do* care? What then?"

"Don't be such a worrywart."

"When it comes to this, I *am* a worrywart. If they catch us…"

I smirk. "Well, who ever said that we're going to get caught?"

5
Ora

THIS IS MY FIRST SPY MISSION WITH ANYA.

Part of me hopes it won't be the last. This is exactly how having a sister is supposed to be. Exciting, enthralling, exhilarating. I'm in *love* with my family's thick English accents. They sound even more English than me. I'm so curious to find out what's in that room. What could it be? A room of hidden secrets or stolen relics? It could be anything, but Veronica's warnings of its danger make me eager to reveal its truths.

We are forced to eat dinner without mentioning any of our scheming. Esme has prepared a delicious shrimp vegetable stir-fry, and it's one of the most incredible things I've ever eaten.

"You're a great cook," I say through a mouthful.

"I'm glad you like it," Esme beams. "Are you enjoying yourself so far?"

I swallow hastily and nod. "Very much. The house is *great*. The food, may I reiterate…"

Veronica raises her eyebrows expectantly.

"Oh, yes, and you all are… remarkable. I was honestly afraid I wouldn't like my new family. It's scary. I thought that you would… I don't know…" I stammer.

"I know how you feel," offers Veronica. "You never know what it'll be like."

"Right. Well, I feel like I'm in the right family now," I say, clearing my throat. "Anya and I are getting on quite well. I've always wanted a sister. A houseful of girls. It's a dream."

Anya looks down, and I immediately regret my last words. How could I be so foolish? Dax has only just gone missing.

"I'm sorry," I begin.

"No, don't be," cuts in Veronica. "You didn't mean it that way."

We finish up our meal in silence, and then Mother and Esme exchange a look before getting up, sweeping up our plates, and pulling out a huge chocolate cake from a white box on the counter. Esme sticks a candle in the middle, and with that, we all proceed to sing happy birthday. Anya glances around with embarrassment, obviously not sure what to do. Then I feel her hand entwine over mine under the table, and a rush of heat spurs through my body. It's joy, I realise. This is what joy feels like.

When we're done singing, Veronica exclaims, "Blow out your candle!"

"Will you blow with me?" Anya asks me quietly. "Please?"

"Of course," I grin. And together, still holding hands, we release a huge breath onto the cake, and the wavering flame goes out. I've never blown out a candle before, as the teachers at the orphanage were never keen on spending money to celebrate birthdays.

After cake — which is the best I've ever tried — Anya tells Esme we're going to sleep early, and we creep to her marvellous bedroom and hide out there. We've made a full-on plan, with a big board and everything, like in the movies. We'll sneak down the basement stairs, and one person will keep watch. With an eyeglass screwdriver in hand, we'll creep upstairs to the secret door, which we'll unlock, and… we'll see its magic that has been kept from Anya so long. I couldn't be more ready.

We both lie in our beds, twitching with anticipation. We close our eyes when Esme comes and kisses us both. When her lips touch my forehead, a twinge of happiness shoots through me. I'm really going to be loved here. Esme disappears after that, and the hallway is plunged into darkness. We wait a couple of moments until there is complete quiet in the house. Then Anya's voice cuts through the emptiness by hissing, "Ora? Are you awake?"

"Absolutely," I reply, grinning.

We both climb out of our beds. Anya pulls on her head flashlight, and she gives me Dax's. It's a little tight around my scalp, but I ignore the itch and follow her down two flights of stairs, to the door leading inside the basement.

"Right, you stay here," she whispers to me. "Keep guard. If you hear a noise, use your walkie-talkie."

I clutch the device attached to my side, feeling a thrill run through me as I do. Real walkie-talkies! I've never seen one until today. She had retrieved them from her drawer earlier on. I guess she and Dax played games with them.

Or at least, they used to.

I watch Anya run down the stairs. After five minutes pass, I start feeling nervous. Is this the best idea? On my very first night? What sort of impression will this set? Kind people bring me into their house, and the first thing I do is break into a secret room of theirs under their noses.

A hand on my shoulder makes me jump. "Anya! You scared me!" I whisper-shriek.

"Well, I'm sorry," she says, "but look what I found! An eyeglass screwdriver!" She dangles it in the air, and it gives a *klink* sound. Anya quickly hides it in her pocket and tones down the enthusiasm. "Follow me."

We trail up the staircases again, to the third floor. I realise with horror that the locked door is only a couple of rooms down from Veronica's. "Won't she hear us?" I ask Anya in a low voice.

Anya winks. "Not if we're quiet."

She shows no fear, but she has no idea how much I have to lose. Is Veronica a light sleeper? If I sneeze, will she come out and catch us? I shrug off the thought and take the screwdriver from Anya. I force it into the keyhole, familiar with how this works. It doesn't budge at first. I have to push, hard, and then I feel the door unlock. Anya's breath catches in her throat. She's more nervous than I am, surely. But, I suppose, we're nervous for different reasons. As anxious as I am about finding out what's behind this door, I'm more anxious about being caught.

"Are you ready?" I ask.

Anya nods and twists the knob. Relief washes over her when it moves easily. She pushes the door open.

We quickly bustle into the room and shut the door behind us. I look around. It's one of the smallest rooms I've ever been in, and at that, one of the emptiest. There is nothing here. It is more like a cubicle than a room, in fact. There are beige-painted walls and a brick wall right in front of us. Nothing else. Nothing between the walls.

Anya's face is full of disappointment. "How is this dangerous?" she whispers.

I honestly can't answer her question. She's right. This is the definition of an upsetting outcome to an adventure. Anya kicks the brick wall in frustration and confusion.

"Anya," I say gently, "I know this is… not what you were hoping for. But we should go back to the bedroom now. It's getting late."

She nods, pressing her lips together. "Sorry for getting your hopes up."

"Honestly" — I shrug — "as curious as I was, I really only came along to spend more time with *you*."

Anya smiles at me, though it's half-hearted. She opens the door gently and closes it behind us. We head to our bedroom. We didn't get caught, but we didn't make any fascinating discoveries, either.

Except I figured out that either Esme and Veronica are lying, or there's something else going on here that truly is dangerous.

The next morning, I wake up late. It is the first day in ages that I haven't forced myself up from the cursed bell alarm in the orphanage.

I'm surprised that I'm the one to wake up Anya.

"That was an amazing sleep-in," I murmur to her.

"Sleep-in?" she repeats groggily, checking her watch and gasping. "Eight thirty! This is early, Ora! I'm going back to sleep. Don't worry. Esme will wake us up if we truly drowse for too long."

I watch Anya turn onto her side and allow her eyelids to flutter shut.

"Well, then," I say contentedly, "I'll sleep as well." I've never woken up too *early*. Everything excites me in the Blackstone household. Everything is a surprise.

I drift off to sleep easily.

After what seems to be only minutes passing, light dances through the room, and I hear the curtains being ruffled and drawn. I open my eyes, feeling very well rested, but Anya groans.

Esme, who has two trays of food in her hands, exclaims, "Rise and shine! It's eleven thirty, you lazy birds!"

Eleven thirty already? How did time pass so quickly? I sit up and rub the crust out of my eyes, but before I can stretch my legs, Esme comes over and sets one of her trays in my lap.

"What's this?" I ask, though it's quite obvious.

"Your breakfast," Esme snorts.

Anya, who is now sitting up, takes her tray hungrily and starts digging in.

With that, Esme leaves.

I look down at the food — a bundle of cranberry crêpes, elegant eggs with a baguette, a divine platter of fruit, and a tall glass of what looks like some kind of fizzy pineapple mocktail with a slab of lemon on the edge. All we got at the orphanage was a couple of pieces of toast, and if we were lucky, a bowl of cereal or porridge with brown sugar.

"Wow," I breathe, chewing on a crêpe. "This is…"

"Delicious," agrees Anya. "Esme is the best chef I know. She always fixes me and D… she always fixes up amazing food. She's so used to doing it now, it's become a routine." There's a sad edge to her voice.

Not knowing what to say, I gobble up the nourishment and guzzle down the drink that tastes like Heaven in a glass.

Anya finishes before me, wiping her mouth daintily with a napkin. She sets the tray on her bedside table. Beside it, she nearly knocks over a picture of a young boy that I presume must be Dax. Anya quickly moves it back to its spot, and her eyes linger on it for a few seconds. Then she shakes her head and turns to me.

"May I ask, what did happen to him?" I ask carefully.

Anya pales. "One day he was here, and the next, he was gone. Dax slept in his bed, the bed you're sleeping in, and the next morning, he wasn't in it. I looked frantically, and there was no sign of him. All of his things remained untouched. I don't know. We were so excited for the summer, you know? And then one week in, poof, he's gone. I'd call it the worst summer so far ever, but then I met you."

"I'm really sorry," I offer. "That must be hard on you."

She nods, clearly eager to change the subject. "I've been thinking lots about the door," she finally says.

"Me, too," I admit. "It's strange that an empty room like that is being kept a secret. And I wonder why it was locked on the day of your father's death, too? The room feels like it should be so much… bigger. More fascinating."

Anya nods, pulling from her drawer the eyeglass screwdriver we used last night. She twirls it in her hands. "I'm going to keep this," she decides. "It'll be useful one day."

I grin. One day we'll find out what's hidden in the true depths of the room. We're both sure of it, or at least I am. "Let's go downstairs and say good morning to your mother."

"She's your mother, too," Anya quickly tells me, and then we both creep down the stairs. We stop at the second flight when we hear whispering from below. Anya raises a finger to her lips. Part of me knows that I shouldn't be eavesdropping on my second day here, but the other part is curious. I reluctantly dip my head down with Anya's so we can overhear the private conversation.

"I've got to do this for Dax," Veronica is saying, her voice wobbling. "I know how dangerous it is, but… I've got to do it. He's my son. He hasn't done a thing wrong. Just because of Harlow… it hardly seems fair."

Anya freezes. "How does this connect to him? Harlow, that's my father's name," she whispers to me, and I wish I could give her an answer. Instead, I gently urge her to be quiet and continue listening.

"You're right. It's *not* fair," agrees Esme slowly. "But I really don't think it's a good idea for you to be travelling all the way to Australia! You could get injured, or worse, *killed*. He's mad, Veronica. He's completely mad. He'll lash out at you."

Who? I look to Anya, whose eyes are wide with fear. She flinches when I lay a hand on her shoulder.

"I've already booked the flight," says Veronica stubbornly. "I'll leave tomorrow. I can fend for myself."

"I know you can, but…"

"Esme, I'm going, and nothing you say will be able to change my mind. I need to find a way to keep Dax safe… without Anya finding out the truth."

"I won't say a word." Esme's voice comes out smoothly.

I look at Anya, or at least where Anya *was*. A door clicks shut, and I run to our bedroom to see her sprawled across her bed.

"I'm sorry," she says into her pillow in a muffled voice. "I couldn't listen to that anymore."

"It's all right," I soothe, sitting on the edge of her bed.

"I thought… that maybe I was wrong about them. But you heard it yourself. They're keeping something big from me. Which means you, too. And Mother's in danger, and I know she'd lie right to my face if I asked her about it. What if she disappears, too? Then I'll be an orphan." She looks at me then, covering her mouth. "I'm sorry. Was that offensive?"

"Not in any way," I assure her, bringing the topic back to her. "I'm sure… I'm sure everything's fine." I can't find a way to make my voice convincing.

Anya draws in breaths slowly. "I don't know what I would do if…"

I interrupt her before she can continue. "Don't think like that." I think of anything to say that may give her support. "How about we take another trek to the secret room tonight?"

"Why would we do that?" Anya demands. "To face the disappointment of nothingness all over again?"

"No. I think we missed something there," I tell her thoughtfully. "This time, we'll look closer. I have a feeling in my bones that there's something special in there. Something… amazing."

"All right," gives in Anya. "But what about Mother? She's leaving tomorrow, and she said her mind was made up."

"I don't know," I admit. When Anya's face falls, I add quickly, "We'll figure it out, though. Maybe we'll find something in the secret room tonight that relates to her sudden travels, and to the man she was talking about. Worst-case scenario, we'll tell them we heard them and they'll have to tell us the truth. We won't let her leave."

Anya doesn't argue any further. Instead, she nods and picks up the eyeglass screwdriver. "Let's do it."

The day passes by slowly, stretching on and on. We read, watch

Netflix — which I've never heard of before — and play soccer in the backyard. Whenever we're in the house, though, around Veronica and Esme, Anya doesn't act "chill" at all. I note that she's a horrible liar. She starts sweating around Veronica, spending as much time with her as possible. When Esme comes near her, Anya pulls away and comes up with some lazy excuse that she needs to go somewhere, like the bathroom. Veronica must pick up on it, because she arches her eyebrows and asks in a low voice, "Is everything all right, honey? You're acting… strange."

"No, I'm not," Anya says quickly. "What would I be acting strange about?"

"Okay," says Veronica suspiciously. "I have to get back to my law papers."

I pull Anya aside and hiss at her, "Act *normal*. They'll start coming up with ideas as to why your behaviour has changed."

"I know that," Anya snaps back, and stamps away from me, back to Veronica.

I hang around Esme, seeing if she'll drop any clues; but, unlike Anya, she shows no difference in her personality. "Did you enjoy breakfast?" Esme asks.

"Yes, I did," I reply carefully. "What did you and Veronica eat this morning? I saw you two chatting with each other."

Esme laughs. "We were having a good talk over some pancakes." She nods.

"Oh?" I don't want to give her the impression that I overheard her, but I do want to see if she lies to me.

"We were talking about you and Anya, in fact. About how well you're getting along," she tells me naturally, taking a sip of tea from the steaming mug clamped between her fingers.

I force a smile and swallow my anger and confusion. "Yes, we're very good friends already," I agree.

Later, when Esme and Veronica are preparing dinner, I share the information of Esme's lies with Anya.

"Hm," she murmurs bitterly. "I couldn't pick anything up from Mother, either. They can both fib, right through their teeth."

We sit down at the dinner table, which has a giant roast turkey and a bowl of potatoes and cheese set in the middle.

"Who's ready to dig in?" exclaims Esme.

I try to look enthusiastic as I spoon the meat onto my plate and push it into my mouth. I have to admit, it's pretty tasty.

"Yum," Anya says through a mouthful. "Thanks so much." The words are exaggerated, but Esme and Veronica continue eating happily. "So," Anya blurts, "what do you have in mind for searching for Dax? You said you had a plan, did you not?"

Esme and Veronica exchange a look, and Veronica clears her throat. "Actually," she says with a gentle smile, "I'm leaving tomorrow to look for him."

"Leaving?" Anya looks startled. "Where to? The police are looking, are they not?"

"Yes, but I have to do my duty as a mother." Veronica chews on a potato thoughtfully. "I'll just be around, hanging up posters, asking people if they've seen him."

Red flushes Anya's cheeks, and I know how angry she is. Luckily, she pulls herself together and says, "Let us come with you. We'd love to help; right, Ora?"

I nod convincingly.

"No, you two will stay here with Esme," says Veronica.

"But—" begins Anya.

"No buts," cuts in Veronica sternly. "You'll stay here with Esme, and I will return… with a very alive Dax in my arms."

Anya huffs and takes a sip of her icy water. "I think I've lost my appetite now. Ora and I will head to bed."

I hungrily take another bite of food, then force myself onto my feet to follow Anya. "Goodnight," I say softly, and Veronica gives me her warm smile that turns my own lips upward. She's so kind, yet she's lying to us. She must be doing it for our safety, but it's too late to turn on our plan now. I reluctantly walk upstairs after Anya, running my hand over the banister etchings.

"All right," says Anya, as soon as we reach our room and the door is shut, "we'll do the same thing as yesterday. We'll be very quiet, of course."

I nod along as she speaks, though I have to admit I'm only half-listening. Part of me doesn't think this is such a great idea. If we really do find something and we get caught, what will Veronica think of me? Anya sounded very sure when she told me I would never get kicked out of this house, but what does she know? She's Veronica's biological daughter, so *she* couldn't get disowned. I have so much more to lose.

"Er, Ora? Are we cool on the plan?" Anya's voice rings out.

I'm startled out of my daze. "Um. Yes."

"Good. Now let's make out that we're going to sleep."

I slip into the silk pyjamas I was gifted with from Veronica last night. The thought of betraying her makes me tingle with guilt, but I try to push it out of my brain. I climb into bed, clutching my headlamp under the mattress. Sweat breaks out on my forehead. I have finally found a place where I feel at home. It's not worth risking everything, but I have to do this for Anya. *This* was *my idea, after all*, I think with shame.

Still, after Esme comes and kisses us each goodnight, and darkness floods through the room, I am tempted not to reply when Anya hisses to me if I'm awake. I remind myself of the sacrifices I must make for my sister.

It takes everything I have to whisper, "Absolutely."

"Good, then let's get going." Anya climbs out of her bed quietly. Her headlight flickers on, giving me a soft glow to pull on my own. She reaches into her drawer and pulls out the eyeglass screwdriver determinedly. "You ready for this?"

I nod and try to smile. My throat is dry with fear. Anya and I make our way out of the room and to the locked door.

"Do you want to try this time?" I whisper to Anya, and she nods. I realise as she presses the screwdriver into the keyhole that her hands are trembling.

The door doesn't budge, so I go to her side, and we push together. It flies open, and we both step in and shut it behind us in awe. Our headlamps don't provide much radiance, but enough to see our surroundings. The emptiness of the room greets us, and Anya looks a bit disappointed again, as if maybe she expected the room would have grown and morphed into the magical place she had thought up in her mind.

"Look around for clues," I tell her, crouching down and feeling the wood of the floor. I'm careful not to hunch over so much to touch the door and make a sound.

Anya feels the walls beside her, and when I get back on my feet, I see her staring at the wall in front of us. I follow her gaze to a wobbling brick that looks like it should fit into something. I'm not sure what, but it might lead us somewhere. I press my palm against the rickety piece. It is hot and smooth against my skin; very different to how it *should* feel. I wait, then press harder when nothing happens.

"Great," snorts Anya. "Why did we think we'd be able to find—"

Suddenly, a bright green glow illuminates the room. A terrified scream slips from Anya's lips.

I'm too intrigued and frightened to scold her for making a sound. I'm frozen as metal digs into my back, pushing me forward. I'm falling into something, and some kind of brilliance is erupting around me, but I don't know why or how. Suddenly, I stop falling, and the light drains from the room. The walls close in again, and I realise they somehow moved, stretching outward into space I didn't know existed. Horrified, I twist my body around. The door is open, and right outside the secret room stands Esme and Veronica, glowering at the two of us. Veronica's hand is up against the side wall, as if maybe she was the one who stopped the expansion.

Anya's mouth falls open. "What is this sorcery?" she gasps. "What is going on here? How… how did *that* happen?"

"You're in no position to be questioning *us*," says Veronica frigidly.

"You went against our orders and *picked* the lock?" demands Esme angrily.

"I'm so sorry," I start.

"It wasn't her fault," interrupts Anya.

"I'm sure it wasn't, but you should both be getting to bed." Veronica's voice is stone hard. She isn't looking at me or Anya.

"Mother—" begins Anya.

"*Now!*"

Anya's face is filled with pain and alarm, but she can't feel worse than I do at this moment. I'm the one who suggested this foolish idea in the first place. I should have kept my mouth shut. Anya slouches off to our bedroom. I'm not sure if I should follow her, so I decide to stay with Esme and Veronica so they can break the news that they don't want me anymore.

A minute passes, and they still don't speak. At least Veronica is now looking at me, but the anger her gaze holds is unbearable.

I force myself to push out some words. "I understand if you want to unadopt me."

Hurt flashes through Veronica's eyes. "We would never do that."

I release a breath I didn't know I was holding. "Really?" I ask in bewilderment. "I broke into a locked, forbidden room that I *knew* I wasn't allowed to be in. I betrayed your trust."

Esme sighs, running her fingers through her hair. "Maybe, but we have no doubt you can earn it back."

"I understand the pain you've been through, like I said at the orphanage," Veronica tells me gently, with pity I don't deserve. "But we're your family, Ora. We're here for you. If you have any questions, we'll answer them."

I have dozens of questions, though I doubt they'd actually give me honest responses. I remind myself they're trying to keep Anya and me safe in their own way, so I nod and breathe a soft thank-you.

"Just don't do anything like this again," says Veronica quickly. "Talk to us instead, all right? Trust us."

"All right." The words come out quickly. "I'll do that."

Veronica's lips are pressed tightly together in a line. Finally, she nods. "Off to bed now, Ora."

I scurry away gratefully. Anya is lying on her bed, completely zonked out. With a sad smile, I pull thin blankets over her body, and she shudders at my touch. I stretch out on my bed, thinking of the green glimmer in the secret room. My eyes are still burning. I was falling forward… but where would it lead to if Veronica and Esme hadn't found us? Is it truly dangerous? If it isn't, then how is it connected to the death of Anya's father? There are so many mysteries; and then, of course, the things we overheard Veronica saying to Esme. What man awaits her in

Australia? How will he be able to help search for Dax, if he's such a madman?

Seconds ago, Veronica told me to trust her and Esme. It's just hard when there are so many secrets buried in this house.

6
Anya

The following morning, Esme comes in far later than usual.

I'm wide awake as soon as the door opens, and I look over to Ora, who's reading a book. She's an early riser, and it's past eleven when I check my watch, so I wonder how long she's been up. Esme places the regular tray between my knees; but today there is only one silvery plate with a slightly too brown bagel and cream cheese. The drink is iced apple, though my glass is only half-filled.

I can't help blurting, "This looks delightful."

"I'm sorry," says Esme flatly. "I had to help your mother pack. It took a while."

"Well, how long is she going away for?" I demand. "I thought she was going *around*. That's what we were told, anyway."

"She is," agrees Esme. "She doesn't know how long for is all. It could be days, possibly weeks if the answers don't fall straight into her lap."

My eyes narrow to slits. "After all that trauma last night, I'm surprised she'd still leave. It's so abrupt. Don't you think so, Esme?"

"She wants to find Dax," she says coolly. She turns to Ora and gives her the tray of the bagel and juice. "How was your night?"

"It was fine," she replies with a smile. "Thank you for the food."

Ora is the best actress I know. She's smooth and confident, and no one would ever suspect a thing. No one would guess how upset and confused she is on the inside. She must have learned to keep to herself in the forlorn orphanage.

"No problem," Esme says. "I'll leave you girls to it. No more plotting to break into strange, unsafe rooms."

"We know better than that now," Ora cuts in, "and again, we're so sorry."

"As long as it doesn't happen a second time."

It already did, I simper to myself. I can't help being angry at Esme, for keeping secrets from me and letting my mother travel to Australia to someone who could kill her. I wish I could squeeze the truth right out of her. Instead of saying these things, I mumble, "Of course."

"Good." Esme perks up. "Now be quick, girls. Your mother wants to leave as soon as possible, so stuff down those bagels."

"Right. We'll do that."

As soon as she exits the room, I start babbling to Ora worriedly. She's much more controlled than me.

"Pretend to be sick," she suggests. "I don't want to lie again, but I will if it's necessary to save Veronica. She'll have to stick around until you get 'better', and that'll buy us some time, and we can form a real plan with her to save Dax."

I shrug. It's not a bad idea, though there are some flaws. Forget the flaws, though. There's nothing else. "What do I do?"

Ora gets right to it, and part of me thinks she may be a bit excited. "Wait here." She returns in a couple of moments with a soaking washcloth. "Put this on your forehead."

I lay it over my skin obediently, and I fight back a scream when it touches me. "Ora, this is scorching!" I shriek. "Take it off!"

She shakes her head at me. "Keep that on for a few more minutes and then start doing jumping jacks."

"What? Why?"

"You need some red in your cheeks," says Ora, hastily rushing around. "Thermometer?"

I dig into my drawers and pass her the only one our house owns. Luckily, I was sick the most recently, so it's in my possession. "What are you going to do? Break it so she can't check my real temperature?"

"No, that would be far too obvious," snorts Ora. "I'm going to heat it up under the tap."

How does she know how to do all this? I watch her leave in amazement. I clench my teeth as real sweat breaks out all over my body.

This washcloth may trigger a heat stroke if I'm not careful. My face burns, and I can't take it anymore. I peel it off me and start exercising. Ora soon comes in.

"This is definitely working." She grins, sliding the thermometer back into its original spot in my drawer. "Good. I'll go get Esme and Veronica. Now get in your bed."

I force my body underneath my sheets. This is the last place I want to be, but I'll do anything to help my family. Soon enough, all three barge into my room. Ora stands behind the two adults with believable fear in her eyes.

"Anya?" says Mother, kneeling beside me and pressing her hand against my forehead. "Darling, you're steaming!"

Yes, and I paid the price, I think bitterly.

I mutter in my frailest voice, "The thermometer is in my drawer."

"Right, good idea." Mother pushes the device into my mouth, and her eyes go round with surprise. "Anya, you're 102 degrees!"

Ora is brilliant.

"Mother," I tremble. "Please don't leave."

She pecks a kiss on my cheek. "Esme is here with you. She will keep me updated. But I really must go, or I'll miss my flight."

"Miss your flight?" I repeat tiredly. "I thought you were going…"

"Around, I know," says Mother, and she nods. "I'm visiting many places."

"Over how many days?"

"I'm not sure, but time will zoom by. Now I must go. Goodbye, Anya."

"No!" I yelp. "No, don't go!" I don't know what to do, and it looks like Ora's run out of ideas as well.

"She's so sick," pleads Ora. "What if she's not okay?"

"She's had plenty of fevers before," Mother says gently. "I hate to leave you so shortly after your adoption, but I truly will miss you. We'll talk over the phone every day, all right?"

"Mother…" I begin, about to confess that we overheard her conversation with Esme.

"Oh, gosh, my taxi's here!" Mother kisses Ora's head hurriedly. "I'll be back before you know it!"

I cry out, but Mother takes no notice. "Goodbye, Esme," she says quickly.

"Take care of yourself." Esme swallows, and I see that her cheeks have gone red. "Please, Veronica, you must."

"I will, of course," Mother says, almost in a dismissive tone. "Goodbye, everyone! Be safe. I'll see you all soon!"

And with that, she disappears through the door.

I hide my face in my pillow, feeling tears well in my eyes. Guilt threads through my insides as I let her go, knowing she's distancing herself from this house by the second.

"Let me go and help," Esme mutters, and she leaves Ora and me alone.

"I'm sorry," Ora whispers to me, joining me on my bed. "I really thought it would work."

"I did, too," I admit, sitting up. "It's not your fault. You only wanted to help. Now you see. Once my mother's mind is made up, there's no changing it. She would've gone sooner or later, anyway. No number of lies will influence her."

"She's stubborn."

"Like mother, like daughter."

"So what do you want to do?" Ora asks, looking to me for direction. "Should we come clean to Esme that we overheard their conversation? Should we try to get the truth out of her?"

I shake my head. "I don't think that would work. She'd deny it or make up some fake story. Plus, it would get you into more trouble."

Ora shrinks. "So… do we have any plan at all, then?"

Do we?

"We can hope that our mother knows what she's doing," I say with a small shrug, though the words sound stupid and needy to my own ears.

Ora sighs. "You're right. She's a smart woman. She's obviously visiting that madman to get some information, and she did promise us she'd come straight back with Dax in her arms." She seems uncertain, though, and I can't help but notice it.

"Yeah. I guess," is all I say in response.

Ora seems to read my mind, because she says, "It'll all work out in the end. Everything. I promise."

I nod, but in the back of my mind, I know we should be doing something. Letting Mother handle it by herself, feels wrong.

Once again, I am sitting back and letting the world damage my family. I am sitting back and being useless.

Yet I lie down in my bed, allow myself to cry, and do nothing at all.

Summer days pass slowly, and they form a whole week. The time is wasted on doing nothing about Mother or Dax. Netflix, more soccer, a whole lot of food, and napping. I feel horrible waking up and going to sleep. Ora is always right by my side to comfort me and make sure I'm okay, and I always tell her I am, but she can see right through me. It's one of her many gifts.

The house feels lonely; like there are pieces missing. No father, mother, or brother. It's terrifying knowing that one of them is already gone, and there's a possibility that the other two won't come back.

Mother calls as often as she can, which is every couple of days. But four days have passed, and we haven't talked to her.

Esme continues being secretive, and I get more and more suspicious of her by the day.

Then, one day, when the three of us are eating dinner, Esme gets a phone call. "It's your mother," she tells us.

"Can we talk?" I ask eagerly.

"Remind her it's been several days," Ora adds.

"Sure, I'll give it to you in a second," says Esme, putting the phone against her ear. "Hello, Veronica! How's it going? What? What…? How…?" Her mouth has dropped open in shock, her face paled.

"What is it?" Ora demands.

Esme shakes her head, getting to her feet. She walks away from us, all the way upstairs where we can't hear.

"Do you think she's all right?" I cry. "Do you think she…?"

"Well, she's calling Esme, so she can't be that injured," Ora says reassuringly, but her voice has a skittish edge to it. "Esme will let us talk, won't she?"

"I hope so," I mutter, my insides fluttering with nerves.

We sit in silence, picking at our food, but not eating.

After about fifteen minutes pass, Esme returns with the phone clutched in her hand.

"Everything okay?" Ora asks serenely.

I can't stay as calm. "You said you'd give us the phone!" I practically shout.

"She couldn't talk any longer," says Esme gravely.

"Why?" Ora presses.

"Is she all right?" I shudder. "What happened?"

"Well..."

"Well?"

"Your mother's been arrested."

7

Anya

"ARRESTED?" ORA REPEATS. "HOW?"

Esme looks at the floor. "I'm not entirely sure how to explain. I didn't get enough details."

Anger rises inside me. "You know," I say, "I've had enough of this."

Esme's eyebrows arch. "That is no way to talk to—"

I explode. "We know you've been keeping secrets! We heard you! We heard everything you said that day before Mother left. Who is she visiting? Why is her life at risk? What's in the stupid room that you've concealed from me for my whole life? You may have listened to Mother, but she's not here anymore, and that's your fault. She's gone! Arrested for a reason I know is false. Dax and Mother are both in grave danger, and I think you know why… so the least you can do is tell us the truth! We want to know about the stupid room. What the hell was that? Why was there some luminous green light? What would we have discovered if you hadn't caught us?" There are tears streaming down my face, and Ora, beside me, clutches my hand soothingly.

Surprisingly, Esme nods and says, "You're right. I owe you both an apology, but you must understand that I did what I did for your safety. There is another world, far more dangerous than ours, that your mother and I have been trying to keep you from. It seems that things have gotten so bad that we're forced to drag you into this whole chaotic disaster."

"Good," I blurt. "We want to be dragged in."

"You want to be dragged in because you are a mere child seeking adventure," spits Esme, her tone icier now. "But when you find out what's behind the locked door, your life will change forever. You will not be ordinary people any more. You will be forced to live with many secrets that could threaten others' very existences if you ever jabbered to a soul. You are taking on big responsibilities, *both* of you. You will hold people's lives in your hands, and you will unsheathe secret after secret. You might want to break under the pressure, but you can't. You have people relying on you. Your brother is relying on you; and now, so is your mother."

"We're up to the challenge," says Ora earnestly. "I swear we'll get the job done."

"You say that now," says Esme with a chuckle, but she leads us up the stairs to the locked door. "You're about to see extraordinary things. You will be shocked. Do not crack, or I will not task you with the mission that must be completed to save your brother. Do not crack now, or you will crack when it is too late, and you will face the monster of death."

The way she speaks is almost hysterical. I would laugh if she didn't look so serious. Her eyes are blacker than ever, and she's shaking tremendously. It's making me nervous.

"We're ready," Ora tells Esme.

Esme closes her eyes, and she thrusts her palm against the door. The door swings open. I catch a gasp in my throat. We are in the empty room again, but I know what she will do next. She finds the unstable brick in the wall ahead of us, and she presses down hard. A stronger green glow than last week fills the room.

Something hard is pushed into my back, and the same falling sensation overcomes me. Everywhere I look, green blinds me. It gets brighter and brighter, and when my stomach is churning angrily, I finally hit a hard surface. I let out a huff of frustration, trying to see, but I'm blinded from the blaze. Finally, after what seems an eternity, my vision floods back to me. I look around dizzily.

Shelves and shelves of books are all I see, reaching upward, far above me. When I get to my feet, I realise there are five floors. Ora's body is stretched out beside me, and she is only just regaining consciousness; unlike Esme, who stands tall on the other side of me, looking more alive than ever.

"A library?" I practically scream, when Ora is standing beside me. "You've been hiding a *library* from us?"

"It's much more than that. This is the Secret Athenaeum," says

Esme, as if that explains everything.

"And this is shocking how, exactly?" I demand, cocking an eyebrow.

Esme ignores me and walks up a flight of stairs, beckoning us to follow. "It's a place of wonders. Of magic," she whispers, as if there are other people here.

"Magic?" repeats Ora. "Magic is just unexplained science."

"No." Esme shakes her head gravely. "Magic is an unleashed monstrosity waiting to swallow you whole and drive you mad. It is something much more irresistible and binding than science. Something much stronger. *Much* more dangerous."

"That word… *mad*," Ora says, curious. "Is this connected to where Veronica's gone? To the man she went to visit?"

"In a way," Esme agrees thoughtfully. "Now, Anya, brace yourself. We're heading to the third floor."

Brace yourself? What is that supposed to mean? We walk up more stairways, and I need to hold the engraved railings to keep myself balanced. When we reach the third floor, Esme walks over to a giant chest. It is long and wooden, with tiny holes dotted along the sides.

"What is this?" I ask, my throat dry.

"You open it," Esme tells me. "There is magic in your bones, clearly. You are a Blackstone."

"And me?" Ora says. "I'm not a Blackstone."

"You are now."

"But, by blood, I'm not biological to Anya."

"But you were meant to be here," says Esme, and she nods. "There was a pull from Veronica to you. You are clearly a child of magic, too. You opened the wall."

"Yes, but…"

"You opened the door to the room as well."

"Yes, but I did that with an eyeglass screwdriver. That means nothing," protests Ora, breathing frantically.

Esme laughs. "The eyeglass screwdriver did not do a thing. It was the power of *you*. You and Anya, I should say. Anya tried picking the lock before you came along — yes, An, I knew all about it; you weren't quite subtle enough — but it was the magic of you *together* that opened the door. You give each other undeniable strength. So, Anya, go ahead. Open the chest. You will be stunned at what you see."

I release a shaky breath. I'm not entirely sure how to do this, so I tug my eyelids shut and prod my fingers to the wood. It sizzles against my skin.

"Concentrate," Esme's voice slices through the darkness. "*Concentrate.*"

I try to close my mind to everything around me, but it's not enough. The wood gets hotter under my touch, and I let out a strangled yell. There is a movement beside me, and I realise Ora is helping me. I feed off her strength and power, and the wood starts to burn. There is a satisfying click, and when I open my eyes, I see that the chest's lock has burst. I pull it away and look at what's inside the big trunk. I gasp at the shallow-breathing body that is lying atop the wood.

"Dax?" I wheeze in disbelief. I turn to Esme, and there is not a hint of surprise in her eyes. "You knew he was here all along? He's here. He's alive. Why have you been keeping this from us? Does Mother know?"

"Of course," Esme says.

"Then… how is she out there, looking for him? How is she risking her life when he's here, healthy and fine?" I demand angrily.

"Well, he's definitely not healthy and fine," snaps Esme. "He wouldn't be stuck in this chest if he were. He's been mentally taken over."

"But… by who?" Ora asks the question now, her mouth tilted open in utter astonishment and curiosity.

"By characters inside the Ash Chronicles," replies Esme.

"What are the Ash Chronicles?" I ask with utmost curiosity. "Another thing I'm quite interested to know — how is my father involved in this?"

"Well… he was the one who discovered this library when we first moved into the house, and he discovered its unusualness. He was the one who found the Ash Chronicles. As soon as he opened its pages, he was teleported to a world of fantasy and sorcery. But once he got in, he was trapped. He got back out somehow, injured. We were never sure what had happened to him, and he refused to tell us."

"What, he just came out bleeding? How is that even possible?" Ora presses.

"I could not describe it, and there's no point interrogating me about it. I tried asking him about it multiple times, but he said he wasn't telling me for my own safety."

"How long did it take for him to recover?" I chip in.

"Too long. But when he awoke, he continued his journey. It took years, but he created his own science with his own hands. We helped here and there, but we didn't have the magic that Harlow did. He made teleporters and hourglasses especially meant for the insides of the Chronicles. There are three Chronicles — the Ash Chronicles — each one very powerful. Harlow travelled back in and out of the books, testing his creations."

"The characters inside the Chronicles... they were alive?" I ask.

Esme nods. "They hated him and swore revenge one day. Harlow had a partner in crime, Atikus. Atikus helped him with all his creations; but one day, he went into a Chronicle with Harlow and came out without Harlow. You see, the hourglasses set a time for you. You have a maximum of five days in one story, and if you take any longer, you turn into a character," says Esme.

"So... is Father a character now?" I ask in confusion.

"We don't know. The pages of the Chronicles are always blank, so you can never know who has morphed into the story and who has died. Anyway, Atikus returned here, and he was broken. He went mad, grieving for power that he could no longer grasp because he didn't have Harlow by his side."

"Where is my mother?" I say it through gritted teeth. It is a plea, a demand.

"Last week, your mother went to search for Atikus to see if he would help. He turned down her plea for help, and she stole something from him called the *Book of Enchantment*. It has spells, and she thought maybe she could go through the Chronicles with its help because Atikus refused to assist her. However, he caught her, and she pushed him away from her. He lives on a cliff, you see..."

"Wait, she pushed him off the cliff?" Ora's face goes white.

"Mother *murdered* him," I gasp.

"Well, no, not murdered," Esme says quickly. "But nearly. You can't wait for her to get out, though. You have to get inside those Chronicles."

"Why would we do that?" demands Ora.

"The characters inside the Chronicles have prophecies that tell the future," explains Esme. "They foresaw that Harlow had children, and they chose the weakest one. Dax. They visited him in his dreams, and they struck him. They bled their darkness into his mind and mentally killed him. There is an artefact in each of the three Chronicles. If you trek into each book and steal each artefact, it'll bring him back. Come."

Intrigued, Ora and I follow Esme to the top floor of the library. There are three leather-bound books that I can only presume are the Ash Chronicles, and right beside them, a wooden block with three carved recesses.

"Once you press an artefact into one of these holes, it melts into a liquid and then solidifies to a round rock. When you put all three objects into all three holes, this puzzle — called the Heart of Stone — will be complete, and it will destroy all the characters in all the Chronicles. That way, they will lose their grasp on your brother, and Dax will be alive once again. But I don't know how long we have until Dax fades away. He is an eight-year-old, after all. One can only do so much to help…"

"Why didn't Harlow destroy the books and characters? Didn't he know how harmful they could be?" Ora asks.

"He began to realise the danger," admits Esme, "but he disappeared before he could really do anything. There's this prophecy, you see, in each Chronicle. I don't know too much about it, but he got his hands on it and told us the rumours that Dax would be mentally overtaken, so we must keep him very safe."

"What exactly happened that night?" I blurt out, voice low.

"We went into your room because we heard screaming. I'm not sure how you didn't wake up. You are certainly a deep sleeper. Anyway, your mother and I grabbed him, and it looked like he was having some sort of seizure. His eyes went red and… and… we just knew. We had taken precautions to keep him safe. We never knew it could happen in our own house."

I wince, but say no more.

"Is there any way to bring a character back here?" Ora cuts in, shaking. "Can they share our teleporters?"

"No. Once a character is a character, there is no getting him or her out. A teleporter will only take a real human being — and only *one*."

I take all the information she has given me, processing it slowly.

"You must travel into each Chronicle and steal away the artefacts. This will be no easy task. Many people will want you dead." She pulls out two crystals and two hourglasses that are bigger versions of the ones I play with in the game *Headbanz*. "Keep these very safe. They will always come back to you because now, they are *yours*. But beware. Ink fire will easily destroy the material of your crystal teleporters. Without them, there is no way back home."

"Ink fire? What is that?" Ora asks.

"Something dangerous."

"How?"

"It will destroy everything in its path," warns Esme. "Including your teleporters."

I'm somehow having trouble piecing together that I'm going to be entering a world of madness, and this will save my brother. I take the two objects from Esme, tucking them into my pockets, and Ora does the same.

"So, can we go?" I question. "I don't entirely know how this all works, but shouldn't we start our adventure now?"

"Don't be impatient." Esme raises her eyebrows as if in warning. "Now, you are tired. You are not ready. You must get a good sleep and gather your strength. Then you can take your leave."

"Fine," Ora agrees. "That's probably good. I think I need to digest this overwhelming amount of material."

"I assumed so. Now, back down the stairs we go, and into bed."

Pulling the door open thankfully requires no magic. We walk back into our hallway easily and head to our room. This much information has made my brain tired. As soon as I reach my mattress, I collapse and let sleep consume me.

The next morning, Esme makes Ora and me big breakfasts and wakes us up earlier than usual. She tells us to eat up, even though Ora insists that she lost her appetite as soon as she stepped into the athenaeum yesterday. But Esme is firm, so Ora eats, and I force myself to do the same. I nibble on my waffle, but as soon as I do, I feel like puking it right back out of my mouth. I would usually find this delicious, but I can't eat today.

Esme gets to it right away. As soon as she sets the trays on our laps, she starts to chatter about the journey ahead of us. "The first Ash Chronicle will lead you to a town called Floe City, the capital of the country, Iciclone. Queen Glacier rules the whole town. She watches over *everyone*. Her guards are everywhere. Now, from what I remember the last time I was in there, she had two missing children — babies. They died thirteen years ago, but she believes it was staged, and they're still out there somewhere. Most everyone thinks she's wrong, but they would never dare say such a thing. She's an evil woman, and in the Frost Palace — *her* palace — lies the first artefact, the Ice Jewel. When you see it, you'll know it. She protects it, and she has watchmen always on the lookout for people who may want to steal it. You will need to get it at any cost. I have an idea that will get you to the artefact quickest. It may sound silly, possibly complex, but you'll have to get the queen to trust you."

"How do you presume we do that?" I snort, but Ora looks fascinated to know, her face twisted in intrigue.

"Well, you could pretend to be Glacier's daughters. You can both pull off being thirteen," says Esme, content with Ora's excitement. "However, she has white hair — hair as white as snow — so, of course, her daughters are expected to look alike."

"But... I have black hair, and Ora has brown-blonde. Our faces don't even look alike!" I protest at her warped plan.

"I'll handle that," waves away Esme. "Come. We're going to the athenaeum right away. Get up and out of your beds."

Curious, Ora and I follow her into the locked room, where we are greeted with the familiar green light and the feeling of falling.

I try getting up as soon as I feel the ground, but my head disagrees and drags me back down until I am completely aware of everything around me. Ora is sitting up beside me, and in front of us stands Esme. Her eyes are closed, her lips in a thin line of concentration.

"Esme?" Ora says warily. "Are you all right?"

Suddenly, Esme's fingers reach forward to my head, pressing down on my scalp. I let out a frightened scream, but Ora is nodding her head approvingly.

"What… what is she doing?" I shriek, but I soon realise. Streaks of white crawl down my hair until my full mop is covered. "How did you do that?"

She ignores me, completely focused on her magic. She rubs her palms over my forehead, wiping them across my skin.

"Wow," gasps Ora, and this time I have no idea what is happening to me. "Your eyes just turned blue. I assume that's the queen's eye."

Esme's eyes flap open. "That's right, it is. As blue as the ocean, she likes to say. Ora, now your turn."

"Er…" Ora shakes off her nerves. "All right."

Ora still looks beautiful with her new hair and eye shade. Her locks are a bit longer than mine, so Esme levels it up with my head and snips a few inches straight off her by the rub of a few fingers. Then, with her nimble fingers, she braids Ora's hair up, then mine.

"Perfect," murmurs Esme, allowing herself to relax. "You look exactly alike. Keep in mind, though, my magic will only work for so long. On your fourth day, the magic will start fading. I know you have five days in the Chronicle, but get the artefact as quickly as you can, or the queen will see you for who you truly are and will make sure you never come back into her palace again. Remember, your names are Meadow and Mabel. Now, look at your wrists, girls. This is very important."

I turn over my arm to see a small, golden snowflake etched into my skin.

"The queen got this engraved in her children the day they were born," explains Esme. "I put it on you so that if she asks how she would know you're truly her children, you can show her your snowflakes."

"How do you know this is an exact replica?" Ora asks sensibly. "The queen will surely know we're fakes."

"Harlow brought back lots of photos from his adventures through the Chronicles in case they were clues to some bigger picture. He sneaked into many places, and your mother and I chipped in once in a while. I've memorised that tattoo, seeing it so many times. My memory is photographic, you do know."

"Thank you for your help, Esme," I say with a grateful smile.

"It's you going into the danger," she says quietly, and I see the plain guilt on her face.

"We'll be fine," I assure her, starting to walk up the staircase. Ora follows quickly until we reach the top floor.

"Do you have your teleporters and hourglasses?" Esme asks us, and we both give firm nods in response. "Okay. Go ahead."

"Do you have to..." — I clear my throat — "go downstairs or something, so you don't get sucked into the book as well?"

"No, my dear. I'm too old now. I don't have that amount of power anymore," says Esme sadly. "But you do. You have the power to save everyone you care about. If you don't complete this, more people will get hurt. More people will lose their lives."

"All right." Ora's voice comes out as a croak, and I realise she's nervous. "And if we can't pull through...?"

"You will."

"If we..."

"You will get the job done." Esme's voice is firm; an order.

I breathe in. "No pressure, then."

"Good luck," Esme whispers. She reaches onto the high shelf and seizes the very first Chronicle. She gives it to me and looks away with a shallow breath. "Open it. Don't let me down."

I gulp and flip the pages, my heart hammering in my chest. My fingers press against a blank page, and Ora joins me.

Light devours me, and I am launched into a vortex of colours. I spin down, down, down, my body rippling with magic.

The adventure is only just beginning.

FLOE CITY

A tale of an evil queen, a battle to perilous deaths, and a jewel holding undeniable power…

8
Ora

The air turns from warm and balmy to crisp and fresh.

I'm plummeting, and then my body plunges into a soft blanket of dankness. My head is throbbing. It takes me a minute to realise that I'm buried by snow.

"Agh!" I gasp in frustration, swiping the icicles from my skin and sitting up. My eyes adjust to the lighting, and I look down in awe. We are atop a miniature frosty hill, overlooking a small part of the city. There is a marvellous array of housing, all made of ice. People are out and about, adults whistling to themselves and children playing Frisbee. No one seems to notice us, so I take a few seconds to admire the residences. Everything is so beautiful that I forget about Anya for a second. When she pops into my mind, I frantically look around and am relieved when I see her figure pushed deep into the snow. I quickly scramble to pull her out into the cool air. I am alarmed when I see the white hair at first, but then I remember Esme's magic and calm down.

Anya's eyes flitter open. Like me, she takes in a few breaths, gathers herself together, and then recollects where we are and why. The information must come flooding back promptly, because she gasps and crawls onto her knees. "Ora!" she exclaims, thankful to see me. "I'm *freezing*!"

"Yes, I know," I reply with a shiver, rubbing my hands over my thinly-covered arms. "But... I think I may be able to use that to our advantage. Come with me quickly. Don't tumble down, or we'll make fools of ourselves."

We make our way down the hill. My boots are completely drenched. I tried to dress appropriately for a place called Floe City, but I haven't had too much time in the Blackstone household to go shopping and pick out some new attire, so I'm stuck in leather boots, a small cream jacket, and some atrocious red velvet trousers, whereas Anya is bundled in thick layers and has a hat and mittens.

As we walk, Anya tells me, "I think we felt like we were falling, but physically, we just appeared in this place, and luckily, no one saw us appear out of thin air."

I'd already figured this out, but I smile in agreement anyway. We reach the slope of the hill, and I hiss to Anya over my shoulder, "Follow my lead."

She nods and starts off after me. I bump into a man on purpose. His book slips from his hands, and I quickly pick it up and give it back to him. "I'm so sorry, sir." I tremble.

"Not a problem," says the man kindly. "Have a good day."

"W-wait!" I call out after him, relieved when he turns around. "I was wondering… where's Frost Palace?"

He looks confused. "Every Floer knows the route to the palace."

"Yes, of course," I tell him carefully, "but we just arrived here. We're the queen's lost daughters. We know it sounds crazy, of course, but we do have proof to show her. Although she'll know us when she sees us." I hold up my wrist to show him the golden snowflake.

The man laughs in disbelief. "Many people pull that one."

I narrow my eyes. "Do we look like we're acting?"

He laughs. "I really don't know, girls. So many people act about this matter."

"I wouldn't walk into my doom willingly," I say dully. "Which way is the palace, please?"

The man surprisingly digs into his backpack and pulls out a map. "I don't know if this situation is real or not, but I want to see how this plays out. Good luck, I suppose."

"Thank you, though we won't be needing luck," Anya says almost snobbishly, grabbing the map daintily and handing it to me. "Your kindness has been appreciated."

With that, the man scurries away, and Anya lets a small giggle erupt from her mouth. "We're really nailing this, aren't we?" she whispers to me, but I've already started on the map.

"We're not too far," I tell her. "I've made a plan." I chatter to her about it excitedly as we trudge through the wet grounds until, many minutes after, we can see a glittering palace just ahead. I've never been in one before. I'm anxious to see the halls and the artefact that is so known around here.

There are two armed guards standing outside the doors.

"Look afraid," I hiss to Anya, but she already has the expression hammered down.

"Rime card," says the guard on the left in a gruff voice.

I breathe in a rattled breath. I assume the card is some kind of ID around here that allows one to enter the palace. "We… we need to find the queen," I say desperately. "We have no ID. We're her… daughters."

The guards don't move an inch, unaffected, and then one lets out a brusque chuckle. "You may have her eyes and hair, but we've had plenty of people like you before. Coming for the money — or worse, to steal something. Like our precious jewels."

I flinch. "We would never do such a thing," I retort, trying to look offended. "Mabel, your wrist."

At first, Anya doesn't react, but then a flash of realisation crosses her face, and she rolls up her sleeve to reveal the tattoo.

The gruff guard inspects it closely, and the other one observes mine. They exchange a long glance and stand there, unmoving.

Finally, Anya demands, "I'm sorry, but we need to see the queen immediately."

"We'll see if she'll see you," says the gruff guard, clearly not believing us. She and her companion open up the door for us and lead us in. As soon as they leave us, I start admiring the palace's beauty. Words can't describe everything — there's a gorgeous rug that has white streaks of glass running through its material; in place of beams, icebergs, climbing to the ceiling so high I have to strain my neck to see; five dangling chandeliers that have tiny frozen ice droplets instead of candles; a gigantic fountain that gushes snowflakes… it's everything I could imagine and more. I'm not done looking when the guards return.

"The queen wants to see you immediately," the female says with a frown. "I must warn you, she doesn't entirely believe it. She doesn't like being given false hope. She will look at your stitched brands very closely to see if they're placed in exactly the right spots and if it has the exact design. When people fake these, they make them look very simple… there is a special embroidery that only she knows. You'd better hope for your sakes that you're not lying, or she'll kill you."

"Hmph, that's no way to speak to a princess," huffs Anya, heedless of the danger. "You'll see that we're true royals after our meeting with the queen. You'll bow down to us and beg for mercy."

But I can glimpse a small amount of uncertainty in her eyes as she speaks confidently. Esme did tell us she had mastered imprinting the tattoo, but is it specific enough? I hope so, or our journey will come to a fast end, and an ugly one, too.

The guards escort us up a glass stairway, through a door, and into a massive room. The walls are shimmery gold, and there is a long white carpet leading to a beautiful throne of twisting trails of ice and looping designs. In the seat sits a flawless woman with a crown atop her curly white hair. She is wearing a silken gown that displays six hues of blue. Clasped in her left hand is a curved staff with a purple gem at the top.

"Guards, leave us," she orders, and her voice thunders through the room, making me shudder.

"Yes, Queen Glacier," they reply in harmony, then rush away, closing the door gently behind them.

"Girls," she says, her voice smooth and cool. "Come to me."

I will myself to stop trembling, but I can't stop. I step towards her and hold up my wrist. Her nail trickles over it. She scratches it, as if she expects it to fall off, but thankfully it stays put on my skin. She looks to the right, and I realise there is a framed photo of this snowflake tattoo. It looks exactly like mine, and I bite back a smile. Glacier inspects Anya, equally as carefully.

But then, when I think we've gotten away with it, Glacier calls out, "The Detector."

One of the guards at the door shuffles in with a black device that somewhat resembles a scanner from the supermarkets. Glacier grabs it and waves the guard away. She takes my wrist roughly and somehow scans my tattoo. Then she does the same to Anya.

"Guard," Glacier mumbles, and the same one scuttles back and takes the scanner.

He taps it twice, and two tiny folds of paper slip from the slit at the top of the scanner. His eyebrows cock. "The papers show positive," the guard says.

"Give me that," Glacier breathes, and her eyes are round. "This is… impossible. My Meadow. My Mabel. How can this… how can this be?" Tears cloud her eyes.

Both Anya and I are familiar with our fake story. "We were stolen, raised somewhere far away. We were whipped and beaten whenever we asked about travelling here, to Floe. We felt a special connection with the place. We did our research and realised the truth. We escaped here. We're afraid our capturers will find us."

"No," purrs Glacier, icy but protective. "Do not be afraid, my children. We will catch who stole you from me, and we will torment them, and we will destroy them. Together."

"That sounds delightful, Mother," I growl lightly, putting my head in her lap and trying not to jerk away when she strokes my hair.

"You have had such hard lives," whispers Glacier. "And… you are wet."

"Yes, we were pushed into a snowbank when we asked a man where to find you," Anya makes up quickly. "It was so awful."

I give her a side glance at the terrible excuse, but Glacier doesn't seem suspicious. She seems convinced and angered.

"You've been mistreated," she hisses. "No one mistreats royalty, especially when they belong to me." There are protective tears streaming down her face, and I wonder guiltily how she will feel when we disappear with the Ice Jewel.

"Oh, Mother." I weep into her arms. "We've finally found home."

"I've been waiting. Everyone secretly gave up hope, but I never did," says Glacier, shaking her head fiercely. "There have been so many children coming in here, pretending to be you. I had to execute them immediately."

Anya winces. "Yes. Of course."

I nod as if I understand.

"We're going to celebrate your return," murmurs Glacier. "We're going to have lots of parties, every night."

"Oh, it's quite all right," I tell her quickly, not wanting to waste any time getting the artefact. "We're tired, and we want to spend our days with you only."

"Well, of course," says Glacier, "but we have years together. We can have a party in a couple of days if you wish."

"But…"

"Perfect! I'll get the servants to start planning. Meanwhile, we must get you into some nice clothes."

"Sounds delightful!"

"Will you show us to our room?" Anya asks eagerly.

Queen Glacier laughs. "Well, the servants will do that, of course."

I set my jaw, but force myself to nod. "But of course. I do apologise, Mother. We're a bit rusty on living royally."

"I would expect nothing more, after how you were treated. Must have lived in a dump, looking at your clothes now." Glacier tosses her head back and laughs, taking a strand of my hair between her fingers. "You have no idea how happy I am to see you, girls."

Anya nods. "We've been waiting our whole lives as well."

Glacier beams and picks up a bell from the small table beside her. She rings it, and right away, two servants rush into the room.

"Yes, Your Majesty?" squeaks a small, mouse-like man.

"These are my daughters, Meadow and Mabel. Don't stand there looking so shocked. Get to it. Change them, bathe them, and get them to their reserved room, the one I've been waiting on. Make sure of it," Glacier orders them. "You are now their maids."

"Yes, of course, Your Majesty. Thank you, Your Majesty," says the man, looking a little dazed. "Come with us, Your Royal Highnesses."

I take Anya's hand, and I can feel the excitement surging through her veins. We follow the servants through frosted hallways to a chamber ten times bigger than Anya's. It's stunning, with two grand king beds, four bathrooms — I don't know what we're supposed to do with so many toilets — and a wondrously big window. It is also positively the most freezing place I've ever been in my life. This whole castle makes me shiver with both the creeps and the cold.

"Meadow?" says the female servant. "I'll take you."

"I can bathe alone," I tell her, my cheeks flushing.

"Queen's orders," she tells me bleakly, and I know there's no arguing.

Anya gives me one last pained glance as the timorous man drags her away.

The woman rids me of my clothes, dunks my body into cool water and scrubs at me with soap. She takes a pitcher, fills it up, and drops it over my head like I'm a baby. I splutter, and she shakes her head but doesn't say a thing. Then she tells me to get out of the tub, wraps a rough towel around me and dries my body forcefully. Luckily, she doesn't try to clothe me, instead handing me a long-embroidered dress. It's beautiful, but it's too much.

"Please," I say, "is there anything else? Literally anything?"

"No. Queen's orders," she says flatly, and turns her back as I change into the long frock.

"Right. I'm changed."

She turns back to me and nods approvingly. "It looks good on you. Come."

Anya is waiting outside for me with two servants, and she looks wonderful in her own dress, which is similar to mine.

"Epic," she breathes.

"All right, you two, we're going to dinner now," the woman who bathed me says sternly. There's a bit of envy to her expression, I realise. She must be treated horribly by the queen, with no respect. Like she's not even a human being. She's just a poor lady who dusts the floors. I shudder that I'm pretending to be such a monster's daughter.

"What are your names?" I ask the servants suddenly.

My bather looks up, surprised. "We're referred to as servant one and servant two." Then she adds hastily, "Or if it's easier, just one and two. I am One. He is Two."

I laugh. "I'm not going to call you a *number*. Who do you think I am? I'll tell you what, names are easier to remember than numbers, anyway." It's not really true, but it seems to do the trick, nonetheless.

The woman gathers herself as if she's forgotten for a second. Then, she says, "I am Charlene. This is my husband, Bertrand."

Bertrand bows.

"We don't need to be bowed to," I tell them, waving my hands kindly, but Anya arches an eyebrow in my direction.

"Yes, you do," insists Charlene, and this time I don't argue. "Come with us to the main dining hall."

Anya comes to my side as we walk and whispers to me, "Don't be too nice, or they'll suspect you're not the queen's daughter."

I shrug, but she's right. We have to act our roles. I should know that.

I feel dizzy as I descend the winding stairs, but Anya takes my hand in hers, and I feel a rush of reassurance.

The dining hall has the same remarkable iced chandeliers as the lobby, but these are far larger. There are only two, swaying just above the long marble table with a top that stretches so far through the room, I have no idea how many seats there are.

There are people gathered around, chatting and laughing, and at the head of the table sits the queen. I find myself wondering about what happened to the king, but I don't have time to ask Charlene before the queen rises to her feet and announces, "Everyone, meet my lovely daughters, Meadow and Mabel."

All the unfamiliar faces stare in disbelief, but then they get up and start applauding. Anya bathes in the spotlight, but I want the floor to drag me under and swallow me whole. I try to smile and make eye contact with as many people as possible.

"Servants one and two," Glacier clips out suddenly, "get out and start serving. Do you think we have all day?"

Charlene turns red, and I feel like embracing her and yelling at Glacier. Instead, I watch her dip into a curtsy and hurry away, out the hall door, followed by a terribly anxious Bertrand.

"Darlings," says Glacier, her voice warm again, "sit. There are two spots designated for you. Every day I left them empty, because they were being saved."

"Oh, thank you, Mother," I reply graciously, sweeping elegantly down into my chair. Anya tries to do the same, but she nearly falls over a chair leg.

"Sorry about that," she sheepishly mutters. "I hurt my knee a couple of days ago, and I'm a bit… misbalanced."

"I bet it was those wretched thieves," says Glacier bitterly. "Mabel, we'll certainly get that checked out."

"Thank you, but it's healing well," says Anya with a nervous smile, as she sits down carefully.

A man in a black suit and white blouse steps in. "Your food is served."

Everything is set on the table quickly. When I think it will end, it keeps coming. Stews, salads, meats, pasta, seafood, even pizzas. It's all here. Every food I can think of is in front of me. More men and women in black suits pour in, loading piles of food onto my plate until it starts sliding over the edges.

I won't be able to eat all this. I feel bad because I know the servants below me must not be eating such a ravishing dinner as this. If I had pockets, I would stuff them with lots of food for Charlene and Bertrand.

"What would you like to drink, children?" says Glacier with a smile.

"Anything will do," I assure her.

Glacier shakes her head. "You've much to learn, but there's time. Servant seven! You! Pour them our best pinot noir, and make it quick!"

Red fills my wine glass that I didn't think was intended for me.

"Oh, um, we don't drink this… stuff," says Anya.

"Nonsense. Of course you do! You are my daughters," snorts Glacier. "This 'stuff' is our finest. I want to see you well fed. Look at how thin you are. Drink it all. I know you must find me cruel by saying this, but I'm doing it for you. You'll realise that when one of you becomes queen."

I force myself to take a sip, but it makes me feel sick. I hurtle food down my throat until I want to vomit. Finally, the black-suited servants come back into the room and clean away our plates. There are red-velvet cupcakes, tiramisu, tartlets, an assortment of gelatos, and a grand apple pie, all laid out wonderfully. I'm not in the mood, of course, and luckily, I'm not forced this time.

Glacier stands. "Hello, everyone. Thank you for coming to this dinner to celebrate my beautiful daughters. I wasn't completely sure they were alive, but God has gifted me for my good deeds. So, a toast. To Meadow and Mabel!"

Everyone clinks glasses and nibbles on their desserts, though I think it's obvious everyone's full. Finally, Anya and I are free to leave. My brain is whirring, and I'm a bit dizzy. I can tell from Anya's stumbling that she's tipsy, too. Charlene and Bertrand escort us back to our room, and I'm sure if they didn't, we would get lost.

"How was your dinner?" I ask them, having to sit down on my bed because I feel so ill.

"You should not be asking us questions like this," says Charlene quickly. "I am your maid. A mere servant."

I frown. "Well, I want to know. How was your dinner? Your stomach is practically growling. What did you eat?"

Charlene's mouth opens, then closes. "I shouldn't be discussing this with you."

"Charlene, you're far more than a mere servant," I tell her, trying to bury my frustration. "What did you eat?"

She gives in at last. "We ate nothing. The queen said to plan the parties, and there was no time for our desires, so she didn't send down any food. But it is all right. I am not complaining. It is a huge honour to be your maid. A lost princess."

I press my lips into a line. "You need to eat. The world shouldn't revolve around me and Mabel."

"But it does," laughs Bertrand. There is no anger to his voice. It's like he's simply stating a well-known fact.

I swallow. "This is unfair." Then I add, because of what Anya had told me earlier, "We're not used to the attention, and now we don't want it."

"You are princesses," says Charlene. "You will get used to it."

We reach the room just then, and Charlene takes me into the bathroom, where she gives me a nightgown to change into.

Then there is a knock on the door, and Queen Glacier steps in. "Flee, servants. If my daughters need you, they will ring their bells."

They nod and scamper off, leaving us with the cold-hearted woman who starved them.

"Mother," Anya croaks, swallowing her hatred, "I missed you for the short time you were gone."

"I felt the same way," she agrees. "I want to spend more time with you. Meadow, may I braid your hair?"

I nod, trying not to cringe when she sits behind me on my bed. Her fingers trail over my scalp, and I can feel her nails as she begins to braid. I'd rather do it myself, but I don't dare tell her that.

"So, Mother," says Anya carefully, "that dinner was wonderful."

"Wasn't it?" she agrees. "It had to be, of course. You are the best, so you deserve the best."

"Yes, of course," says Anya. "I just have a question."

"Hm? Of course, darling," murmurs Glacier.

"Whatever happened to the king?" Anya asks.

I feel Glacier's hands stiffen in my hair, and she pulls too tightly. "Pardon me?"

"I'm sorry, I didn't mean to step out of line," says Anya hastily.

Glacier raises her hand and begins to talk. "The king was a bad man. He was a horrible ruler, too. Flimsy. Too soft. He was caught having an affair with my very own maid, Karly. He told me he loved me, and he betrayed me. You could imagine how ashamed I felt!"

"So what did you do?" asks Anya.

"I was given no choice but to get rid of both him and Karly. I guess your research wasn't very thorough."

"No. Sorry, Mother."

"Yes, hm, well, not your fault, is it?"

"No, Mother."

She tugs on my hair silently, making me wince. Finally, she tightens a band around the end and slides off the bed with satisfaction. "Mabel? Ready for your turn, dear? I think, for you, I'll do a nice bun."

"How about in the morning?" Anya moans. "I'm so exhausted from everything that has happened today."

"Oh. Of course, I'll let you get your beauty sleep. Anything else before I leave?" Glacier asks, making her way to the door.

"Actually" — I perk up — "one thing."

"Yes?"

"I'm starving again."

"Of course, my Meadow." She beams at me. "I'll send your maid up right away. For you as well, Mabel?"

"Um…"

I arch an eyebrow.

Anya catches onto my plan and nods.

"Then I'll send both your maids," decides Glacier.

"Perfect. Thank you. Goodnight." I grin until she disappears through the door, and then my mouth quickly deepens back into a scowl. "She's awful."

Anya collapses into her bed and agrees. "This place is super nice, but certainly not the people inside."

Soon, Charlene and Bertrand come in with trays of stunning dinner.

"For you," I whisper.

Charlene looks tempted, but she shakes her head grimly. "If the queen ever found out, Your Highness…"

"We'd be fired. Eating our mistresses' food," tuts Bertrand. "Please, do enjoy. Though the thought was kind."

"We don't want it," says Anya stubbornly. "We only got it for you."

"But… it's against the rules," wails Bertrand, though I can see how desperate he is to eat.

"Well, you work for us, so we command you to eat," I say sternly. "I… I know how you feel. I know what it's like to be hungry and be filled with neglect."

"When you were kidnapped?" Bertrand asks anxiously.

"Of course," I stumble, heart pounding as memories flood back into my mind. "Now follow my instructions and eat. It'll be our little secret. Okay?"

A smile spreads across Charlene's face. "Okay. Thank you," she breathes, and bites into a chicken leg.

Anya and I triumphantly watch them savour every bite. There's so much food that they can't finish half of it. After they're done, they slip away, sparing us one last grateful glance before they take their leave to bring the remnants down to the other servants.

I get up to turn out the light when I see Anya has dozed off. I burrow under the blankets, feeling a sense of unfamiliar homesickness. This much moving around has made me tired, and I long for the same place to sleep every night. At least I have Anya, but what if something happens to her? What if I lose her, too?

I try to rid myself of the thought and let sleep swallow me whole.

I have to be well-rested for what's to come.

9
Anya

I KNOW I HAVE TO WAKE AS SOON AS I HEAR FOOTSTEPS.

A warm hand rattles me, and a voice whispers, "You have slept in! It is nearly eight thirty! I'm on strict orders from the queen to get you down and ready as soon as possible."

"Bertrand," I murmur. "Is it possible to get a few more minutes of sleep? In my other home, this wasn't sleeping in."

"No, you must get up now. Look, Meadow is already awake. If you want to prove yourself to Her Majesty and become the next queen, you will need to look sharp."

I nod. "Yes, I do want to be queen," I mumble, because I know that's expected.

"Of course," says Bertrand, shaking me once more.

"I'm up. I'm up," I groan, stripping myself from my comfortable bed. "What do I need to do?"

I am forced into a crimson dress, and then Bertrand does up my hair surprisingly nicely into a bun atop my head. "This is good." He hums. "You're ready."

I stand next to Ora, who looks dazzling in her own clothes: a sky-blue blouse and a ruffled matching skirt, rippling like ocean waves.

"Wow," I say approvingly, "that looks great."

"Thanks," Ora beams. "Back at you."

"Let's go down now. We don't want the queen to get angry," says Bertrand hurriedly.

I roll my eyes, but follow them down to the dining hall table, which is covered with breakfast. Honestly, I'm still stuffed from yesterday, but I force myself to sit next to Ora. It's just us and the queen.

"Leave us," Glacier snaps, and Charlene and Bertrand bolt away.

"Mother," says Ora, curious, "where is everyone else?"

Glacier laughs. "Well, it's not like you *know* them. We'll do proper introductions tonight at dinner, I was thinking. Today I want to give you a tour."

This sounds bland to me, but Ora perks up. "Oh, Mother, that sounds brilliant. I'd *love* to get to know the place."

Is she serious? She's more interested in exploration time than saving Dax?

"Sounds delightful," exclaims Glacier. "Everyone dreams of living here. You haven't seen our gatehouse, or the pond, or the library... the dungeons, too."

"What about that Ice Jewel I've heard so many rumours about?" Ora asks subtly. "I'd love to see what everyone is marvelling about."

Glacier says, "Well, you are my daughters, so of course, I must show you. It lies in the Glass Chamber. We have so many people protecting it, it's impossible to steal. So many people come in here for the sole purpose of taking the thing. It really is a pity. Whenever I catch a thief, it's off with their heads." She laughs, shrill and hyena-like. "But, truly, we can go in whenever you'd like and see it. I trust you completely."

I swallow my excitement. This is why Ora wanted a tour. This will be perfect. We can go in, snatch it up, and teleport ourselves home before the queen can catch us. It'll be perfect. I'm so looking forward to it that I eat a whole omelette.

"Mother, can we do the tour now?" I say, once she's finished a lobster roll and is wiping at her mouth with the corner of a napkin.

"Oh, don't be impatient," she tells me coldly. "Meadow is much more patient than you. Learn from her."

I want to growl and spit something back, but I make myself nod obediently. "Right. I apologise, Mother."

"Hm," she mumbles. "Well, I think it is about time we begin. Keep in mind, *I* am giving the tour, and this is very rare. It's an act to show you how much I love you. Especially you, Meadow, may I add."

I might be offended if I actually cared what this woman said. If anything, I feel bad for Ora, as Glacier seizes her hand and drags her forward. I follow them.

She brings us to the dungeons first, which is an awful place. People behind bars moan, and some are lying on their backs, looking very dead.

"Most of these people are waiting for their executions," Glacier explains lightly in a matter-of-fact tone. "They are traitors, or they disobeyed me, or they left the palace."

"Left?" I repeat bluntly.

"Yes," she replies. "If someone has a job here and they quit, why would I want them in my city? They'd probably try to escape to some other town, try to start 'fresh', but how is that beneficial to anyone?"

I nod. "You said *most* people," I point out. "What about the others?"

"If they're lucky, they can stick around before I decide what to do with them," says Glacier. "Or if they really did something horrible, they suffer. They suffer for an eternity, until death feels like a gift." She chuckles, and I cringe.

Even Ora, the best actress of them all, flinches.

Luckily, the queen leads us back upstairs to the main lobby. "Where would you like to go next, my children?"

"Hm. What about the Glass Chamber? The idea of the Ice Jewel intrigues me," says Ora with a hint of a smile. "I just want a glimpse."

"You can get more than a glimpse, my darling," replies Glacier. "Come."

We are led to the sixth floor, and my legs are hurting by then, but I don't let a complaint slip from my lips.

The Glass Chamber takes up the whole storey. There is a crystal door with guards crowded in front of it.

"Let us in," commands the queen.

The door opens, and as soon as I step through, my insides tingle with something unfamiliar. A magical pull, perhaps. There are glass crates everywhere, and each one has some kind of treasure inside. In the centre, in the biggest case of all, is a glittering stone. It flashes with brilliant slivers of white, gold, and blue. It takes everything in me not to run right to it and smash my fist through the glass.

"Isn't it splendid?" purrs Glacier happily.

"It truly is," agrees Ora, and I can see her glowing eyes fixated on the artefact. "May I hold it, please, Mother?"

"Of course." Glacier presses her fingers to the glass, and the jewel rises into her hands. She gently gives it to Ora.

I catch my breath. This is it. Once I see her raise her teleporter, I'll do the same, and we'll be out of the queen's grasp. But Ora just stares at the icy treasure, unmoving. "Wow. This is magical," she whispers.

"Isn't it?" Glacier beams.

"Wow," Ora repeats. And then, to my horror, she hands it back to Glacier.

"Wait," I plead. "It's my turn."

"You sound desperate for the power," tuts Glacier. "Darling Mabel, don't be impatient. Wait for it to come to you." Then she sets it atop its glass crate, and it falls silently into its spot.

I tremble with anger and surprise, but Ora doesn't seem to notice. She keeps moving, her hand clasped in Glacier's. Does she want to be here?

I participate in the rest of the tour grimly, horrible thoughts passing through me.

When Glacier finally announces it's over, she tells us we can go back to our rooms to tidy ourselves. I don't talk to Ora the whole way there, and then she plops next to me on my bed and asks me, apparently oblivious to my feelings, "What's going on? You're acting so… strange. Angry, I dare say?"

"I *am* angry," I growl. "You had the Ice Jewel in your possession, and you didn't do a thing. You gave it back to her like it was nothing."

Ora opens her mouth to protest, but I keep going. "Are you soaking up the power? Do you want to live here and be a fake princess for the rest of your life, Ora? Or shall I call you *Meadow*?"

"What are you talking about?" Ora exclaims. "All I want is to get out of this place. But what did you expect me to do, Anya? Just teleport away? As soon as I withdrew my crystal, the queen would've known. She would've hailed her guards and killed us. She'd know we're *fakes*. Then what would happen? We'd be doomed. Dax would be doomed."

I want to argue with her, but I know she's right. I want to get that artefact as soon as possible, but I can't rush it, or we'll all die, and then, so will my brother. There's still time left for him. I hope.

"I'm sorry," I mutter. "I over-reacted."

Ora shrugs, her face softening. "I understand. You want this all to be over. You want to return to your normal life of getting trays of cranberry crêpes and pineapple mocktails without a worry."

I sigh. "We have three days left, but really it's two before we start transforming back into ourselves. We can't waste time."

"We won't," Ora reassures me. "And really, Anya, all we need is contacts and a hairdresser. We could get our hair dyed. Then we'll have our full three days, okay?"

She's right again, of course. I don't think to inquire where we will get these things or if they even *exist* in this world, but honestly, I don't want to start asking more questions. I want everything to be perfect, so I just mumble lamely, "Okay," mostly to myself.

The day passes by slowly, and despite Ora's words, all I can think about is how we're wasting time. Dinnertime comes, and as food is loaded onto the table, I can only hope that the servants below us are getting some kind of meal. We are presented to many people whom I don't remember the names of: Glacier's nasty brother and sister, some dukes, an ambassador, a poet somewhere in there, I think.

I nod and smile for the whole time, even when the queen announces Meadow will most likely reign as the future queen.

I push food down my throat, and soon, Ora and I are back in our room. Charlene and Bertrand do our hair and help change us into our nightdresses.

"Did you eat?" Ora asks them, and they both nod, genuinely.

"She was happy today," says Charlene. "Good mood."

"Have a good sleep, girls," Bertrand whispers, as we climb into our beds.

"Thank you for your help," I say, practically already snoring. "Goodnight."

Then they slip away, turn the lights off, and let us sleep restless sleeps.

The next morning, I have no trouble waking up.

Today is another adventure; another day to steal the artefact.

Another chance at the prize.

Bertrand doesn't insist on bathing me today, which is a huge relief, because yesterday was one of the most uncomfortable experiences, I've ever been in. "Thanks," I tell him with a grin.

"It is a little weird looming over your every action, let's be honest," he says with a wink, and I laugh back in agreement.

"Bertrand, no matter what the queen says, you will always be my equal," I can't help blurting out in a low voice. "She can call you a servant, but you… you're my friend when she's not around."

He flushes red. "Friend?" he repeats, stunned. "Equal? You are a woman of change, Mabel. I've never been called those things."

"Well, get used to it," I say, and he chuckles. *Get used to it for two more days. Then I'll be gone, and so will you*, I think guiltily.

"Come now, Your Highness," says Bertrand, most likely mistaking my silence for regret at talking to him.

To reassure him, I loop my arm through his. He beams but pulls away. "If the queen saw," he tuts, "I would get in trouble."

Ora, dressed beautifully once again, awaits me alongside Charlene.

"Morning, Mabel," says Ora, a delicate smile playing on her curled lips that only I can understand.

"Morning, Meadow." I wink back.

"Come, Her Majesty is waiting to have breakfast with you," says Bertrand hastily.

"We got our tour," I tell them proudly. "Let's see if we know the way."

"Hm," replies Charlene dubiously. "It's a large place, and we don't want to be late."

"So you don't think we can do it!" Ora teases playfully. "I assure you, I pick up on new places *very* fast."

"This is Frost Palace, the biggest of them all," Charlene says, allowing herself a laugh.

"Well, fine, we'll lead the way and see if we can get down to the dining hall in *half* the time you took us," I bet.

"Fine, then," Bertrand chimes in, much to my delight. "Let's see if you can do it."

Ora leads, and it's a good thing, because, honestly, I'm not sure I've memorised the way. Luckily, she has. She nimbly zigzags down staircases and through halls, and Charlene, Bertrand, and I have trouble staying with her. Soon we reach the dining hall, where the queen is sitting at the table.

"Hm," she mutters when she sees us, "you're actually early. Good job, servants one and two. For once, you're doing your job right."

They bite back smiles, bow, and leave.

"Mother!" Ora exclaims, sweeping her way towards Glacier. "What a marvellous day it is. Is anyone joining us? William, maybe? Duke Ivan? Mm… that writer, Prithi? They were all quite nice."

I can't quite remember any of these people, but I nod along anyway, not wanting any more one-on-one time with the queen. Unfortunately, she shakes her head.

"I want to spend breakfast *only* with you," she informs us. "Dig in — the food has already arrived."

We finish our meal faster than yesterday, and right away I want to start planning to get the Ice Jewel.

"Mother," I say carefully, "Meadow and I would quite like to go to the spa. Would that be all right?"

"Certainly," says Glacier with a nod. "I want you to relax. I'll come with you."

"Um…" I don't know what to say. "All right. We were thinking of getting our hair dyed, actually. I'm getting black, and Meadow's getting strawberry blonde."

"Definitely not," Glacier answers brusquely, dropping her fork in surprise. "You are my daughters. Your hair will stay white."

I swallow. Tomorrow our hair will begin turning back to their original colours, and Glacier will know that we're fakes.

"Mother, we have something to tell you," blurts Ora suddenly. "I don't know why we didn't tell you earlier."

I look at her with curiosity. What is she doing?

"All right," mutters Glacier, "what is it, girls?"

"Back when we were kidnapped, the thieves used their magic to dye our hair different colours permanently so no one would suspect we were the princesses. They made my hair brown-blonde and Mabel's hair black. When we realised we were the lost princesses, we questioned the men, and… they told us the truth. That's when we ran away, but not before dyeing our hair white. We knew your hair was white, and we wanted to look like you in case you didn't believe us. So we want to let you know our hair is going to start draining its colour quite soon. It's already started," explains Ora.

She is a genius. An utter, genuine genius. I want to hug her. The eye colour dilemma doesn't even cross my mind.

Glacier seems very understanding about it all. "Ah, of course," she murmurs. "I'll use my magic to make your hair a permanent white then. Thank you for telling me, darling."

I gulp. I don't want white hair forever, but it is a small price to pay for an extra day at stealing the artefact. Plus, I'm sure Esme can pull something off to get our hair back to their normal colours after this whole adventure.

"Thank you, Mother." Ora smiles, and she sounds so sincere, no one would stop to think that she actually hates the queen. "We'll go tidy ourselves, and then we were thinking that maybe we'd explore."

"Of course." Glacier nods.

"Goodbye now."

"Oh! Would you like me to come with you?"

"We'd love it," Ora cuts in quickly, "but we want to take it slow, really. And you must get ready for the gala this afternoon. We'll be there."

"Well, all right, if you're sure," Glacier says bitterly, much to my delight.

"Thank you," I beam, biting back my excitement.

"I spoil you, I know," she chuckles, watching us leave.

As soon as Ora and I get to our room, I start freaking out about the eye colour. "It'll change, too, and then we'll be toast!"

"We just need to find a way to change our colour with magic," says Ora. When she notices my look of pure horror, she shrugs and adds, "There's really no other way."

"How is that even possible?" I groan.

"It's like what Esme did. We're touching up on it again." She stands in front of her mirror and gazes closely. She squeezes her eyes shut and clenches fists by her side. She begins to go pale, her forehead scrunching up in concentration.

"Ora!" I whisper a warning, but she doesn't stop. A small, tired smile appears on her lips, as if telling me she knows she's close.

She finally opens her eyes, and shockingly, they're a fresh crystal blue.

"You are incredible," I moan. "How do you do that?"

"Just picture it in your head," she says, looking satisfied with herself. "It's a good look! Your turn."

I face the mirror, clench my fists, and close my eyes. I try to muster something, anything, but there's no response.

"Feel it, Anya," Ora encourages me. "Picture it."

I imagine myself with blue eyes, the same as Ora's. I open my eyes hopefully, but my eyes are still the fading dusty blue shade. "Can't you do it?" I beg Ora.

"I can see if I can help," she says carefully, laying a hand on mine. I repeat the process, trying to focus as hard as I can, and it seems as if minutes pass until my eyes reach the same shade as Ora's.

"You look gorgeous," she tells me.

"You are astonishing," I breathe. "You've got something in you."

"Don't be silly, you're just as powerful as me," Ora says matter-of-factly. "Now, since Glacier's not coming with us, we should use our time wisely. We can easily sneak into the Glass Chamber and take the Ice Jewel. We'll teleport away, leaving that monster of a Glacier behind us." Ora nods with a naughty glint of pleasure in her eyes. "One step closer to completing our mission."

I look at her victoriously. "And who would've thought we could pull this off on only our third day?"

"Definitely not me."

I laugh, playing with the threads of my bed, when suddenly, with a lurch, I realise that wasn't Ora's voice. My heart leaps with fright as I slowly look up to see Queen Glacier in the doorway, her beady lashes twitching with anger, her lips pressed into a thin line.

"Looks like we've got ourselves some *imposters*." She takes one step closer to the bed, making me flinch.

"Please," pleads Ora. "It's not what it looks like."

"I've certainly heard that one a lot." Glacier's voice goes unforgiving and cold.

"Let us explain ourselves," I beg, starting to create a story in my head.

"You are imposters," spits Glacier. "You can explain yourselves on your *deathbeds*."

Then, something hard smashes into my head, and all I feel is numbness.

10
Ora

MY HEAD HURTS.

My legs hurt.

My arms hurt.

Everything hurts.

I groan and roll over, expecting to feel the palace bedroom's blankets beneath me; but instead, I am greeted with the touch of cold flooring. Everything rushes back to me that I thought was a dream. The queen overheard our conversation. She hit us with her staff, and we blacked out. She brought us here.

Us.

I blink my eyes open, my vision blurry for a few seconds. Then everything falls into place. It is dark, but not enough that I can't realise where we are — the dungeons. Anya lies beside me in our cell, unconscious. She will be devastated when she wakes up. Because now we are trapped, and there is no way to the artefact. Now we will die, and so will Dax.

When her eyes flutter, she clutches her head, sits up, and looks around. Then she hangs her head in my arms and cries. She cries until her eyes are swollen, breathing shallow, unsteady breaths.

"It's done already," she sobs. "Esme told us not to let her down, but look at us now. We've left her alone."

I gently lift her face from my knees and rub my hands together. Just as I am about to try and break out of the jail, a voice stops me.

"Magic won't work here in the dungeons." Queen Glacier steps out from the shadows to our prison, and I wonder how long she's been there. She has two drinks in her hands, a plate of four slices of brown bread, and a slab of butter with some brown specks in it that look like cinnamon.

She slips the food through the bars.

"Why would we eat anything you give us?" I demand, though my stomach is growling.

"Well, you choose." She shrugs innocently. "If you want to starve and then get your heads chopped off, it'll be even more fun for me."

I shake my head, though my stomach growls in disagreement. Unsure what to do, I take the food and sniff it. Normal, I suppose. It's tempting, and it's not like it's a choice. Reluctantly, I take a bite — it tastes rubbery on my tongue, but it doesn't taste toxic. Beside me, Anya tastes it, too.

"You have no idea what's at stake here. You need to let us out before it's too late," Anya says, barely giving herself time to digest.

"I don't *need* to do anything," Queen Glacier snaps coldly. "I don't owe you. You lied to me and gave me hope. You attended my parties, slept in my beds, earned my love. I made plans for us."

"The *servants* made plans," Anya corrects, and her voice is stronger than before. "You should've known this was all too good to be true."

"I would watch your mouth if I were you. I'm not the one getting killed, am I?" snarls Glacier, and that shuts Anya up.

I sip the liquid in the glass, cool and smooth. "What is this stuff?" I splutter. "It's disgusting. It's, like, *sticky*."

"Hm. Yes, that's how it's supposed to be. In your world, you'd call it... a truth serum," she says, arching an eyebrow with a chuckle.

Anger rises in my throat. I know I can't fight it, no matter how hard I try.

Everything in me wants to restrain, but there's something stopping me from doing that. I cry out, but Glacier doesn't take any notice.

"Don't," Glacier says shortly. "So tell me, little ones, what are your names?" she snarls, her voice cutting a tear inside me. "Your *real* names."

"Ora and Anya." The words are pulled from my throat, and I grimace.

Glacier's mouth tilts open, and then she smirks. "I should have known. Blackstones. The prophecy mentioned you — if only it had pictures. You are powerful, and you are on a mission. What mission?"

I can't share this information. It'll ruin everything. I clench my jaw, but as my mouth opens, the information spills out of Anya. "Our brother… he's been seized by the characters of the Ash Chronicles. We're collecting all three artefacts from each book."

Glacier bares her teeth. "People were never supposed to be able to enter until your wretched father, Harlow. You're just like him. Greedy. You deserve to suffer. You deserve pain."

Anya's fingers curl into fists, but she doesn't say a word.

"You have his fiery temper, too," says Glacier with a laugh, and then her voice goes hard again. "You'll rot in this prison. I'll torture you, and you'll die. I don't care about your stupid brother. I want Harlow's whole family dead." She turns to leave, but stops midway. "One more thing to add. In your bread, there's *cricynine*. That's the deadliest poison in Iciclone, if it doesn't ring a bell. It'll put you to sleep for a good couple of days, and then your bodies will start to decay. Soon, you'll become a figure of my chronicle, and I can hurt you all I like without any worries. Next time, don't take the food. You should know by now I don't care about personal needs. This is justice, my children. This is revenge."

As soon as she's gone, Anya punches the ground beneath us, screaming in frustration.

"Come back!" she yells after Glacier, even though we both know that she's long gone. "Face us, you coward!"

"Anya…" I whisper, "just stop. There's nothing we can do. She won. The characters won."

With that, darkness sweeps into my mind, and the poison kicks in.

11
Anya

"WAKE UP." HANDS SEIZE MY SHOULDERS AND SHAKE ME.

Realisation of where we are and what has happened floods through me. I keep my eyes pressed shut.

"I don't want to wake up," I decide.

"But I *need* you to wake up," Ora's voice cries into my ear.

I force myself onto my bottom, trying to ignore the ache in my stomach. We are in the same spot where we were when poison consumed us; in the same filthy dungeons. "How much time do we have left?" I whisper.

She takes her hourglass from her pocket and shrugs sadly. "Maybe a couple of hours."

I nod, and her hand takes mine. Her eyes are watery, and there are bags underneath. She looks dirty, in desperate need of a bath. I probably look worse. I feel terrible. But I know treatment isn't coming any time soon. We'll be stuck here. Like Glacier told us, we'll rot. Be tortured. I wish we could bring out our teleporters and just go home. At least then, we'd survive. But there is no magic in the dungeons, so it simply wouldn't work.

"Anya," Ora whispers.

"Yes?"

"I'm scared."

"I know."

"What do we do?"

I suck in a strangled breath. Usually, I'm the one to ask this question, but honestly, I have no idea if there is anything we *can* do right now.

Ora closes her eyes and takes a huge gulp of air. "Magic is the only way, right?"

"But the curse…"

"I don't believe that for one second," Ora says. "All it takes is a little concentration and imagination." Then her hands shoot out to the bars of our cell, and the metal glows a dark hue of blue. I watch in horror as she is sent flying backwards, crashing into the back wall of our prison.

"Ora!" I cry, rushing to her. "Are you all right?"

She gets up onto her knees with a wince. "I'm fine."

"What just happened?"

"The queen wasn't lying. We're stuck. We can't get out," she mumbles bitterly, slumping back against the wall.

"I can feel my insides chipping away," I whisper, my hands trembling. "I can feel the poison at work."

"Me, too."

I put my head on her shoulder, willing myself not to cry again. Too many tears have been shed here already. I sigh when a body steps out of the shadows. The body becomes two. Guards? They are both shorter than the queen, with long blades at their sides.

As they step into the light, I realise they are dressed as guards, but silvery masks veil their faces instead of the usual steel.

"Who are you?" Ora's steady voice hisses. She's so strong, but I feel weak. The poison is exhausting me.

"Shh," a familiar voice squeaks. "It's us."

I grit my teeth, trying to dissolve the shivery feeling that my body holds. "Charlene?" I whisper into the darkness. *Bertrand?*

Charlene nods, lifting her mask for a second and then putting it back on. "It's us," she repeats with a nod.

I stare in utter confusion, but Ora speaks up.

"How?" Ora wheezes. "How are you here? How did you get past the guards, into the dungeons?"

"We did things that will get us into lots of trouble later on," admits Bertrand, his voice shaking. "We, too, are pretending to be different people. We attacked, stole, and sneaked in. We're pretending to be the Head Guards. They always wear these masks."

"But you never do anything that gets you into trouble." I frown. "Why would you risk everything for us? We lied to you. Grasped identities that weren't ours. Took advantage of you and everything in the palace."

Charlene allows herself a shallow laugh. "You're the first people that ever treated us with respect, and I know that much was real. You were kind to us. You used manners. We're not going to stand back and let you get slaughtered by the queen. It's time she gets a taste of her own medicine for once."

"But you'll die," Ora says quietly. "We can't let you do this."

"It's our choice," Charlene replies fiercely. "We would rather die serving you today than die later on serving the queen."

Hope rises inside me. "Do you have the key?"

"We've come prepared."

To my delight, Bertrand smiles and pulls it out. He fits it into the keyhole and twists it to the side. The door swings open with a creak, and relief washes over me as soon as I step out of the cramped cell. "Thank you," I croak.

"It'll be our little secret."

I let myself smile.

"So we hear you need to get to the Ice Jewel," says Bertrand, picking at his nails nervously. "Head Guards are allowed in the Glass Chamber. We have a plan."

"Then we'll follow your lead," Ora grins.

Charlene grabs her by the arm and marches forward. Bertrand does the same with me. His grip is surprisingly strong. We exit through the dungeon doors. My heart skips a beat when I see all the guards.

"Riki. Haru. What are you doing with the imposter prisoners?" asks one.

"We're on strict confidential orders from the queen to go to the Glass Chamber. I'm not sure why," says Bertrand thoughtfully in a gruff voice. "Perhaps she's waiting there. She's very keen on beginning the torturing. Page the guards upstairs and tell them that we're coming up. I don't want them to be too shocked when they see the imposters."

"Of course, Haru, sir," agrees the guard right away. "We'll get that done immediately."

"Hmph," grumbles Bertrand, jerking me forward roughly and

stamping up the stairs grimly.

As soon as we are in the stairwell, far from the other guards, I nod approvingly. "Nicely played," I whisper. "You're a better actor than I thought, Bertrand. Or shall I say Haru?"

He remains scowling and hisses, "You can't talk to me. Someone may see."

"Oh, all right," I snort.

We reach the floor of the Glass Chamber. Bertrand and Charlene hold up their Rime Cards — or, rather, Riki and Haru's. I can't imagine them stealing ID from the Head Guards, but somehow, they managed it. I want to jump with excitement when we enter the Glass Chamber.

Bertrand releases my arm, and Charlene does the same with Ora. Ora and I run up to the Ice Jewel's crate.

"You have magic, don't you?" asks Charlene. "Get it open! We'll keep watch. You need to be quick."

I wonder just how much the poison has slowed my strength, but I force the thought out of my mind and press my fingers next to Ora's against the glass.

"Let it all out," she murmurs.

I push harder.

There is a knock on the chamber door, and it swings open. Behind me, I hear, "Haru, I thought you said the queen told you that she'd meet you here, but she's getting ready for the gala — hey! The imposters! The Ice Jewel! *Guards*!"

Fear surges through me. If we don't hurry up, we'll get captured again, and our time will run out for good.

"Anya," Ora whispers to me, "keep using your magic to try to open this thing. I'm going to fight, or we'll all get killed."

"Wait!" I wail. "I can't do it without you. I'm not strong enough!"

I feel more power drain from my body, and I scream in fatigue. Everything in me wants to stop, but I keep the strength spilling from my fingertips.

Meanwhile, Ora has taken Bertrand's sword and is slashing at any guards in her way. Suddenly, someone lunges at her, swiping away her weapon. The guard's dagger flies out, and Bertrand jumps between it and

Ora. She lets out a horrified shout as Bertrand is impaled and falls to the ground.

Gone.

Another one. And it's my fault.

"No!" Charlene cries, trying to fight off a guard. Her face crumples — she's barely even defending herself.

A dagger slashes across her cheek, but she doesn't scream. She's slowly giving up, staring in agony at her knifed-through husband.

"Anya, faster!" howls Ora, as a sword strikes her arm, and she screams out.

"I can't… I don't know how…" My mind hurts, but I keep drawing out whatever I have left inside me.

"*Anya!*"

"I can't, I can't…"

"They're coming. Anya, *watch* out! *Anya!*"

The glass crate shatters, and the Ice Jewel rises into my hands. I turn around to see three guards charging at me.

"*Anya! Teleport! Now!*"

I fumble in my pockets and bring out my crystal. I press it with trembling fingers, and my body begins to fly, but not before I see a sword plunge through Ora's stomach.

12
Ora

PAIN AND POISON CONSUME ME.

All I see is red.

I clutch my gut, and as soon as I do, I wish I hadn't. A scream of agony escapes my lips. Where am I? Did Anya make it home? I realise numbly that I'm being carried, but I'm too tired and weak to open my eyes and see whose arms I'm in. Am I going back to the dungeons? Has my time run out? Is Queen Glacier going to torture me further? What does she have in store for me now that I'm weak and defenceless?

I am set on something soft. A mattress. A bed. This is no jail. There is a sound of a door locking, and then a cup is lifted to my lips.

"Drink," a gentle voice orders me, soft and familiar.

Everything inside me protests as a cool liquid is forced down my throat, but this time it doesn't taste strange or speckled. I'm quite sure it's not poison, again, but if it is, I'll die. I'm already dying, and all I need is something to speed the process.

The drink gives me some kind of strength, so I keep guzzling it down until there's nothing left. I open my eyes and crane my neck painfully to see my bedroom at the palace surrounding me. Charlene looms over me, holding the glass with bloodied fingers. Her blood or mine?

Or someone else's?

"What…?" I moan, not knowing what to say.

"Hush," she whispers. "We got away from all the charade at the Glass Chamber, but soon enough, the queen will find us. You need to move fast. I know that you must be in a lot of pain right now. You were… stabbed."

I grimace at the word, but I have a vivid memory of what happened. I try not to think about it and change the topic to what's really important right now. "Reach into my pocket, Charlene, and bring out the hourglass."

She digs into my soaked red dress and hands it to me. I'm surprised that there's still sand slipping. Little sand, but still sand.

Hope.

"What does it mean?" she asks me.

"There's time." Excitement rises inside me, but as soon as my lips move to a smile, pain comes shooting back.

"I have no magic," says Charlene sadly. "You'll bleed out, but if there's still time, you can go back to your home. Your friend already has the Ice Jewel, and I'm sure she'll figure out some way to heal you. I've tried covering the wound, but it's barely doing a thing. I don't know… I don't know what to do to help you."

"You've helped."

"I've tried," she corrects guiltily.

I can feel the blood seeping out. "Well, at least there's that," I mutter with as much warmth as I can muster.

"Can you get home with this?" Charlene holds up my teleporter in shaky fingers. "I… I saw your friend use it back in the Glass Chamber, and then she disappeared into thin air. The guards started looking everywhere for places she may be, but I knew she was gone. I seized that moment to get you here."

I nod gratefully, taking the crystal in my hands. "I might be too weak to do it. I might die on the way there. It requires energy and strength, two things I certainly don't have right now. I just want to maybe have a small sleep…"

"Mead — Ora, this is the only chance you have. Your time will run out, and I won't live to see the pain that will be inflicted on you."

I shudder, but I know she's right. "When I leave, you're going to die. You'll have no protection. After all you've done for me…"

"I understood the risk coming into this. I'm not even sure I want to be saved any more, Ora. I want to join Bertrand, and I will."

"You can't mean that." My lower lip wobbles. "You can't desire death. That's what she wants. You have to fight back."

"Ah, but I'm tired of fighting now," says Charlene calmly. "Here, I will never be treated with true respect. I will always be thought of as a servant."

"But you're not. There's so much more to you than that."

She sighs. "You and I both know this, true, and I've tried not to let their comments change what I think of myself, but they will never understand. You understand, and I never thought anyone could. I will take my love for you to the grave. My husband and I will watch over you every day."

I wish I could throw my arms around her, but I can hardly move. I can only muster a small goodbye.

"Goodbye to you, too," says Charlene, and a peaceful smile is on her lips. "Thank you for everything."

Gentle tears roll down my cheeks as I press down on my crystal, and all of Floe City evaporates into nothingness.

I land on hard ground. My eyes recognise the athenaeum. Anya is running towards me, but she's fading away. Why is she fading away? Blood leaks from me. Esme stands over me, asking questions I can't make out. What is she saying? Why can't I hear her properly? I made it. I finally made it back.

Right?

"Ora? Are you awake?" a voice speaks into my ear. "I don't want to put you under. I'm afraid of what might come from that."

I feel dizzy. I can't open my eyes or move my lips.

"I'm going to start now, Ora. I think you're asleep. Stay asleep."

It's Esme talking, I realise. As soon as the thought occurs, I shudder. My brain hurts. It is too exhausting to think.

"Ready?"

No.

A sizzling liquid is spread over my wound. As it sinks into my skin, it begins to sting. Now it's burning. Burning. I feel like I'm on fire. The liquid keeps coming.

No.

Stop. Stop. Stop.

I want to scream, but my throat is dry. Pain devours me. I want to sleep. I want to never wake up again. Anything. I will do anything for this to stop. My body shakes in frustration and agony, protesting and trying to fight off the burning.

"Is she okay?" a concerned voice shrieks. "Oh, my God. Is she having a seizure? Esme, what's happening?"

That voice.

"Anya." The word leaves my lips, but I know it's me talking. She's alive and healthy. She's the only person I want to see, but I still can't open my eyes.

"It's me!" Anya chokes. "Are you okay? What...? How...?" She's crying, I figure out, kneeling just beside me, her fingers intertwined with mine. She's as cold as ice, and I can almost feel her numbness. Her hopelessness.

I want to reassure her that everything is fine, but I'm not sure if I would be lying if I said that. I want to hug her, but my body refuses to let me move. I want to at least see her, but my eyes won't let me.

"Hey... you're strong. Use your strength. I know you can."

"Anya." I wheeze again, starting to shake.

"Ora! What's happening to you?" Esme's stressed voice cuts through the air.

I don't know.

I don't know.

I don't know.

All I know is that I want it to stop.

My wish comes true, and a familiar darkness, floods through me.

I wake again, but this time there are no familiar faces. People in blue trousers and shirts crowd around and over me. Scrub suits, I realise. These are doctors. Why doctors? Where is Esme? Where is Anya?

"Ready to begin?" asks a woman.

"I suppose."

"It's necessary, Dr. Smartin."

"Let's hope we don't lose her."

"At least she'll feel no pain."

No pain. That sounds good. A fuzzy feeling crosses over me. I try to move my neck to see what's happening, but I am frozen in an uncomfortable lying-down position. All I can see is a white-tiled ceiling.

Let me stand, I want to beg. Heal me, and let me be free.

"Come on! She's slipping away!"

"Harder! Harder!"

"Save her!"

Voices are screaming all around me. Stressed voices. Stress is something I want to be rid of for good.

"She's slipping away! She's slipping away!"

Good. Let me slip.

"Ora, can you hear me?"

"It hurts," I groan. The words are slurred, but at least they come out.

"I know. But you're alive. You're going to make it," Esme whispers to me.

I let my eyes open and search where I am. My bed. *My* bed. Not at Corkwood Orphanage, not at Floe City, not at any hospital, but in the Blackstone household. The comforting scent of pineapples and cranberry greets me. I wasn't dreaming. I'm here. I move my hands to my stomach. My skin is greeted by something rough. I strain my neck to see my middle completely wrapped in a brown cover.

"Anya," I mumble. "She's okay?"

"She's okay," repeats Esme, smiling faintly.

"She has the Ice Jewel?"

"She does."

"But now… how will I travel? I'm weak. Injured. Useless." The words ring of truth.

"You'll heal. My magic will speed the process. When you are ready, you and Anya will go to the next Chronicle, to the Realm of Monsters. You will collect the Shadow Ore. I feel it."

"I'm slowing her down. What if Dax…?"

"You just have to worry about yourself for now," says Esme soothingly. "I believe in you. I know you're going to complete the mission. I know you can save Dax."

I want to tell her that she shouldn't place her trust in me; that I'll let her down. But I just force a nod and close my eyes. "How long have I been out?" I ask, terrified of the answer.

"A week."

"A week?" I splutter. "That's so much time wasted! I'm going to cost Anya everything. Everything she loves. Shouldn't she go without me?" But I know, as soon as I say it, that we have to do this together. I know I can't send her into an unsafe Chronicle without me by her side. If she went in and never came out, everything would be lost, and I would never forgive myself. I would lose my sister.

Esme seems to read my thoughts. "She needs you. Now, Ora, you've got to rest. Your body will heal, and I'll keep applying magic. The bleeding has stopped, and you're all bandaged up."

I want to jump out of bed and go straight to the Realm of Monsters, but I'm too worn out to head into that danger. I'd die straightaway, and then I really would be useless. I allow myself to fall asleep, and for the first time since the day we found out about the Secret Athenaeum, I feel at peace.

I wake up what seems only minutes after that, but when I check my watch, I realise it's already the following day. All my weariness dissipates as soon as I see Anya, sleeping beside me.

"Anya?" I say.

She immediately wakes and grins at me, but there's sadness piercing her eyes. "I thought you were dead, Ora."

I try to sound stronger. "Look now. I'm okay and alive. I'm healing. I've gotten all the help in the world."

"But... I *left*." It's almost a squeal, a plea for forgiveness. Her voice holds guilt and culpability I didn't think she could possess.

"This isn't your fault," I tell her right away, because it's true. "You're the one who pulled through. You're the one who saved us all. You're the one who got the Ice Jewel."

"Only from your protection," she protests.

"Anya, stop. Don't blame yourself. Everything worked out. Even if you had stuck around, those wretched guards still would've stabbed me."

"But if I'd hurried up" — she wheezes — "you would've never

gotten stabbed in the first place. We would've teleported home *together* like we were supposed to."

"Hey." I touch her shoulder. "Please, Anya. It's important to me that you don't take responsibility for the accident. Because it doesn't matter how we got here, what prices we paid… we're here, about to journey into the second Chronicle."

She chokes down a sob. "I'm so happy you're alive." She leans over and gives me a tight hug around my chest, careful to avoid my wound.

"I'm happy, too," I whisper. "We have our Ice Jewel. That's one down, two to go. We're on the right track."

Anya smiles half-heartedly. "I never thought it would be this cool… this *thrilling* to have a sister."

I laugh, though it hurts as soon as I do. "I never thought I'd be so close to my adoptive family, but you're my best friend."

She smiles at me and takes my clammy hand in her warm one. "I'm here for you. No matter what."

"What about you, though? Dax's time is being wasted away because of me, slowly but surely. Every second that passes is a second that we should be spending somewhere else, trying to get at the next artefact."

She winces, but says, "I'll wait. I want to. If I hurried away without you, we all know what would happen. I would turn into a character. Then I'd have no Dax, no Mother, no Esme… and no you. Everyone I care about would be gone because of my rash foolishness. I really don't want to make a place called the Realm of Monsters my home."

"I can imagine that, can't you? I mean, if you close your eyes…"

"Oh, shut up."

I snort. "I'll try to recover fast."

"Yes, by resting and regaining strength," murmurs Anya. "But I'll stay with you. Whenever you wake up or feel afraid, I'm here."

13
Ora

THE DAYS THAT FOLLOW PASS IN A BLUR.

I never know what the date is because the same happenings occur from Monday to Sunday and repeat. Esme thrusts more and more magic at my body each day, until I reek with her power. She feeds me some kind of medicine that strengthens me, but at the same time makes me want to gag. Even though I am constantly drinking it, my stomach doesn't get used to it.

Eventually, I go back to the hospital, and a woman named Doctor Shilling removes my stitches. She's under the impression that I was in some kind of car accident. I'm not entirely sure *what* Esme told her, but she doesn't seem suspicious.

I'm afraid the removal of the stitches will hurt, but there is only a faint tugging near each knot. She announces that there is no infection, the wound is closed, and I'm basically healed. I have a nasty scar, but that doesn't matter, because Shilling tells me that as long as I take it easy, I can travel and move around. I'm certainly not going to "take it easy", but I nod and thank her. I go back home alongside Anya and Esme, and we start planning as soon as we get there.

"Can we go now?" I ask eagerly. "To the Realm of Monsters?"

Esme sighs. "I suppose if you feel ready…"

"I do. I've been waiting for this moment for days now, and we can't waste any more time," I point out.

"Very true," Anya agrees. "Plus, Esme, all the information you've given me, I've passed on to her. We're going to get it done quickly. And I'm stronger now, too. Ora, Esme's been training me to control my magic while you've been recovering."

I nod approvingly. "Esme, if she's been trained by you, we're going to be fine. I won't get stabbed again." I wince, but at least we've convinced Esme.

"All right," she shrugs. "You know what you're collecting?"

"The Shadow Ore."

Esme rubs her temples, and I don't think I've ever seen her so upset.

"Esme," Anya says gently, "what's wrong?"

"Nothing, nothing, I'm fine," she says quickly. "I'm just scared for you."

"We'll be safe. Or, as safe as we can be."

"It's not only that, it's the fact that…" Esme takes in a shaky breath. "Nothing. It's nothing. Let's just go to the athenaeum."

"Esme? Tell us, come on," I coax.

"No. Let's go." Esme's voice is stern now.

"All right," Anya says, puzzled at Esme's sudden response. "If you say so."

Esme opens the door that was once locked, presses her hand against the brick wall, and summons the green light.

As I fall, I pray that this trip won't be like the last. I pray not to suffer like I did before. I hate the feeling of being afraid. I've never been afraid of an adventure, but the guards scarred me in some way, and not just from the dagger remnants carved into my skin.

I nearly land on my feet, but topple over because of the impact. I'm getting more used to the athenaeum.

Esme, a perfect lander as always, begins walking up the stairs. A bit dizzy, I follow, and Anya trails just behind me. Right away, she runs to the chest on the third floor to see Dax. She places her hand on his heart. "His breathing is shallower than the last time I felt him," she observes quietly. "Esme, he's dying."

Esme purses her lips. "That's why you must hurry, girls. Who knows how much time he has left?"

Anya flinches, crawling back to her feet. "I have never desired an adventure more than I do right now."

"Don't let that craving, that hunger, get in the way of your actions," warns Esme. "Be smart. Ora will help with that. You've gotten stronger, you know, Ora. After the incident, you gained irrefutable strength. In fact, you're stronger now than before. It's astonishing, really, how you've improved."

Anya looks to me, her eyes glimmering with admiration.

My throat is dry. They have such faith in me, but what if I've lost hope? What if I don't believe I'll make it through the remaining two Chronicles?

"Ora?" I hear Anya's startled voice.

I snap my mind back to reality. "Sorry. I'm ready."

"If you're in too fragile a state to do this…" murmurs Esme.

I look to Anya. She's trembling, but looking at me with reassuring eyes. She's willing to give up even more time for me, but she's already risked too much; made far too many sacrifices that could cost her a great deal.

"No," I tell Esme, sounding braver than I feel, "I'm ready."

She looks concerned, but finally nods with a sigh. "Please be safe, girls. Tell me you'll be safe no matter what."

"We'll be safe, Esme," I vow. "You don't have to worry."

"Yes. I don't have to worry, even though you just got stabbed." She tries to put on a smile, but it falls right away.

I give her a hug, but as soon as I touch her, I realise how much she's shaking. What is so horrible that awaits us in the Realm of Monsters? What is Esme not telling us?

"You have your teleporter? Your hourglass?" she asks, her voice so small and mousy, I barely hear her.

"Yes," Anya assures her, feeling in her pockets. "We're ready."

Esme watches us as we reach for the fat Chronicle and flip it open.

"Let's do this." I whisper to Anya, digging my palms into a blank page.

Then shadows carry us away from our world.

THE REALM OF MONSTERS

A story of a treacherous land, shattering secrets, and an eerie ore of shadow and gloom…

14
Anya

"UGH!"

"Anya? Is that you?" a voice whispers.

I rub my eyes. I can make out the silhouette of someone sitting beside me, but other than that, all I see is darkness.

"It's me," I whisper to Ora. "Where are we?"

"I don't know, but we're definitely going somewhere."

I realise then that the floor beneath us is moving. I am sitting in some kind of crate, and it's rattling tremendously. I try to push myself out, but my bottom is stuck.

"Hmph," I grunt with frustration. "What are we even in?"

"I don't know."

Something rests on my shoulder, and I realise it's Ora's hand. It trembles slightly.

"I preferred waking up in snow," she admits.

I sigh. "At least we're together. Unseparated."

"Yes, I suppose there's that. This would be a whole lot scarier without you by my side."

I grin into darkness. We sit in silence, riding over rutted bumps, thinking up ideas of where we could be going and who could be taking us. Have we accidentally landed in the back of a truck? Does the driver even know we're here?

My bottom is starting to ache, clasped in some crate's grasp. Whenever we arrive — and *wherever* — I'm going to somehow have to get this off.

Finally, after what seems an eternity, the floor beneath us stops moving. I hold my breath as light streams through where we are. In a car. Well, the *boot* of one. So maybe my prediction was near to right. Maybe we landed in the back of this car accidentally?

The boot opens up, and a man smiles as he sees us. He has brown curly hair and is wearing some strange purple jumpsuit. One of his eyes is green, and the other is blue. I've never seen anything quite like it. "Girls! We've arrived!" he announces.

"Um…" I stammer in confusion. "Arrived where?"

"At the Slay Arena," says the man, cocking an eyebrow. "Sebastian. Pleased to be at your service, Miss Ariana and Miss Jade. We talked over the phone?"

"Right. Of course."

"Tell me, what are your stage names? You do have those, don't you?"

"Stage names? Yes, indeed," Ora croaks. "Um, I'm… Snowblaze. This is, er, Sunstar."

"Snowblaze and Sunstar," he repeats to himself. "Perfect. Are you ready to meet Diablos, the Master of Monsters?"

"Yes," exclaims Ora, trying to sound pumped.

"It's a rare opportunity to actually work with him," Sebastian agrees. "The first show is tonight, so start warming up."

"The first show?" I ask.

"Yes, of course," he says hurriedly. "He's excited to have you as the Opening Act to the Executionists!"

Ora and I force smiles.

"Follow me," he instructs, not picking up on our oblivion.

Somehow, I manage to get my bum out of the crate and crawl out of the boot after Ora. The sky is grey above us, and there are lots of trees. We stop at a gate. Sebastian merely flicks at it, and all the trees behind it dissipate into nothing. I watch in awe as a massive fighting arena is revealed. There is a staircase that leads to rows of seating, and a man in a tall red-feathered hat and a furry yellow jacket is walking towards us.

"Sebastian," he barks. "These the acrobats?"

"Yes, sir."

"Hmph," grumbles the man. "They're qualified?"

"Only the best for you, sir."

"Hmph," he says again. "Leave us. You can head to your tent and get ready to help work the show."

"Of course, Diablos."

"Nice work."

Sebastian smiles and hurries away.

I strain my neck to see where he is going, and I realise there are an abundance of tents set up behind the whole arena. There's a big field there, in fact.

"You're familiar with performing, I reckon?" Diablos asks in his thunderous voice.

"Of course," says Ora smoothly. "We know our first show is tonight, but we're awfully tired."

Diablos lets out a roaring laugh. "Just because you're tired doesn't mean the show won't go on. Most everyone in the realm is coming. We get a large audience with the Executionists, but we'll get even more people with acrobatic openings. Especially since you're magic acrobats. At least, that's what Sebastian told me."

"Of course we do magic," says Ora quickly. "Can we rehearse?"

Diablos waves dismissively. "There will be no time for that. I need to show you your tents. Where are all your sleeping things?"

"Our sleeping things?" I repeat. "What do you mean?"

"We're like a circus. We move around, sleep in tents; do lots of performances. You'll be doing this for at least a good thirty years. You look so young. How old are you?"

"We're both fourteen, but very experienced."

"Well." He looks wary. "Your parents?"

"Dead," I say quickly. I'm barely lying.

"Hm." I suppose he decides not to inquire about it further, because his face brightens again. "Come, come. Let's go to your tents and get you ready. You'll receive new clothes if you have none."

We are forced to follow him to the field behind the arena, where Sebastian went. There are tents dappled all over the field, and we are led to two, one yellow, one pink.

"You'll sleep here," says Diablos.

I take a peek in. It's nothing special. Just a normal tent with a sleeping bag.

Then we are led to a purple tent, bigger than the rest, in the centre of the field.

"Go ahead in there," orders Diablos. "You'll find your outfits, and you can do your hair, I presume. Unless you want me to send the hairdresser?"

"No," Ora and I say at the same time. We need to talk to each other privately.

"All right," says Diablos. "Then I'll leave you to it. Come to the arena thirty minutes before your opening. That'll be at six."

"Of course," Ora says, dipping her head.

"I've never seen or heard of you before. I'm taking Sebastian's word for your talent," he snarls, a warning edge to his voice. "This is a big day for the company. Anything you do reflects on me, so you'd better be good. You know what the penalty will be."

I swallow and watch him disappear back in the direction of the arena. "We need to get out of here," I hiss. "I have no idea what this Diablos man is talking about, but I certainly don't want to wait and find out. We need to focus on finding the Shadow Ore. *That* should be our only concern."

Ora looks ahead thoughtfully. "But don't you think we may have been sent here for a reason?"

"No! We got picked up by a random stranger who thought we were acrobats! Which, clearly, we're not."

"Anya," says Ora calmly, "we can't simply run away from this circus. He'll find us. In the last Chronicle, we knew exactly where the artefact was. But this time, the Shadow Ore could be anywhere in the realm. We need to think strategically. Apparently, Diablos is a well-known, powerful man. Our adventure would end straightaway if we fled. Everyone would be on the hunt for us, and we'd probably end up in another prison. This time, though, there'd be no saviours risking their lives for us."

I stare at my toes, feeling silly. Ora's right, of course, as she always is. "So, what? Just go through with the show? Diablos will be disappointed, and then what'll he do with us? He has high expectations that we clearly won't be able to live up to. We'll fail," I whine.

"Failing isn't an option," Ora insists. "We need to pull through so we can stay here and figure out some clues."

"How will we blow away the whole realm?" I whisper, nerves getting the better of me.

"We have a connection," says Ora firmly, cocking a grin. "Our magic will tell us what to do. We'll put on an enchanting show for everyone."

"If you say so," I mumble.

We step into the purple tent. The inside is much fancier than our sleeping tents. There are racks and racks of dresses, all shades, all sizes; all colours. Then, at the front, there's a row of seats sitting in front of mirrors. There are shelves crammed with hairbrushes, hairspray, elastic bands, make-up — all things to dazzle ourselves.

We glide to a rack labelled *ARIANA AND JADE, OPENING ACT ACROBATS*.

There are two identical dresses hanging from the bar. They are fiery orange, adorned with thousands of sparkles. There is golden thread gilded through, a black monster claw symbol imprinted in the top right corners. Right beneath the costumes are two pairs of red-laced shoes.

I check my watch, realising it's already 5.30. If we want to get in any practice at all, we'd better hurry up. Ora slides her rusty clothes off straightaway and slips on the dress. It's short, a bit showy, but there are shorts built in, so her underwear is covered.

I pull on my own outfit. It's too tight around my hips, but I suppose I couldn't expect a perfect fit. "This is… very bright," I say, arching an eyebrow.

"Itchy, too," she adds with a laugh. "Come. Let me do your hair and make-up."

I gratefully sit down as she runs a comb over my scalp. She sweeps my hair onto my head, weaving strands together with her nimble fingers. She showers the style in a coconut-scented spray, then spots small butterfly jewels on a shelf. Before I know what's happening, she's pinned all the studs into my locks.

"Voila!" Ora grins at me. "A Dutch-braided bun!"

I look at it closely in the mirror, gazing at the intricate twists through my hair. "Wow," I breathe, impressed. "It's stunning."

"You're not done quite yet," tuts Ora, grinning. "We have to make you look like a doll. Lots of make-up is necessary for big performances. It'll make us look bold."

"Really? Because, see, I was thinking maybe a bit more subtle than bold…" I start, but Ora has already begun loading blush onto my cheeks. Blue and green eyeliner, bronze eyeshadow, and lavender mascara follow, and then she paints my lips a glittery crimson red with gloss.

"Now you're done," she says.

I inspect myself. "A good definition of this would be bold, I agree."

Ora hides her excitement and starts doing herself. I watch in awe, wishing I could help in any way, though I know I'd mess it up. When she finishes, she comes and stands next to me. We look nearly identical. My stomach clenches thinking about what we're going to have to do next.

"Are you ready?" Ora says enthusiastically, not noticing my uneasiness.

"Not really," I admit. "I'm no gymnast, let alone an acrobat. I know what's at stake here, but…"

"But nothing. You'll be amazing," she says, taking my hands.

I draw in a shaky breath and check my watch again. We don't have much time. "Let's try conjuring up a few objects. Like how we did with our eye colours."

We practice focusing and imagining objects. Sometimes it comes, sometimes it doesn't. Ora does it with more ease.

When it's time for us to head over, we hobble through the grass in our elegant shoes. Just as we are about to make our way up the staircase to the seats, we realise there is no way to the centre from the seating area. Luckily, Diablos appears behind us.

"Follow me," he says in a low voice. He guides us back to the field, and I realise then that there is a door leading into the arena. "It's concealed, just in case."

Just in case what? I think with curiosity.

We step through, into the backstage, which is a small area behind red curtains. I peek through to see the thousands of seats being filled.

"You shouldn't be doing that," a low voice booms behind me.

I spin around to see a fully dressed-in-black man behind me. A mask covers his face.

"Who are you?" I demand, drawing back the curtains.

"I…" He clears his throat as if embarrassed. "I am the ringmaster."

"So, what, are you two a duo? The ringmaster and the Monster Master?" I snort.

"We work together, though he is the main face of the Executionists," he says stiffly, and then turns away from me. "I must rehearse. If you'll excuse me."

I watch him join Diablos.

Ora jumps from foot to foot. "This is going to be so… exhilarating."

"I just want to get it over with," I admit anxiously.

"When you hear the music, you'll never want it to end," she promises, squeezing my hand reassuringly.

"How do you know?" I ask childishly.

"I did plenty of acrobatics at the orphanage. There was a programme there, and I loved to dance. Once, when I was caught trying to sneak off, Gertrude kicked me off the team, but I still danced in my room when no one was watching. Silly, I know, but it was a hobby." She chuckles. "I stopped after a while. I'm out of practice for sure."

The black-dressed man steps past the drapery, and the crowd roars with hunger. For us, or for something else? We are an opening, I remember. What for?

"Hello, everyone," the ringmaster says into a mic, and I shiver as the words leave his mouth. "You were all promised a Magical Grand Opening, and now you're going to get it! Presenting… Snowblaze and Sunstar!"

People cry out with excitement.

We step through the curtains. My heart hammers louder when I see everyone. How are we doing this? Are we simply making up an act on the spot? I look around. Rings line the ceilings, hula hoops are scattered in the corners, and ropes hang from a red platform above us.

Ora doesn't waste a moment. She climbs up a rope and flexibly curves her body over it. Whoops arise from the audience. What do I do? Thinking fast, I take a hula hoop, place it on the ground, and strike a pose in the striped band.

"Who's ready for the most special act you'll ever see?" growls the ringmaster, getting a series of shouts in response.

The light dims, and a spotlight is shone upon each of us. That's when the music starts. It's a crossover of jazz and pop, a perfect circus song.

I freeze, not knowing what to do, but Ora spirals down the rope, landing elegantly on the ground. Then she slides to me, takes my hands, and does a flip right over me. My hands remain in that position, so Ora seizes the moment.

"Do something," she whispers.

She's right. I'm barely moving. I grit my teeth and hold my ground as Ora launches herself onto my hands. I grab her feet to give her support, and she stands there, barely wavering, as the crowd hollers, intrigued. Then Ora jumps. I push her toes up with all my might, and I must have done something right, because she shoots all the way to a ring on the ceiling. She glides through them cleverly. She looks down at me, and I nod, taking the hula hoop from below me and holding it out in front of my body. Everything in me wants to drop it and run away, but I stay in my spot. I try not to close my eyes as Ora springs off a ring and jumps easily into the hoop. The crowd gasps in surprise.

"Come on, Anya, do something," Ora hisses again, standing beside me.

My body sways with the music, and I let myself loosen up. I place my hands, on Ora's chest and somersault over her head. Then my hands propel me forward, and purple fire erupts onto the rope. The magic echoes through me.

Magic.

I climb the rope, and Ora joins me, catching onto the trick. The spectators are bellowing in disbelief now. I take Ora's hands, and together, we jump. We spin and dance through the air, and when we reach the bottom, we unhinge, experimenting with our power. Ora rains confetti down on the whole arena. We hula hoop and twirl and climb rhythmically, always in harmony with each other. We do this until darkness falls into the arena. The crowd cheers as we hurry back out the curtains. Diablos gives us each a clap on the back.

"Nicely done." With that, he and the ringmaster step into the arena. "Hello, everyone! Who's ready for another game of the Executionists?" announces Diablos, clapping his hands together.

The crowd shrieks.

The ringmaster throws out his arms, and two gates appear beside him.

"Terry, our man-slaughterer for today!" he calls.

A gate opens, and a measly man stumbles into the arena.

"And... the monster for today, the Prickle Pickle!"

I nearly laugh, but when the creature stomps into the arena, all humour evaporates from my body. It's a green, lumpy monster with a spiked coating. Its eyes are like coal: beady black vortexes.

"Begin!" roars Diablos.

The Prickle Pickle edges towards the terrified Terry. Soon enough, its body is on top of his, and the monster is attacking the poor man.

"Stop!" he screams, lying in his quickly forming pool of blood. "Stop! I'll do anything!"

"Unfortunately, Terry, you know how the Executionists show goes. It's a battle to the death!" says Diablos with a chuckle.

I stop peeking through the curtains. I don't want to see any more. Ora is looking straight ahead, shaking. "*This* is what the opening was for?" she whispers angrily.

I swallow, interlocking my fingers over hers. "We really need to get out of here."

Terry's screaming echoes off the walls, and I have to cover my ears. Finally, the sound fades, and I know it's over.

"Well, I guess we still await a winner!" says the ringmaster thoughtfully. "Who will reign as the next champion?"

"Thank you, everyone!" Diablos clamours. "Have a good night!"

The squealing from the audience doesn't stop until Diablos and the ringmaster join us backstage. I am frozen in shock.

"Are you all right?" the ringmaster surprisingly asks me. "You seem startled."

"I'm fine," I force out, clenching my jaw. "Snowblaze and I are tired, that's all."

The ringmaster backs away. "Of course. Sebastian will be waiting at your tents." It sounds like he wants to say something else, but he stops himself and nods firmly. "Get a good rest for tomorrow's show. You did well tonight."

I take Ora's hand, and we run out the backstage door to the purple tent. Unfortunately, Sebastian is already there.

"Girls!" he exclaims. "I watched the show, and you were *fabulous*. You didn't mention you do Blackstone magic."

I eye him curiously. "What do you mean?"

Sebastian cocks an eyebrow. "It's powerful stuff. You... *created* things. You related to Harlow or something? Because that's where it originated from. You know of Harlow, of course. Who doesn't?"

I gulp. "Of course we know him, but we certainly don't have his blood."

"So you learned it then." He shrugs. "You're more talented than I thought."

"It took a long time," I tell him. "Years, in fact, locked away trying to learn. But after a while, it started happening easily."

"Hm." He grunts. "Very impressive. And to think you're only fourteen! You probably are related to him, I'd say. Distant, perhaps, but still connected by blood."

"I... I have a question," I blurt. "The Executionists... how are those victims chosen? Those man-slaughterers, or whatever."

"You disobey Diablos, you get put in the ring. You win and defeat a monster, you earn his respect and get a high prize of luxury. Very few survive — about a half percent. It depends on the year, though sometimes there are no winners for decades on end."

I suck in a strangled breath. "When do we leave this area?"

"A week more," says Sebastian. "The crowds are good here."

"All right," cuts in Ora. "We're going to change now. We're exhausted."

"Of course," he says quickly. "I just wanted to congratulate you."

Congratulate us for an amazing opening to a dance of death, I think, but I plaster a smile onto my face until he leaves.

"Ora, what are we going to do?" I ask right away.

"I'm not sure. Maybe we should stay another day; see if there's any clues that may lead us to the Shadow Ore. I think there's lots of fishiness going on around this place."

"But that could be wasting time. And if we stay, won't the real Ariana and Jade find out what's going on? Won't they come to seek out Diablos?"

"But would he believe them? We've earned his respect, haven't we?"

I huff thoughtfully. "I don't know what the right thing to do is here, but I really can't do another magic show for… that."

"It's not like *I* want to," she snaps.

"So what do you presume we do?" I ask impatiently.

"One more day, and if we find nothing, we'll run away, and I assure you, we'll make a plan to get the artefact."

"That sounds too vague to me. It's too risky to wait around for an answer to fall at our feet and fix all our problems."

"Our whole lives are risky right now. We have to take chances, or we're doomed for good. Do you have any better ideas?"

We stand there, and when it's become clear that I haven't a clue what to do, we silently enter the grand purple tent. On our rack lies two folded pairs of grey pyjamas. There are monster claws sewn through the material, and I wish that I could rip them out as soon as I change into the nasty attire.

Ora helps me undo my hair, and then we head to our sleeping tents.

"Goodnight, Ora," I whisper.

"Goodnight."

Just as I'm about to go off, she stops me with a hand.

"Tomorrow, we're going to do something. Find something. Discover something," she tells me in the most confident voice she can muster, but I'm quite sure she's only saying it to convince herself. "Maybe everything will be all right in the end."

"Yes. Maybe your plan will work." But as soon as I say it aloud, I know what a tiny chance there is that the idea will do us any good.

We stare at each other, breathing shallowly, eyes drooping.

"I'm tired." She finally yawns.

"I won't be able to get to sleep," I admit.

Ora frowns. "We're going to get the ore."

"Yes. Of course."

I say these words serenely, trying to look at ease, but everything inside me protests frantically. How can she sound so sure? I watch her dip into her tent, so I do the same. My sleeping bag is rubbery and far too large, so when I climb into it, I'm freezing.

The night only gets chillier as it stretches on. I can't stop looking back to feeling Dax's chest, so light and trifling. What if we don't find the ore soon enough? What then?

The thoughts swallow me into a sleep of nightmares.

15
Ora

THE NEXT MORNING, WE HAVE SOME KIND OF LESSON PLANNED WITH DIABLOS.

"Diablos told me he's waiting, so you'd better hurry up," Sebastian says, when I get out of my tent after being poked multiple times by him.

"What is this, preschool?" I groan. "Can't Sunstar and I just relax and rehearse all day?"

"He's training you," Sebastian says sternly. "Sunstar's in the tent, so go meet her there. Clearly, you're not a morning person."

I actually *am* a morning person, just maybe not in a place called the Realm of Monsters. Or maybe I'm just hangry, since I haven't had any food since our arrival.

He leaves then, and I look up at the crisp blue sky. Clouds still hang in the blanket above, but I wonder if that's how it always is here. I join Anya in the purple tent, who is brushing at her hair aggressively.

"Good morning," I mumble.

"Not really," she sighs back. "The Shadow Ore could be anywhere in the whole realm, and because we've been trapped at this killing circus our whole time here, we haven't been anywhere else. I know you have a *feeling* about this place, but I think we're wasting time."

Maybe she's right. Maybe we do need to get out of here. "I'm sorry, Anya. I know this is tough for you, being so confused."

She shrugs. "It's not your fault."

"Maybe," I say under my breath, taking some bland brown clothes from our rack and pulling them over my body. "Do you want me to do your hair again?"

"No, I'll just put it into a ponytail for now," Anya says with a sigh. "I guess since we'll be here for the show tonight, you can do it up then."

I purse my lips together, but don't say a word.

"Ready to go?" Anya asks after a couple of minutes when she's changed, and I've finished braiding my locks.

"Sure."

We walk to the arena in silence, an awkwardness spreading between us that we haven't yet shared before. We've known each other for only a month or so now, but it's seemed like forever. We reach the large stadium, where Diablos and the ringmaster are waiting in the middle.

"You're late," growls Diablos.

"And starved," Anya blurts.

Diablos narrows his eyes. "Are you complaining?"

"Let them eat," says the ringmaster. "They didn't have dinner yesterday. What do you expect? They'll learn discipline as they grow; but for now, they are untrained children."

Diablos sighs. "You would have gotten lunch anyway, but after the lesson, *if* you follow through, I suppose I can get Sebastian to bring some snacks to your tents."

He looks at us as if he expects gratitude, but I'm not about to thank someone who watches people die at his feet.

"Fine, then." Diablos crosses his arms over his chest. "Let's begin. Today, we'll be experimenting with your magic, making you grow and become more comfortable with it. Sebastian told me you've learned Blackstone magic. My partner over here—"

"This wasn't what I had planned for the lesson," the ringmaster interrupts sternly. "I can take over. Isn't the Penumbra coming out today? Make sure she's ready. If she falls apart on stage, you know what'll happen. We'll lose members and fans. The Penumbra is something everyone is looking forward to. There are high expectations that must be met. I know this has been taking years, and the day has finally come. Do you want to waste precious time on *this*?"

"I suppose you're right," grunts Diablos. "You'll take care of the acrobats?"

"Yes, of course."

I watch Diablos trudge back into the field. He draws his fingers through the air, and a door appears. He glances around before stepping through the entrance, and then the opening, along with him, disappears into thin air.

"What happened? Where did he go?" I demand.

"Only Diablos, Sebastian and I know the way to the Monster Making Room," the ringmaster replies. "That is where the magic happens. That is where Diablos creates his monsters."

"He creates them?" I gape.

I expect the ringmaster to tell us we should know this already, but he nods instead. "You know Sebastian, yes? He's the controller. Most anyone can control, but he's grown to be good at it."

"A controller?" repeats Anya. "So, what, the monster is merely a robot?"

"Precisely."

"Then how can it be destroyed? That gives the man-slaughterer no chance of survival," she protests.

The ringmaster grimaces. "There is always a way to defeat robots. They all have some kind of…heart. A pair to its death."

I shake my head furiously. "Do the fighters know that they're fighting robots? Does the audience even know?"

The ringmaster shakes his head. "I've given you too much information." He grits his teeth as if angry with himself.

"Fine," I growl. "What do you want from us? What shall we even call you? Do you have a name?"

"It's better not to know for now."

Anya rolls her eyes, and I can't help doing the same. Secrets always have a way of coming out, so why wait?

"Call me…" The ringmaster's voice trails off as he thinks.

"Sir," Anya says rigidly. "We'll call you *sir*."

He winces. "Just call me Ringmaster."

"We'll stick with sir," Anya insists coldly.

"Well… as you wish." He swallows hard and clears his throat. "Now, let's get started. Across the field, there are targets. You'll be aiming your magic at those. I'll tell you to make something, and you'll shoot that object towards the target. This will help with aim and accuracy."

I turn to the targets vexingly.

"Glass shards," he announces.

It takes everything inside me not to turn to him and shoot them in his face, but I focus on spilling them from my fingers towards the target, like how I miraculously did in the show. The magic is strong in this realm. The shards don't go nearly far enough, and Anya's land even shorter than mine.

"Well," the ringmaster says, humming, "it seems like we have much to work on."

I stifle a groan. The hours that follow are exhausting, and I can sense Anya getting more irritable by the second. This is a whole waste of time, she must be thinking. The hard thing is that she's right. We're getting nothing out of this. I don't know how much time passes, but I'm starved and worn out when the ringmaster lets us leave. If we could only slip away… but we can't. We'll be discovered as frauds, and all will be lost.

"Please remind Sebastian about the food," Anya says stormily.

The ringmaster nods and watches us go.

"That was a bore," groans Anya.

"I know," I mutter, and for what it's worth, I apologise.

Once again, she replies, "It's not your fault."

We reach the tents, and Sebastian hurries towards us with two sandwiches in hand. "I was told you were hungry." He grins. "Is prawn mayo okay for you?"

I snatch it from him, unable to return the smile. How can I smile at someone who massacres people every day? Everyone thinks it's the monsters who kill, but now I know that it is the cold-hearted man beside me.

"Thanks, you can go," I force out, before Anya decides to blow his head off.

Sebastian looks confused. "Did I do something wrong, or are you just hungry?"

"We're just hungry, of course," I say as kindly as possible, although now I'm considering using my own magic on him to put a knife into his neck. "We need to discuss the show tonight between ourselves."

"I'll leave you to it, then," he says politely, but he still looks puzzled.

I watch him go before biting into the sandwich aggressively. Part of me wants to throw it at the back of his head, but I'm too hungry to do that. I'll have to eat whatever food I'm given by whoever gives it to me. There's no other choice. My stomach is practically wailing.

"He's… just… so…" Anya growls, tearing off a piece of bread and throwing it into her mouth angrily. "What the hell are we even doing here, Ora? Learning magic isn't doing us any good to help us find the ore."

"I know. I'm sorry. I guess I was wrong. We'll escape tonight, when no one's awake and lurking," I tell her sadly.

"Then what? What do we do? We have no idea where the stupid artefact is," spits Anya spitefully.

I nearly tell her to calm down, but her brother's life is on the line. Everything, everyone she cares about, is on the line. I'm not going to yell at her for being a bit stressed.

"I don't know what we'll do," I admit guiltily. "I wish that we had some outline of where it may be. Then we wouldn't be scurrying around, doing… I don't even know what."

Anya's shoulders slump, and she finishes her sandwich in silence. "Even if we do escape tonight, that's another useless day gone by. Remember, our time is limited."

"I know that." I lower my voice. "One more show. I promise."

She shrugs. "I don't know if we'll ever find the ore if we keep up at this rate."

I clench my jaw, but I can imagine why she's thinking such thoughts, seeing as we've made absolutely no progress.

"Anya…" I start, but she silences me with a firm shake of her head.

"Don't tell me you're sorry. There's nothing you could do. I'll keep saying that out loud."

Except I could have agreed to run away last night, or not do the show at all, or tell Sebastian we weren't the acrobats he was looking for in the first place.

"I've made mistakes, and it's cost us time," I admit. "I'll make it right."

"*We* will."

"Right."

"I'll go for a rest now, I think," Anya groans. "Maybe it'll help me get my mind off everything that's going on."

She lays her head in my lap and dozes off.

I stay in that position for what seems hours. Whenever she wakes up — breathing hard, beads of sweat dripping down her forehead — I tell her I'm here, and it's all going to be okay. I hope that I'm not lying.

When she wakes up for good, well rested, we get lunch, eat in silence, and rehearse in the field. Then Anya finally breaks down and sheds some tears, and then, before we know it, we're back in the purple tent, getting ready for the show tonight. Today, our dresses are taffy pink with tiny cherry rosebuds embedded into the silk, and there are honey-coloured leather boots to match.

I decide to do French twists as our uniformed hairstyles, and I throw some sparkles on top for decor.

We head backstage, where Diablos and the ringmaster are waiting.

"Are you ready?" whispers the ringmaster. "Use the skills I taught you."

"Yes, sir," grumbles Anya.

He tenses but says, "Good luck, girls."

"I'd say the same to you, but it seems you've been doing this for a good amount of time," I glower. "To be honest, *sir*, I don't know how you get used to it."

He opens his mouth, then closes it. "It just happens."

Then he slips past the red curtains, and I hear the audience roar.

"Hello, everyone! Who's ready for the magical acrobats?" he thunders, more confident now. He gets delighted screams in response.

"Ready?" I whisper to Anya quietly. "Last show."

"Last show," she repeats, and we step into the ring.

Today, both Anya and I decide to start on the ground in a pose.

The music begins, and light starts spinning through the arena. I climb the rope and slip, twirling through the air. Anya catches me in a hula hoop, and I focus my mind on lightness. I feel the hoop lift me into the air, and Anya whirls me around. Then she releases her hand and launches me upward so I'm clutching a ring.

The crowd is going wild by now.

I stretch my arm down, and Anya jumps and joins me on the ring. We whirl to the ground, creating confetti, rings of fire, bubbles that we can fit into, and cotton candy bunnies.

The lights fade, and I am angry at myself for not wanting to step out of the spotlight. How can I enjoy something like this? An opening to a killing?

Anya and I join Diablos and the ringmaster backstage. They give us impressed nods, then go into the arena.

"Close your eyes and cover your ears," I whisper.

"Don't need to tell me twice," she replies with a wince.

I can still hear Diablos' resounding voice, and the faint click of gates sliding open. Suddenly, I feel Anya move away from me, and the curtains open. I flip my eyes open to see her gazing out into the ring.

"What are you doing?" I demand. "You enjoy this stuff now? Don't you think...?" My voice trails away as I realise what's happening.

"This is impossible," breathes Anya.

I can feel the pull of magic, but why? I edge to Anya, joining her in looking out through the drapery. There is a man, far more muscular than yesterday's, but he is still getting demolished. However, that's not what holds my attention. It's the monster.

The Penumbra that Diablos and the ringmaster were talking about this morning. It's massive and so dark, you'd think it could be a shadow. It turns in our direction as the man moves, and I stifle a gasp.

Beneath all the iron and metal, I sense its heart. I *feel* it. It's strong, angry, enchanting. It's there.

I turn to Anya, and she takes the words right out of my mouth. "The Shadow Ore."

16
Anya

THAT NIGHT, I HAVE NO NIGHTMARES.

Now, there's a sliver of hope. There are only three days left, but we've located the artefact. Step one is complete. The only thing left to do is get it.

I think as dusk stretches to dawn, trying to come up with ideas as I stare at the roof of my tent. I don't know what time I finally fall asleep, but when Sebastian peeks in and light streams through, I'm completely exhausted.

"Rise and shine, Sunstar!" he hoots, and a part of me hankers to kick him in the gut and go back to sleep.

"Sebastian…" *Would you get the hell out of my tent?* "I'll be out in a few," I force out instead, resisting the urge.

"Perfect," he says, beaming contentedly. "You and Snowblaze will be getting private lessons today."

"Private?" I repeat, startled. "Why?"

"You have different skills; different weaknesses. I suppose Diablos and the ringmaster want to focus on each of you."

"But… why?" I splutter. "Who's teaching me?" As much as I despise Diablos, there's something disturbing about the ringmaster. I know he has his secrets, and I don't want to be around that spook alone.

"Instead of asking questions, sweet-face, why don't you just get out there and see for yourself?" says Sebastian, resting his hand on my shoulder.

It takes everything in me not to burn the flesh off his palm. I gently sidle out of his grasp with a smile. "You're right. I'll go join Snowblaze."

"I'll drop by with some snacks again," says Sebastian cheerily. He winks. "For now, I have some work to attend to."

I watch him go and stop midway in the field. Like Diablos, he outlines a door in the air, and as soon as he walks through, he disappears altogether, leaving no trace that he was ever there.

I feel my mouth drop open in disbelief and a slight touch of anger at the sheer stealth of everything in this place. I force myself up and into the purple tent, ignoring the cracking of my tired bones.

Ora stands in front of a mirror, plaiting her hair.

"Morning," I say.

She jumps and spins around. "Oh! You scared me."

"Did you hear that we're taking lessons *privately*?"

"Sebastian told me," she says resentfully. "But after that, we'll have time for the action before the show."

"It sucks that we have to do that again," I mutter, but there's a small part of me that wants it. A part that wants the attention, and the social recognition. I force it out of my mind and change the topic hastily. "Anyway, I was up all night, thinking."

"Figured as much," admits Ora. "So was I."

"I made a plan," I tell her, and her brows shoot up. "I know. I'm not the one to usually organise what we'll be doing."

"No, that's not what I meant at all," she apologises quickly, but I know she's lying. I've always been the one to ask *her* what to do. To be honest, I've never been a good schemer, but maybe some of Ora's skills of strategy have rubbed off on me.

"I was thinking that perhaps — and I know it sounds crazy — but it might be our only shot. We should fight the Penumbra."

A wave of uneasiness floods over Ora's face. She stands there, looking a bit shocked, and when she realises, I mean it, she demands ferociously, "Are you serious?"

"Of course, I am," I say, gritting my teeth and pulling myself together. "I wouldn't kid about something like this."

"Do you… do you know how *dangerous* that would be? It's a robot, Anya. Sebastian is controlling it. If he saw you going for the heart, he'd kill you. He may be bringing us snacks and playing nice now, but he'd lose his job if we won. Take my word for the fact that if there are any threats in his way, he will destroy them without a doubt."

"I know that," I bite out too harshly. "I *know* what's on the line here. But there's no other way. Only we can fight the Penumbra and steal its heart. We're strong. We have magic. We'll use it."

She laughs roughly. "You think it's that easy? Have you considered everything that factors into the plan? How do you think we'd even fight the Penumbra? You think that Diablos would let his most prized acrobats, who are getting him so much publicity, merely waltz into his arena? You think that he'd let us fight and be killed?"

"He doesn't know we're after the heart," I offer lamely, but I know my idea could never work.

Ora must sense the despondency in my voice, because her face softens slightly. "Anya, I know how desperate you are to get the ore, but like Esme reminded us, we can't let the hunger get in the way of our actions, or we'll lose our lives foolishly."

"We need to find a way to get into the ring," I whisper in anguish. "There's no other way."

"We'll find one."

"What if we don't? What if this is all we can do, and we sit back for three days, hoping for a solution to pop up and solve all our problems? And what if—"

"After the lessons," she murmurs, taking my hands, "we will do something. Anything. I promise you."

I swallow and force a nod. I change into the bright green-and-blue outfit laid out for me, and I let Ora do my hair. Then we make our way to the arena, aware that we won't be getting breakfast today and not truly caring.

Diablos and the ringmaster await us.

"Even later than yesterday," mumbles Diablos. "Sebastian hopefully told you about the one-on-one time?"

I shrug, wishing I was anywhere but here right now.

"Sunstar, you'll be with the ringmaster over here, and Snowblaze, you're with me." Diablos flashes a grin, and I can feel Ora shudder beside me.

"So where are we going?" I demand of the ringmaster in my least whiny voice. "To the field?"

"Actually, yes," he says with a laugh, but I don't return the cheer. He doesn't seem to notice, because he continues talking lightly. "There's plenty of room for us to practice there. Sunstar and Diablos will be in the arena."

"Fine by me," I grumble, and Ora shoots me a look from the corner of her eye. I sigh and make an effort to look happier. "Let's go."

I throw a miserable glance back at Ora one last time and then follow the ringmaster to the large field strewn with tents.

"Who do the rest of the tents belong to?" I ask.

"They're extras. More workspace. If anyone decides to come, they act like guest rooms."

"Hm. And some personal questions. How'd you get into this... job? This living?" I add, trying to keep my voice even.

The ringmaster turns to me, his face dark. "Sometimes, you must learn to keep your mouth shut."

"Well, I..."

"Anya, enough."

The world seems to go silent, and I can hear my own heart hammering loudly in my chest. "You... how do you know my name?"

"What?" He looks at me, puzzled.

"You called me Anya," I squeak.

He shakes his head. "No, I didn't."

"Yes, you did. I know what I heard. Why did you call me that?"

"I don't know an Anya," he says. "Why would I? You have two names, Sunstar and Ariana. Isn't that right?"

I gulp. Had I really misinterpreted what he said? Had I imagined it? Am I paranoid? I try to gather myself and say as politely as I can, "I must have misheard."

"Yes, of course," he says curtly. He waves the subject away as quickly as it came, much to my surprise.

He stops abruptly just then, raising his hands above his head. He closes his eyes in concentration, and some kind of air wave ripples over the whole field. All the tents vanish in the snap of a finger.

"Just for the lesson," he says, and winks, all uneasiness forgotten. "Plenty of space."

"Perfect," I force out. The thinning tops of the grass waver in the breeze, and targets appear across the meadow grounds.

"Ready to get started?" he asks, bringing me back to reality.

"I suppose." I shrug, rubbing my hands together to ready them for the tasks ahead. "What do you want first? Glass shards?"

The ringmaster chuckles. "Ah, but that was the lesson of *yesterday*."

"Well, I see targets," I say, before remembering that I should probably tone down the sass. "What exactly are we doing?"

"You're impatient, Sunstar," he tuts. "Today is a day of telepathy."

"Telepathy?" I repeat in disbelief.

"The communication of magical peculiars." He emphasises the words far too sharply, making a shiver climb up my back.

"Right." I try not to laugh at his seriousness.

"Trust, and close your eyes."

I press my lids shut. Something surges through me. I desire to understand it but I don't know what it's trying to tell me. My arms are tossed from my sides.

Coolness erupts from my fingertips, and I open my eyes with alarm. "What was that?"

"Hm," the ringmaster murmurs thoughtfully. "You let me into your mind. I poured my emotions into you, and you felt it. You felt my orders. Your brain accepted them."

"That makes no sense," I stammer. "I'm not a Telepath."

"Maybe, but you know how to connect with others. You know strong connections."

He's talking like Esme now, all powerful and knowing. "I don't have a strong connection with *you*," I growl.

He flinches, but doesn't speak.

"How did you get to me, anyway?" I demand. "Inside my *mind*?"

"I know you. I feel you. I connect to you." He swallows and hurries on before I can interject with any questions. "Stand up, Sunstar."

"But—"

"I said *stand up*."

I sulkily climb to my feet, and the ringmaster nods.

"Comprehend me. Close your eyes."

"Will you read my thoughts? My secrets?" I ask carefully, the concern only now occurring to me. "I'm not sure I'd like to participate in this activity."

"I will not invade your privacy," he says firmly. "There are two layers of the brain when it comes to telepathy. The first, the outer layer, is where you communicate. The second is the inner layer, containing dark thoughts and memories, and that takes a lot more energy to get into."

"I'm still not sure about this..."

"It is not a choice. Close your eyes."

I reluctantly obey, and the same rush of magic floods through me. This time, the voice is clearer. *Comprehend me. Comprehend me.* The words stream through me.

The booming voice keeps thundering, but I can't focus my mind any further. Exhaustion takes over. I try to maintain attention, but I can feel the power sinking; the sensation evaporating. My eyes burst open, and I realise how fast and shallowly I'm breathing. I pant, drawing in inhales and letting out exhales slowly. Just like Esme taught me.

Inhale.

Exhale.

Inhale.

Exhale.

"Sunstar."

I rub my eyes, adjusting to the lighting. I'm sitting in the grass, the ringmaster crouched in front of me.

"I did it," I gasp. "It drained me."

He nods. "Some things do that. Pull yourself together." He rests his hand on mine, and power engulfs me.

I let my body absorb the light, and then he lets go. I'm not as tired. I feel fresher; more alive. "How did you do that?"

"Years of practice," he assures me. "Your turn."

"My turn?" I ask. "Can't we... wrap it up?"

A chuckle escapes him. "After your turn, yes. Reach me. Talk to me. I'll be easier to grasp."

"I don't know how."

"Yes, you do."

"I don't know how," I repeat, vexed.

"Your mind will guide you. Your magic is with you."

I close my eyes, searching deep within myself for anything. Light glimmers within me, and I reach for it, but it's hard to grab. Gritting my teeth, I dig deeper and push with all my might. It doesn't quite hurt. It aches. Magic bites into me greedily, pulling away everything I have inside me.

"Sunstar."

I breathe hard, returning to reality. "What?"

"I felt you."

I look at him in shock. "Really?"

The ringmaster frowns. "You filled me with your gloom. I didn't know you possessed that."

"Neither did I," I whisper, getting up, desperate to do anything else. "What were the targets for, anyway?"

"An activity I don't think we have time for any more," he says softly. "I think your friend will be done soon, so if you'd like…"

"I'll go." I smooth my skirts and walk away, a bit dazed from the bewitchment of the whole lesson. Suddenly, something rises beneath me. I scream in confusion as I'm hauled over a tent, landing on the hard ground. My knees scrape against the grass, and I wince in pain.

"Sunstar, are you, all right?"

The ringmaster rushes up behind me, and I feel him pull me to my feet. "I'm fine," I tell him firmly. "Just give a warning before you create a whole field of tents as I walk across."

"Right. Probably should've done that," he says, and winks.

"What's your name?" I blurt. "What's beneath the mask you wear all the time? And how *old* are you? Because, no offence, but you seem far older than me. Thirties, maybe? Forties? What's so… off about you?"

He stares at me, and for a second, I think he's going to tell me to shut my mouth, but then an easy laugh escapes his lips. "Under the mask is my face."

I glare at him. "Yes, I figured," I shoot back sourly.

A smile plays on his lips, and he continues talking as if I haven't said a thing. "Showing my face could be dangerous in my case. You're right about the age. I'm somewhere in between. Now, run along. Look, I see your friend has returned to her tent."

Although I could interrogate the mysterious ringmaster all day, I'd rather plot a plan with Ora. I look at him warningly one last time, then rush to her.

"An… Sunstar!" she corrects herself, spotting the ringmaster down the field. "How was the lesson?"

"Fine," I admit. "Good, even."

"Well, I'm glad that one of us had fun," she says with a laugh.

"He said my name."

"What? He called you Anya?"

I shrug. "Maybe. I might've imagined it. I demanded to know why he called me that, and he had no idea what I was talking about."

"So… does he suspect now?" says Ora with a troubled frown.

"I don't know. I don't think so."

"Well, then. Be careful."

"Yeah. Let's get back to business."

We slip into Ora's tent, and I immediately start chattering. "I think we have to do this. I think we have to give my plan a shot."

"Anya," she groans, massaging her fingers against her temples, "it won't work. It's impossible."

"It's *improbable*. Nothing's impossible."

"That's for children," she says practically. "Like I said this morning, you can't just throw your life away."

"Ora, if you could stop bossing me around for once," I hiss under my breath.

A mixture of hurt and surprise crosses her face, and then her eyes go stone hard. "Fine. Go. Talk to the ringmaster. See if you can get us into the ring."

"Fine. I will."

"It won't work," she warns.

I ignore her and step out of the tent, but part of me thinks she may be right. What if I'm holding on to false hope? How would it make sense if the ringmaster said yes to my proposal?

Not now. Now is not the time to think of everything… wrong.

I trudge on determinedly until I reach the opening to the shadowy dark tent that belongs to the ringmaster. I'm only just realising what a grand size it is, at least ten times bigger than mine. I'm not sure how to knock, on tarp, so I just barge through the opening. Inside, there's a whole kitchen and a bed. Not a sleeping bag, but a *bed*.

The ringmaster stands at the shallow counter, his back to me. I can see that his mask isn't strapped on.

"I need to talk to you," I tell him nervously.

"Sunstar." He sounds hollow and dark, even more than usual. "You need to leave. You need to leave right now."

"No need to be rude," I snap defensively, but a shiver shakes me from his sharp tone.

"You shouldn't be here. My mask is not on." He stays in his position, facing away from me. "Leave the tent, and I'll meet you out there."

"You're so careful no one sees your face," I say. "Why?"

"You can't see me. It's dangerous."

"I can handle danger. More than you know."

"You need to *go*."

I jump at the thunderous sound that he's never addressed me with before. Part of me wants to scurry away, but I force myself to stand my ground. I urge my voice not to quiver as I speak. "Tell me. Tell me why."

"I can't. Don't you understand, Anya? I *can't*."

I release a terrified breath. "You did it. You said Anya again."

"No. I didn't."

"Don't deny it," I cry out, and I can hear my own anguish. "Don't! Stop lying. I've been told too many lies."

"*Leave.*"

"Tell me," I continue. "Who are you? What are you?"

"I can't. You'll hate me." His voice is suddenly softer, and his back, which was so straight, seems to sink.

How does that make sense? How will his name affect how I think of him? "Show me. Show yourself," I order.

He warily turns around.

He is older.

He is hollower.

He is angrier.

But I recognise him from all the frames sitting on shelves around my house… because he is still my father.

17
Anya

NO. NO. NO. IT CAN'T BE. IT ISN'T. IT'LL RUIN EVERYTHING.

But as I look more intently at him, I know I can't deny the truth. This is why Esme was so worried. Because she thought we'd never come back, just as he didn't.

His face shows such pain and guilt, but I can't stop gaping. I finally get my lips to move. "You… you're lying. You're his twin. Something. Anything. This is all wrong."

Harlow nods. "I know. It's all wrong. But it's me."

"No!" I scream, willing this to be a nightmare. "It's not you! You're lying!"

He watches me, unmoving.

"I'd rather you dead than alive like *this*. You're a monster. You happily let people die. You are everything the father I knew wasn't. He was kind. Honest. He would throw himself in front of a car to save other people. He would read me stories. Sing me lullabies. He would never, *never* do this. You're just as well a killer." I'm shaking violently, and I don't know if it's from fear, shock, fury, or maybe all three.

The ringmaster — Harlow — winces with each word, but he never intervenes; never argues with me. Finally, when I'm finished insulting him, he talks. "Please, Anya. Sit. Let me explain. I know nothing will make up for… *this* — but let me tell you why I'm doing it. How I got here; how it all happened."

I'm still trembling, but I crouch down on a small cylinder seat, and Harlow squats beside me.

"I travelled here with my friend, Atikus. We had grand adventures, but the only problem was that we were wanted. Everyone was on the hunt for us. Mainly me, though. I took the blame for everything when we were found, so they let Atikus go. However, they captured me. I was jailed, and Diablos put me in the ring against his prized robot. Like the Penumbra, but less modern. It was then that Diablos and the audience learned I had a beautiful kind of magic they had never seen before. When I won, they were astonished. I wanted to go home, of course, but my time had run out, so I was forced to live here. Diablos studied me and named my power Blackstone magic. I was 'upgraded' to being his partner in crime, the ringmaster."

"So you stayed." I shake my head, breathless and ashamed. "You stayed in your job and settled into your new life because you felt you had no other choice. Who does that? You didn't fight! You let innocents die!"

"I missed you every day," he says fiercely. "I didn't know another way to live."

I look away. That doesn't change what he does every day. How he takes pride in it, in front of millions. "You should've tried to make a change," I tell him.

"It's hard sometimes."

"You're a coward!"

"I'm a coward."

"When you saw me," I whisper, "you knew. You knew I was your daughter, and you continued on like I was nothing but a dancer who worked with you. Like I wasn't special to you at all. But am I? Or am I something worthless that earns you money? Did you get so used to living like this that you stopped caring?"

"No! I..." He struggles for words. "I thought it would be better for you if you didn't know the truth. I'd rather have you love me dead than hate me alive. I knew Esme and Veronica must've sent you for some strange reason, and hopefully you'd be gone in five days."

"You knew we weren't the real acrobats, but you didn't say anything. Why? Was it you being selfish?"

"I liked being around you," he admits. "Even for a short amount of time. I told the real Ariana and Jade not to come because we'd found replacements."

"And you didn't tell me the truth. You weren't even planning on it. How could you do that to me? Your own daughter? Your own flesh and blood? You were going to let me walk away, never knowing about you being my *father*. You were going to watch me leave, oblivious to everything.”

“I know. I just thought it would be best. Look at how… upset you are.”

“But I *deserve* the truth. You’re not who you were at all. There’s no resemblance any more to the idol I grew up with.”

“I know. I’m sorry.”

“Ha. What good that does.” I fiddle with my watch and gesture to it. “You remember this?”

His face softens. “You still have it.”

“Take it.” I throw it at him.

He takes it gently and hands it back with a shake of the head. “Keep it. Please.”

“I don’t owe you anything!” I smash it onto the ground, and a part of the glass shatters.

“Keep it,” he repeats, picking it up and slipping it onto my wrist. “I’m cracked like this watch.”

“You’re cracked, we know. I don’t want any of you on me.” But I keep it. I sit there and stare at it.

Harlow clears his throat. “How is Veronica?”

“She’s in jail because she had to go find your mental friend, Atikus,” I snap, not being able to hold in my anger. “Dax has been mentally kidnapped by your characters, and there was nothing left to do. We were told the truth and sent away.”

He gulps. “You’re collecting the artefacts, then.”

“Yes. We are.”

“The prophecy warned us people may come searching,” Harlow says, “but we simply ignored it. The prophecy is wrong very often.”

“Not this time,” I say shortly. “Ora — my adopted sister — and I are out lurking in the Chronicles.”

“That’s your adopted sister?” Harlow says, and his breathing seems to slow. “Of course. Orabelle.” It looks like he’s piecing things together in his mind.

“Yes,” I say slowly. “Is something wrong?”

Harlow shakes his head. "Everything's fine. Please, go on."

I consider pressing for an answer, but I can tell he won't give, so I continue. "We have the Ice Jewel. We need the Shadow Ore next. And I know where it is. The heart of the Penumbra. This is what I wanted to talk to you about. Let us fight. Ora and I will destroy the robot and take its heart and teleport away."

"That's dangerous."

"Dangerous? You're going to talk to me about dangerous?"

"Diablos would never allow it, either," he adds quickly.

"Then convince him," I practically shout. "Don't you owe me that much? We'll betray him. We'll weaken our performance. Anything."

"He adores you. You win him love from his fans. He would never put you in a ring to fight and potentially lose your lives."

"Make him. Tell him that two girls have never won before, let alone one female. It will draw a crowd. It will get him cash. He's focused on the money, and his greed will drive him to say yes. That's all he cares about. You can persuade him. You *will*."

"You'll die, and he'll… God knows what he'll do."

"Then you fight. You've won before, so do it again. Steal us the heart. Everyone would be yearning to see you battle." I'm desperate by now, coming up with anything, anything at all to get us the ore.

"Even if Diablos agreed to that, he wouldn't put me against the Penumbra. He loves that thing. It took years to make."

"Let us fight," I plead, confidence draining. "We're strong. Together, we'll survive. We always do."

"Even if I convinced Diablos, I don't think I'd be able to let you into that ring. You're still my daughter," he says sadly. "Forgive me, Anya, but you'll have to find another way."

"Your son is at stake here!" I yell, getting up, wanting to shake his shoulders and draw a solution from his lips. "Everything is at stake!"

"Anya, please."

"Your family! Everyone I care about! Everyone you *used* to care about."

"I still love them," he says. "I always will. And I still love you. You, Dax, and your mother mean the world to me. Trust me when I say I want to help."

"Then help!"

"Anya."

"What? What do you want from me?" I shout. "What can I do to get you to help me?"

"Just… just wait a second," he says quietly.

I watch him intently, my impatience growing stronger by the second.

Harlow swallows, his fingers thrumming against the small table. "What if… what if, instead of Sebastian, I controlled the Penumbra that night? I would let you steal the heart, and afterwards tell Diablos the robot wasn't working properly because of some mechanics. The Penumbra would be smashed up anyway, so he wouldn't be able to argue. And once you're gone, Diablos can't come after you. You can collect the artefact and go to the third Chronicle."

"You think that could work?" I ask, a small flame of joy rising inside me. "You think we could pull it off?"

"I don't know," he admits. "I'm trying to figure out how I could convince Diablos. If the plan doesn't work, I don't want you to do muscle magic later on. I need you to go home the day that you're supposed to."

"What's muscle magic?" I demand. "There's a way to stay here longer?"

"Oh, God, no, I'm not explaining this to you," he says, almost frantically. "You should go, Anya."

"No, no, no. What is it?" My voice is stone cold.

He hesitates. Then, "When I discovered the Athenaeum, I travelled into a book and didn't know how to come back out. I used my power to get back to the library, but it drained everything inside me, and I was near to death. I was, supposedly, the 'inventor' of muscle magic. It is where you muster up all your strength and concentrate your mind on where you need to go. You would die. Your mother and Esme healed me, helped bring me back to life, but it took months. If you want a shot at finding Dax, I don't recommend trying it just to stay a little longer, because chances are, you'll die, or by the time you recover, he'll be gone."

"So that's how you came back," I whisper, mostly to myself. Esme had lied about not knowing what had happened to him, and for obvious reasons.

"You should go." My father sniffs.

It's true. I need to go fill my sister in. "Tell me the date once you've negotiated with your little friend," I finally say, getting to my feet.

Wide-eyed, he watches me leave. My heart is dancing with fear and hope by the time I reach our tents. Ora is waiting.

"You took an awfully long time," she says, and I can tell she's still frustrated from our argument.

"Ora." I take in deep breaths. "So much happened. I think we have a way to the artefact now."

She looks at me with curiosity, and I tell her everything — every detail, small and large. Ora follows along, making shocked comments here and there and gasping at Harlow's brilliant idea.

"Wow," she says when I'm finally finished. "So I suppose you were right, then."

I laugh. "Though it definitely didn't occur the way I thought it would."

"Your father is alive."

"He's a beast."

Ora shrugs. "But he still has a good-ish heart."

"Not so sure about that."

"He's helping us, isn't he?"

"He's not the person he was."

"Well, he changed. He's lived in a place called the Realm of Monsters for the past ten years, so what did you expect?"

I sigh. "Anything better than this."

"He may not be the perfect person," says Ora with a snort, "but he's still your father. Say goodbye for the final time. Say goodbye before we leave."

I shiver. "I hate goodbyes."

"Yet you can't ignore them."

"When I make an effort, perhaps."

"He's your father, Anya. Your *father*."

I change the topic hastily, and although Ora seems a bit irritated for a second, she settles down and joins in. We spend hours chattering in that tent, and finally, it's showtime once again. We change into sequined crystal-blue leotards and silver-bowed shoes, and with that, we head backstage, where Harlow and Diablos are already waiting. When I meet Harlow's eyes, they are filled with grief and worry. I look away, and Ora takes my hand. It usually comforts me, but right now my body feels frozen.

Harlow steps into the ring and makes his usual introductions, but today he is barely enthusiastic. The audience doesn't seem to particularly notice, because they roar and cheer at their usual volume.

Ora and I perform our regular show, which the spectators are quite content with. The Penumbra isn't fighting today, so we don't bother peeking through the curtains. The grunts and screams can be heard from a mile away.

When a man has been killed, Harlow and Diablos join us.

"I'm sorry," Harlow whispers to me, as we begin to leave, resting his palm on mine. "I can't… I don't know what… I'm sorry."

I ignore him, shrug his hand off, and hurry away, with Ora a step behind me. We change into our pyjamas and slip inside our tents. I curl into my sleeping bag, and suddenly power rocks me. I fight off a scream as heat fills me. What is Harlow doing? I realise he's saying something, repeating a word over and over. I grit my teeth and reach for his mind. *Tomorrow. Tomorrow. Tomorrow.*

"Tomorrow," I say aloud, and as soon as I do, the word disappears.

I will fight tomorrow evening. I don't know how my father pulled it off, but I hope he knows what he's doing.

Because if he doesn't, both Ora and I will die.

18
Ora

ANYA RATTLES ME AWAKE THE NEXT MORNING.

"What is it?" I moan. "Why are *you* waking *me* up?"

"It's a big day!" she exclaims.

"Celebrate by yourself," I grumble, nestling into my sleeping bag.

"Oh, so you want to be awakened by Sebastian? How about, on our last day, we play a prank on him?"

I flap my eyelids open, all weariness gone. "What type of prank?"

Anya grins as I sit up. "Well, I was thinking perhaps we could work our magic. Literally."

I snort. "Where's his tent?"

"I've tracked it down, don't worry," she assures me.

We excitedly make our way down the field to a large tent, a little smaller than Harlow's.

"So he gets a bigger tent than us." Anya pouts playfully. "How unfair is that?"

A grin slips onto my lips. My arms reach out, and the tent shrinks downward. We sneak in. Sebastian is peacefully sleeping in a bed. A *bed*. Why does he get such a fancy area? He murmurs in his sleep, and I freeze, but he doesn't stir, and his eyes remain shut.

Anya's fingers flick gracefully through the air, and Sebastian's face turns bright pink. Polka dots erupt over his cheeks. A blue moustache ripples over his upper lip.

Anya winks at me. "It'll wear off in a couple of days, I'm sure."

"Let me have some fun, too," I smile, spiralling my arms. Giant tarantulas pop into the air and start crawling atop him. "If he gets a few bites, it's nothing compared to what he does to other people."

We flash one last look at the obliviously sleeping Sebastian and head back to our tents. We're lucky he's a deep sleeper.

"What do you reckon we do now?" Anya asks, scratching her chin thoughtfully. "I really would love to do a trick on Diablos, but I feel like that's not such a good idea."

"I feel like he'd definitely notice," I agree.

"Oh." Anya perks up. "I did tell you that we're fighting the Penumbra tonight, didn't I?"

I freeze. "Um. No."

She laughs nervously. "Slipped my mind, I suppose. But Harlow is going to control the robot, so it's all good."

"An, I hate to ask you this, but are you sure we can trust him? I know he's your father, but he still works with Diablos."

"I don't think he'd ever deliberately hurt me. I'm his daughter. And if he hurt you, he knows how furious I'd be."

"I'm just scared. That's all," I say quickly, not wanting Anya to take offence.

"You have every right to worry after all we've been through." She frowns. "I know Harlow doesn't seem entirely trustworthy, but I suppose our lives are in his hands. We have no other chance at getting the artefact."

"You're right," I sigh. "Trusting people can be…"

"Tricky. Warped." Anya laughs. "I've had my fair share of betrayals."

"Oh. I suppose that's true."

We talk until Sebastian pops in. He's bubbly as usual, and I resist a giggle. Clearly, he hasn't seen himself.

"You woke early!" he exclaims. "How are you?"

"We… are fine," Anya says, suppressing a smile. "It was a lovely night."

"Good, good! Why don't you go meet Diablos and Harlow — he told me he revealed his name to you, so it's okay to mention it — in the arena?"

"Hm. Sounds great." I nod along. "Hey, what happened to you? Midlife crisis or something?"

"What do you mean?" He looks genuinely confused; so clueless.

"Have you looked in a mirror lately?" asks Anya, doing a great job at keeping a serious face. "Is it some kind of disease? And… those spiders on your back…"

"I have no diseases," he says, feeling his lumpy cheeks. "What *spiders*? *I hate spiders! Get them off! Get them off!*" His scream is so high-pitched, I can barely suppress my emotions. He runs off into the field.

As soon as he's gone, Anya and I erupt into laughter. "He had no idea! Can you imagine the look on his face when he sees himself?"

"I can only dream of it!"

We make our way to the tent cheerily. The prepared outfits are bright and sparkly, a match to our moods. We make our way to the ring.

"Morning, girls!" says Diablos, who also seems more sprightly than usual.

"About tonight…" Anya begins, but her voice is cut off. Her mouth opens a bit, and she trembles slightly as if in pain. Then she continues on as if nothing happened, "We're so excited for the show."

"Er… are you all right, Sunstar?" asks Diablos warily.

"Yes. Why wouldn't I be?" She cocks an eyebrow and I look at her, curious.

"Shall we make a switch? Sunstar with me, Harlow with Snowblaze?" asks Diablos, waving away the subject.

"Yes. Let's do that," replies Anya earnestly, and I frown at her hastiness.

"Hm, so you want a taste of my teaching?" chuckles Diablos. "All right. Snowblaze, why don't you head to the field with the ringmaster?"

"All right," I stammer, trying to reassure myself with the fact that this is our last day in the realm.

We walk to the tent area in awkward silence. Harlow raises his arms, and everything disappears around us. I stare in bewilderment.

"Do you… want to learn how to do that?" he asks, fiddling with his fingers as if nervous.

I clench my jaw. "I know what you did. You know what you did. Why are we ignoring it?"

"What did I do?"

"Well, more like who you *are*. Anya's idol. Her father."

He gulps. "A disappointment."

"I suppose you could be called that." I shrug. "But honestly, I want you two to get along. Father and daughter. You'll likely never see each other again after tonight."

He winces. "She'll never forgive me."

"If you don't fight for her, you'll never get the chance to find out what an amazing person she's become."

"You seem great, too," Harlow offers. "What's your story?"

"Oh, please," I snort. "You already have one relationship to worry about."

"You're not a burden to me. I *want* to get to know you."

"Well, maybe the feeling isn't mutual."

"Right," he says, though he looks a little hurt.

"What happened to Anya back there in the arena?" I demand, ignoring him. "She froze up. She changed her wording."

"We've found a way to share thoughts," he explains thoughtfully, running a hand through his hair. "I had to tell her to stop."

"Why? Why couldn't Anya ask about tonight?"

"Diablos doesn't exactly… *know* about it."

I gape at him. "You lied. I can't believe it. We're not fighting the Penumbra. You lied to get to Anya."

"No, I didn't," he says. "You *are* fighting tonight. We're going through with the plan. Only without Diablos' consent."

"How do you think that's going to work out?" Threads of hope waver inside me.

"I know it will. I'm a man in a position of power, and for once, I'd like to use it for the better. This is happening."

I sigh, and I'm not sure if it's from relief or disbelief. "Well, then. Aren't we here for a lesson? Are you going to teach me telepathy?"

"No, actually." He frowns. "I planned the lesson for Anya. So it's a step up from that, but I'm sure you can handle it."

"You don't know me."

"But Anya does."

I roll my eyes, but stop talking.

Harlow goes on, "Today, we are learning the second T. Transportation."

"Like, what, making a train?"

"No. More like speeding. Sprinting at an astonishing pace. Faster than the fastest animal."

"This sounds like it will be quite useful to me, then."

"You've got quite a tongue there, Snowblaze."

"It's Ora. Please, just get on with it and teach me already."

For a second, I think he'll scold me, but then his face softens, and he shrugs. "I deserve all this, I suppose. *Ora*, concentrate your mind on the rapidness of a cheetah. The lightness of a feather. The strength of an ox. Focus, feel, feign."

"Um. All right, then." I try to obey his strange requests, and as soon as I do, my body tingles with energy. A painful, overwhelming kind of energy. I let it drop.

"The more you do it, the more you'll get used to it," Harlow promises. "Do it again."

Everything inside me wants to stop as soon as the power returns to me.

Focus.

Feel.

Feign.

I steady my mind on rapidness, lightness, and strength. I imagine speeding, and my feet start to move. I open my eyes, thinking it may have actually worked, but when I look down, I realise my feet are moving at a normal — even a *slow* — rate.

"It didn't work," I huff.

"Well, you didn't really think it would work on your first try, did you? Not even I, as an adult, could do that."

I roll my eyes, but I can't deny the small amount of comfort it provides me. At least I have a chance of learning. "Show me. Harlow, the most powerful man known in the realm. Show me."

He doesn't hesitate to do so. He closes his eyes and stiffens. Then he zooms across the whole field and back to me in only a few seconds. It's like he never even moved. His body whirrs, a giant blob of a blur as it bolts. He doesn't even seem tired when he turns back to me.

"You're ridiculous," I breathe. "Your *sorcery* is ridiculous."

"The sorcery is yours as much as mine," he chuckles. "You are connected to my family. Related, maybe."

"That's impossible." I swallow. "I'm just rare."

"We'll see."

The certainty in his voice makes me unsteady for a second, but then I wave it away, and look at Harlow expectantly. "Teach me."

"There's nothing to teach. There's only to learn."

"All right, *poet*, what if I *can't*?"

"You'll learn," he assures me, and there's something soft in his voice. "Keep practising."

"I don't have time for that."

"Then try again now."

I exhale sharply.

Focus.

Feel.

Feign.

I feel my body fizz, and then I'm moving. I can barely see anything, but then my feet stop. I am breathless. I'm halfway across the field, not too far from Harlow. "What happened? I barely went for a second!"

"Your power ran out. This requires… a lot of strength." He nods. "But you got it, and even that's an outstanding achievement."

"Well…" I blush a little. "I want to get better."

"Good, and I'm sure you will," he tells me firmly. "For now, however, I think our time's up."

I open my mouth to argue, but wisely close it with a grunt. The tents reappear, and I can see Anya making her way into one.

"I'll see you at the arena," I say shortly. "Be sure to see that Sebastian brings snacks. I think he's gotten some kind of… illness. But we're still starved."

"How did this 'illness' happen?" he asks, but a smirk tugs at his lips.

"I'm not sure." I arch an eyebrow.

"Serves him right, however the form." He winks knowingly. "Though I guess then I have some karma coming my way."

"You're doing the right thing tonight, Harlow." Then I turn on my heel and join Anya behind the tarp.

"Well? How was the lesson?" she asks right away.

"Much better than yesterday. Your father teaches well, you know." I flex my arms out tiredly. "Which brings us to you and Diablos."

She rolls her eyes. "We both know how that went. First, tell me everything."

I do, chattering quickly, but I want to get to something. Anya must sense it, because she raises an expectant eyebrow.

"You were desperate to get away from Harlow," I say quietly. "I thought... I thought that you'd want to soak up the small amount of time you have left with him. I thought you'd cherish and savour it. He's your family, and no matter how many mistakes he's made, you have to find a way to forgive him."

Anya looks away from me, breaking our locked gaze. "He hasn't been with me for nine years. I barely remember him."

"We both know that's not true."

"You know, Ora," she says, stealing a glance at my face, "a part of me wonders... do you want to find your birth parents? Do you wish you had your very own father, connected by blood? Your very own sibling?"

I shake my head at the silly thought. "You are my very own sibling. As for my birth parents... they abandoned me. Left me as a baby. I have no interest in them."

"You must."

"I don't," I admit. "I had plenty of years in the orphanage to process what I wanted. It was a nightmare. Maybe I dreamed of having a true place to call home once. Maybe I dreamed of having normal parents. But the wishes wore off after a while. I got used to being treated roughly, like I had no feelings. I started believing what they said, because who else was there to believe? No one was there for me. No one."

Anya swallows, a distressed expression crossing over her. "I'm sorry," she offers.

"Not your fault. Just... don't leave him in the dark, okay? You'll regret it."

She shrugs. "When you put it that way, maybe I'll reconsider."

"Good. You should."

Sebastian suddenly scuttles into our tent. He looks the same, maybe even worse, and my urge to laugh returns. In his hands are two bowls of noodle soup.

"Harlow told me to whip up something special, and this is the best I could find," he grunts, setting them down.

"Sebastian, you look *terrible*," says Anya sympathetically. "What disease is it? Maybe I can help with my magic?"

"No. It won't work. And I have *no* diseases, for the last time," he snarls viciously, his lip curling in anger. "I don't know how this happened!"

"Hm," I mumble thoughtfully, spooning broth down my throat. "I could only imagine, but I truly hope you get better."

"That's kind of you." Sebastian bobs his head. "Get ready for the show in a couple of hours. I guess you'll see me tomorrow morning, hopefully in better condition than now."

This is going to be the last day I see him, I realise, and I'm definitely not sad about it. I wave my hand. "Goodbye, Sebastian."

He grumbles something under his breath and leaves. Anya and I explode into giggles as we down our cold soup.

"You ready for tonight?" I sing.

"I've never been *more* ready."

"Good. Because if Harlow doesn't pull through, we're going to need to save our own butts. We're going to need to know how to attack the Penumbra and get its heart ourselves."

We discuss our strategies, and Anya takes a nap. Once again — but this time for an unknown reason — Sebastian pops his head through the tent.

"Oh!" I force a smile. "It's been a while."

Anya shakes awake, and as soon as she sees Sebastian, she grimaces. Then she takes a breath, musters some positivity, and exclaims, "You again!"

"Yes, with my charming face," he murmurs, and then looks up, as if he's just remembered that we're here. "Right. Harlow wants you to change for the show now and go to the backstage, where he'll be waiting."

"Now? There's still a good hour left."

"Well, don't ask me. I have my own matters to attend to. Have fun tonight, girls."

"We plan on it!" As soon as he leaves, I mutter to Anya, "He's obnoxious even when he's in his best moods."

Anya yawns. "And now we need to get ready. Do you think Harlow's having second thoughts?"

"Or this is where he betrays us," I growl. "But there's no other chance of getting the artefact, so I guess we'd better go."

We head to the purple tent, change into violet gem-stoned costumes, and meet Harlow backstage. He is clicking his tongue impatiently, but when he sees us, his lips quickly pull into a smile. "Girls! Thank you for coming so last minute."

"It's not like we had a choice," I snort.

"I wanted to prepare you," he says.

Relief floods through me, but I stare at him angrily. "You wasted our time to give us tips? For a *pep talk*?"

Harlow doesn't move a muscle. "It's important, you know. You're taking on the Penumbra."

"No, we're taking on *you*," corrects Anya. "Unless you've changed your mind."

"I would never." He sounds sincere, but I know I can't afford to trust someone like him, so I cross my arms stubbornly.

"If you're planning on betraying us, we can—"

He raises his hand to silence me and shakes his head firmly. "You're my blood. I would not hurt you."

"Would you hurt me, though?" I interject warningly.

He pauses, pressing a finger to his lips. "You're my blood, too."

"I don't know what you're talking about."

"It is impossible to learn Blackstone magic by just being *rare*. In fact, despite other people's words, you cannot even learn it. You're family, Ora. You're a Blackstone. One day, you will *realise the truth*." I open my mouth to argue, but he keeps going on. "In case anything does go wrong, however, you're going to need to do something for me. You're going to need to promise me something.”

“What would that be?”

“You need to step out of the ring and forfeit if things go haywire.”

I laugh coldly. “Once you’re in the ring, you’re in the ring. You fight until death.”

“Don’t throw your lives away foolishly,” says Harlow. “I’m the one letting you fight, so you’ll do as I say. I will not watch you die. Promise me that you will back out if it gets too dangerous.”

Anya and I mumble pledges under our breaths, but I don’t know if I’ll actually be able to keep to my word if it comes to that.

“I wanted to go over some skills with you for the beginning of the battle. It may take a bit of time for me to get to Sebastian and start controlling, so you’ll need to be able to fend for yourselves. If it gets very bad…”

“We’ve already made the promise,” Anya scowls. “What do you think you can teach us?”

He goes over what to do when the robot acts up. This is dangerous, but I’m desperate.

Diablos joins us soon enough. “You’re all here. Girls, why did you come so early? I usually arrive before you.”

“It’s a big show for them tonight. You’ll see,” Harlow says, but I can sense something tense in him.

“You know how much I hate surprises,” sighs Diablos, “but I trust you.”

Well, I suppose we’ve both instilled our hopes in Harlow, then. He’s going to be backstabbing one of us.

“I’ve promised the audience something special tonight, so there’s going to be a big crowd today.” Harlow winks.

“Hm,” Diablos snorts. “And that something special is my surprise, I’m going to assume?”

“You’ve always been a smart man,” Harlow smiles, but I can tell it’s forced.

“Hm, well, this is your cue.”

“Good luck, girls.” Harlow looks over his shoulder, his eyes sorrowful. This could be the last time we ever see him.

"Wait!" Anya says abruptly. "Just… I'm so nervous. Can you give me one of those… er… magic hugs that you were teaching me in our lesson? To… give me strength?"

"What magic hug?" asks Diablos, but Harlow completely ignores him this time. A huge grin sweeps over his face, and he scoops Anya into his arms. I notice tears in her eyes as she sinks into him, embracing him tightly.

"What is going on here?" demands Diablos angrily.

"This magical hug got somehow very emotional," says Harlow. "I guess my emotions sank into her."

"Well, we'll work it out tomorrow," Diablos says carelessly. "Now, get off my ringmaster and let him do his job."

Anya's shaking when he pulls her weak arms off him.

Harlow gives a feeble smile. "I'll see you. One day."

"After the show," corrects Diablos with a snort. "This hug has some serious effect. Even on you, Harlow."

"Yes," he replies. "I'll work on it. Goodbye, Sunstar. Snowblaze, you're special, and you have such potential. Kill it tonight."

"Thank you," I stutter, because Anya can't bring herself to speak.

"Yes. It… it was my pleasure." Then he walks through the curtains. His voice drops when he speaks. "You've all been promised something special tonight. But first, the acrobats!"

The audience cheers as we walk out. I dance, and Anya forces herself to do the same, but we can feel Harlow's wistful eyes on us, and all we care about is the artefact. That is the only reason we perform. Our hunger drives us.

When we finish, we join Diablos and Harlow backstage.

"It lacked a little something, don't you think?" Diablos tuts thoughtfully. "Do better next time."

"Come. Shall we?" Harlow says. The two men go back into the arena. Harlow's voice is thunderous when he speaks now. "What you've been promised… some very special slaughterers! Two females, Sunstar and Snowblaze!"

We readily walk into the ring, and Diablos' mouth tilts open in surprise and anger. "What the hell do you think you're doing,

Blackstone?" he hisses at Harlow. "We have the man-slaughterer. We're not putting up our acrobats."

"Trust me," I wink. "We'll put on a good show."

"Don't make a scene," growls Harlow to Diablos. "They're ready. Continue on, or we'll lose fans. Do you know how many more coins came in today? I knew you'd say no, but Sunstar and Snowblaze completely convinced me."

The thought seems to put Diablos a bit more at ease, but he still looks uncomfortable. "I…I suppose…"

Harlow raises his voice for everyone to hear. "Presenting the Penumbra!"

The dark creature emerges from the wall, slithering across the floor viciously. Diablos steps forward, but Harlow shakes his head.

"I need to do something," he whispers, "but I'll be back."

I watch in amazement as Diablos shrugs, and Harlow escapes the stadium. He must be going to control the Penumbra. A part of me is surprised.

"Harlow had some business to attend to," Diablos coughs. "Who's ready for the Executionists?"

The audience roars, clapping their hands together. I lean in towards Diablos. "Trust me. We're going to win."

"Okay… and… commence!" he shouts.

My heart hammers in my chest as the Penumbra makes its way over to us. It looks unbelievably real. I wouldn't know that it is a robot if Harlow hadn't told me. Unfortunately, we don't get any warm-ups. Right away, the Penumbra lunges, and an earth-shattering scream erupts from its wiry mouth.

Anya jumps back, trembling.

"Snap out of it," I hiss to her. "This is the key to the ore."

She looks ahead to the Penumbra's heart and steadies herself. The monster is circling the ring, baring its teeth at us.

"Now," I whisper through my teeth. "What we practised."

We focus our minds together, and long, dangerous blades sprout from our fingertips. The Penumbra jumps at me, and I attempt to pierce it, but it dives under me easily. "Anya! Do it!" I shout.

Anya waits for the robot to come closer, and when it's about to attack, she launches herself onto its sturdy back. It howls again, trying to claw her body off, but it can't. It runs around the arena, screaming, as Anya digs her daggers through its metal body.

As it wildly gallops, I jump in front of it and concentrate on its heart. I hold out my hand, trying to stop it from shaking. "Stop. Please, Sebastian, I know you're there. Stop."

It pauses, and for a second, I think my words have worked, but then its claws reach back and tear Anya off its body. I scream in horror as she falls to the ground in a crumpled ball. The spectators gasp. I try to take our promise to Harlow out of my mind.

The monster takes a step towards Anya, reaching outward.

Harlow, stop this. Save your daughter. I can only pray.

But there is no hope. The Penumbra saws its nails through Anya's body. The wounds go deep, and anger rises inside me as her blood drips onto the floor beneath us.

I let power seep from the tips of my fingers. Blue magic shoots towards the Penumbra, strong and angry. It rips through the iron, and the Penumbra screeches.

"Anya! Get up!" I beg.

The monster, its back torn open, throws itself back and forth as it edges towards her. One more blow and she will die. One more blow and I will lose my sister, permanently this time. I can see her chest shallowly rising, but I don't know how long that will last.

As the Penumbra's talons go down, I jump in front of Anya's body, bracing for pain. But nothing comes. I realise that Diablos has raised a hand. His voice is quiet when he growls, "Stop now, Sebastian. Stop. Don't kill my dancers."

I freeze as the Penumbra obeys. Maybe I could cut through its heart now, steal it, and teleport away. But Diablos won't let that happen.

Anya shudders, and I feel something light up inside me.

I'm here.

I'm here.

I'm here.

It's Harlow speaking to me. He's finally taken over. Finally.

I will run. You will attack.

His voice rings through my ears. Anya squirms on the ground. Part of me wants to rush to her and try to heal her with my magic, but the other part knows what needs to be done. The Penumbra starts to bolt at me.

"Hey! Sebastian, stop that," commands Diablos irritably. "I said stop! You work for me, and I order you to *stop!*"

Harlow doesn't stop moving. If anything, he speeds his pace. I hurl my arms out, looking the Penumbra in its eyes.

"Stop." My voice is serene and sure in my own ears. "Stop."

Diablos watches as the Penumbra listens to me. "Good. Stop, Sebastian. Leave now."

The audience looks utterly confused as I take a step closer to the monster.

Do it. Do it. Do it.

"Not so fast, Diablos," I say calmly. "Maybe I want something more."

He watches in horror as I jump onto the Penumbra's stomach, clawing through the metal. I feel a surge of power. I look down to see Anya still lying on the ground, her quivering fingers in front of her. She's using her magic, despite her injuries; despite the red pouring from her body.

She gives me a weak smile. "You didn't think I'd let you have all the fun, did you?"

A whole load of confidence gushes through me.

"Girls! Don't kill my monster! Sebastian, fight back! They're trying to destroy you… and I'd rather have you than them!" Diablos is frantically looking back and forth between us, his eyes round with fright. "All of you—"

"Diablos, it's over." Anya's voice comes out strong, stronger than I know she's feeling. It must be hard, dangerous even, for her to be doing this in the state that she's in right now.

I try to stifle my gasp of relief when wires begin to fall, when the electricity starts sizzling into my palms.

Keep going.

This time, when he says the words into my mind, he sounds weaker. I ignore it, grasping harder. The large stone falls to the ground. "Anya, grab it!" I screech.

She moves slowly, inches away from the Shadow Ore. But Diablos is already there.

"*No!*" I shout out as Diablos gives Anya a hard kick in the gut and takes the artefact in his hands. A loud yelp of agony erupts from her lips.

"The prophecy was right," he glowers. "It's time for your end now. You will never get the Penumbra's heart."

I jump from the large creature as it falls. Before I can rush to Anya's side, I notice that there is a door inside the robot.

Don't open it. Please.

Harlow's voice is even more sickly than before. Exhausted, I pull my arms around the opening and jerk it open. I nearly choke when the body rolls out. Then another. Two bodies. Sebastian and Harlow.

"Oh, my God!" I wheeze, ignoring the audience's breaths of realisation. "How? Harlow, you told me that you moved it from the Monster Making Room."

He rolls over with a groan and rasps out, "To control it, you have to transport inside the Penumbra and do the work from there. It's some weird magic, but once you master it…"

"You lied," I cry. "Why did you lie?"

"Once the monster dies, the controller does, too," sighs Harlow. "It's better not to know sometimes."

I look back. Anya is unconscious on the floor, and Diablos is staring at us in bewilderment, because we've just ratted out all his secrets to the realm.

"You traitor!" he screams. "I always knew you were a traitor!"

"But I'm good as dead now, so what does it matter?" Harlow chuckles, though he grabs his stomach as soon as he does. "Now everyone knows the truth. There'll be no more Executionists from now on. Ora, bring Anya to me. As for you, Diablos, you'll need to stay put."

He starts to run backstage, but with the snap of a finger, Harlow has frozen Diablos. Agog, I lift Anya to my chest and lay her down in front of Harlow.

He lays his hand on her, and the wounds disappear. He leans forward and gives her a kiss. "Goodbye."

As soon as Anya's eyes open, I already know what to do. I grab her teleporter from her pocket and hand it to her. "Stop, Ora—" but I have already jabbed her fingers into the crystal. She screams in protest as her body shimmers away.

"You've done well, Ora," whispers Harlow. "Keep protecting her. Complete the mission. I know you are capable."

Then he's gone, his mouth tilted open, his eyes shut. His magic wears off, and Diablos is free again.

"You're not going anywhere." As small as I feel on the inside, I won't let him get away with this. I decide that I'm too tired to use my power on him, so instead, I sprint to him, springing my body over his so he is on the ground.

"I will never let you have this," he pants. He throws his hand out, and the ore disappears.

I watch in terror as it gets flung over the ring and into the millions of seats. The audience squeals, and they lunge at it.

"*No!*" My voice is shrill as I hastily get to my feet. "You've got to give that to me!"

"They've read the prophecy," sneers Diablos. "They know you want to destroy them. Why would they give up their lives to you?"

"You give up lives every day," I snarl back. "This is for a good cause."

"You want to eradicate our land," an audience member yells, throwing her fist into the air. "*Good cause?*"

"I need to." I swallow. "I have no choice."

"Yes, you certainly do," growls Diablos. "Stay. Work with me. I'll treat you with luxury. We can forget this ever happened."

"I would never," I tell him haughtily. "You are a beast."

"*You* want to crush my whole world," he scoffs. "And *I'm* the beast?"

I sniff, ideas piling into my mind.

"Are you really considering it?" asks Diablos, reading my mind. "You're considering killing the whole audience and taking the ore."

"They're all going to die anyway," I plead. "I hate… war. But I need this. I need it. You are *characters*. You aren't people."

"Don't. There are other ways to do this."

"No." I jab a finger at him. "You must end."

"And all my people," he breathes, taking a step towards me.

"Stay there!" I swing my fist at his cheek and he stumbles back in surprise. I look at my knuckles, shocked at the sudden strength, but this is no time for regret. I focus my mind, and waves of water gush through the ring. They creep through the whole place, build around me. I stand in a bubble of resistance as chaos spreads everywhere else.

Diablos sinks into the sheet of water. "You are a monster." Then he collapses, his body lifeless and swept away.

"Give me the ore," I shout at the audience, "or I'll flood the arena." The words sound wrong, but I remind myself that the characters are not real. They are simply illusions.

"We'll die either way, then," hollers back a spectator. "We'd rather die fighting you. Diablos at least embraced his depravity. You think you're doing the right thing."

"I am! You don't understand!" I don't know why I sound so desperate. I don't know why tears cloud my eyes. They are illusions. That's all. I grit my teeth as power rushes from me to them. I pull away their air, so they are all gasping. The sounds make me want to apologise that I am inflicting this pain on them, but this is what must be done. I am suffocating them. Killing them slowly.

"Monster!" The word rings out several times, and each time it does, I shrink a bit inside. The voices fade away.

Soon, all the men and women have fallen. A sob rises in my throat, but I push it down. I focus on being weightless as I leap over onto the seats. The pull of the magic makes it easy to locate the artefact. When I pick it up, it glows brightly, and a small thrill, rushes through me. I take a second to look around to see what I've done. There is a countless amount of bodies scattered around, and it's hard to believe that this is my doing. I breathe in slowly and pull out my crystal. Tears run down my cheeks as I disappear.

Illusions, I keep telling myself. But it's not true, because Harlow had been a *real* person. So I may have just killed hundreds of humans.

19
Anya

"ORA."

Her body is thrown in front of me. I look around to see the familiar walls of the athenaeum. Esme, by my side, looks at her with concern. "Are you all right?"

Ora swallows. "I have the ore. Put it into the Heart of Stone."

Esme takes it from her fingers and presses it into one of the holes. It liquefies immediately, melting in its spot.

There is only one more to go, and then I will have Dax back. I've already checked his heartbeat. It's slower and hollower, but it's still there.

"Ora," I repeat. "You brought me away without my consent. You tore me from my father. He's dead."

She shivers. "I'm sorry. I thought it was necessary."

"What even happened out there?" I can't help asking.

"I did what I had to do." But as she says this, tears leak out of her eyes. And then she vomits into a bookshelf.

Esme grimaces and goes to her side, patting her back gently.

"You should've let me help," I say quietly.

Ora clears her throat and wipes the sides of her mouth. "Your father… he died. I didn't think you'd be able to bear it."

"You know I would've had to kill him either way. The whole realm was destroyed, and if he weren't already dead, he would be by now."

"Yeah." She pauses and gets to her feet. "I was lost in the moment. I wasn't acting properly, I guess."

"Well" — I sigh — "good job, anyway. Thanks for getting it. Thanks for doing what you had to do."

She shrugs. "It was necessary, but… I'm a monster."

I stare at her in shock. "What? Who told you that?"

"Everyone," she whispers meekly. "A whole realm. I killed them all. I took away their oxygen to get the artefact."

I take her hand, searching for the right words. "They didn't understand. All they sought was havoc, watching those nasty shows, and they deserved what came their way."

"No one deserves what I did to them. Even... *illusions*."

I shake my head. "What's done is done. It's in the past."

She buries her face in her hands, murmuring to herself. Esme sets a hand on her shoulder. "Are you okay to go through the next Chronicle?"

She looks up, her face wet but determined. "Of course. I took away all those lives; they had to be for a reason. We're going to do this. And after, we'll get Veronica."

Esme sighs. "Yes, so there's quite a list, but you're over halfway done. One more book is nothing."

"Right," I snort. "Nothing."

"You know what I mean." Esme breathes in sharply. "The third Chronicle is dangerous, of course. The Stardust Crown is what you'll be looking for. In the Fairy Tale Land. All the stories you've been told — everything you've read in the stories — exist there. All the characters are within those pages. But beware: people are not what they seem. You may expect Snow White to be very kind, but she's quite the opposite. What you've been told... lies. This Chronicle holds the truth of the characters. Some villains are quite amiable, to be honest with you. Some fairy tales have endings that never appeared in the books. Hansel and Gretel were prince and princess, and their father, who you thought was Wheresmeine, the woodcutter, was truly a king. Each king and queen had a crown that proves them royalty. They are their most prized possessions."

"And let me guess," I say. "One crown is the artefact."

"Yes, that's correct." Esme frowns. "It's going to be hard to get. The crown belongs to King Wheresmeine, a selfish man. Once that person finds out that it's gone, they'll do anything to get it. Kill, even."

"Yes, we've learned that many have no mercy," mutters Ora. "When can we leave? Just because I'm 'shaken up', doesn't mean we're waiting another week. I want to go. Right now." Suddenly, she reaches up to the third Chronicle, but a hard hand slaps down on her arm, making her pull away in pain and shock.

"Foolish," Esme mutters. "You are so desperate, so careless. You don't consider the consequences. You thrive on thirst."

"Maybe," she retorts. "But I'm ready."

"No. You say that now." Esme shakes her head angrily. "Rest is what you need. You just arrived from a Chronicle, so you must be wise."

"She's right," I admit meekly. "Sleeping will do us good."

Ora studies me, her eyes blazing, but then she gives in with a sigh. "If that's what you want. Maybe I am a little… rusty right now."

Scarred. That's what she is. I know that, and I think she does, too, but neither of us dare say it aloud.

"Come. Let's go out of the athenaeum for now, and you can tell me about all your adventures," Esme says, beckoning us warily. I realise that she's afraid we'll try and hop right into the Fairy Tale Land without warning. That she may want to check if we're still sane after how Atikus lost it after he exited the second Chronicle.

I throw one last glance back at Dax's shivering body in the chest before following Esme down the stairs, Ora at my side. We reach our bedroom, and I collapse into my fluffy pillows. "I've missed this," I murmur dreamily. I sit up to see Esme looking at me, her face twisted with guilt.

"Yes. A child always misses home," she whispers.

"It's not like I went unwillingly," I protest hastily. "I wanted to help, and I got to. I wouldn't want to be in any other position. Not really."

Esme just shakes her head. "This is your childhood — *childhoods* — and I…"

"Stop," Ora interjects, raising a hand. "I've already told you, this is pretty much a paradise for me."

Esme sighs. "No. Watching people die, having to worry about being slaughtered or turning into a character in a book is no paradise. You are grateful because you don't understand what's really happening. You don't use your eyes to see what a nightmare I've handed over to you. A part of me wishes that I never showed you the athenaeum. That I never set you into the grave danger you are now in."

Before I can argue, Esme hurries on. "Anyway, children, I should leave you now. Let you relax, maybe plot a bit."

We watch her quickly go, clicking the door shut gently behind her.

"If we die, she'll feel responsible." Ora swallows. "She'll break."

"Well, we won't die," I tell her shortly, as if it's that easy. "

Ora laughs forcedly, her eyes exhausted. "I can't believe what happened today. How many people I murdered."

I frown, wishing I could have been there for her. "Next time, let me fight by your side. It will be easier."

"If you were with me, it would have given me strength, but it wouldn't be *easier*. I'll always carry that sorrow in my heart. I'm glad you didn't witness what I did."

I breathe out softly, and a part of me wants to jump out of bed and wrap my arms around her; but when I look at her, she's asleep. I don't know what time it is. I could check my shattered — cracked, as Harlow would put it — watch, but even that seems like such an effort right now. Instead, I settle under my covers and close my eyes.

"Anya. Anya, wake up. *Anya.* My God, you wake up, or I will dump a pail of water over your head. Don't doubt that I mean it. Yesterday I wiped out a part of a realm with my skills."

I groan and force my lids open to see Ora looming over me. "What time is it?"

She rolls her eyes. "It's already noon."

"Noon?" I nearly choke. "Why didn't you get me up earlier?"

"Ha!" She lets out a small chuckle. "We've tried. At nine o'clock, Esme came in with breakfast, and when we shook you, you didn't react in any way. I waited and finally gobbled up your food. I was hungry. Tried again at eleven, and you threw a pillow at my face."

I huff. "Sorry."

"Can't say I blame you."

I sit up. "Well? Let's go now. Where's Esme?"

Ora fiddles with her fingers. "Downstairs. But… she says that we have to wait another day to leave for the next Chronicle."

"Are you serious?" I gape at her. "We don't have time for that!"

"I know." She shrugs. "It's not in my hands."

Right on time, Esme barges into the room. "Did I hear you talking?"

"Yes," I snap. "And I hear you want us to spend *another* day locked up in this house."

"Locked up?" Esme asks with a chortle. "That is a bit of an exaggeration, don't you think? I mean, this place isn't so bad."

Ora looks around. "*Locked up* may not have been the right phrase," she agrees unhelpfully.

"Certainly. I have an objective to this plan, of course. I think that, last time, you rushed into the Chronicle far too quickly."

I snort. "Far too quickly — meaning what? We waited weeks to go. We waited for Ora to recover fully."

"Yes, well…" Esme pauses. "As soon as the stitches were removed, you fled."

"I was cleared," points out Ora. "I was fine to travel."

"She told you to take it easy," corrects Esme, arching an eyebrow. "I would hardly say teleporting to a mad world and fighting against monsters in an arena is *taking it easy*. What do you say?"

Ora shrugs. "I'm stronger than most. Shilling was just being careful. She's not aware of or used to my power."

Esme releases a shallow sigh. "I just don't want you rushing into the Fairy Tale Land the following day after everything that happened."

"You don't… that's not *fair*." I sound like a baby saying those words, and they ring falsely in my ears.

"Life isn't fair." Esme frowns. "Today, you gain power. Tomorrow, you put it into practice. Understand me?"

I roll my eyes but don't bother protesting. She, after all, is our guide amid all this mayhem. Ora keeps her mouth shut, too, though the look in her eyes doesn't make it hard to know that she wants to say something.

"Perfect." Esme gives the smallest smile. "I'll leave you to it then."

"It's not like we have a choice," I grunt, taking Dax's photo and running my fingers over his outline. *Soon.* Soon, I will be reunited with my brother. Except… "Mother. When is she coming back?"

Esme's voice turns hard. "She's been brought to London, but we are not allowed to visit her right now." Then she disappears into the corridor, not bothering to close the door.

I gulp nervously. "I hope she's okay, but we both know that we won't be able to get anything out of Esme."

Ora gives me a reassuring smile. "It'll all be fine in the end."

I can't return the smile, as hard as I try. Instead, I mumble, "We can hope."

"Dax is so close."

"Sometimes, things seem within grasp, and then…" I cut myself off, refusing to finish the sentence. "You're right. We'll get to him."

Ora studies me, her face screwed up in concern. "You all right?"

"There's just a lot of pressure." I shrug. "So many things could go wrong. I want this day to be over already."

"Well, we'll do something fun," Ora replies. "We'll…"

An idea pops into my mind. "We'll go to the forest."

"The forest?"

"I don't know why I haven't taken you out there before." I shrug thoughtfully. "It's my secret hideout place, where I go when I want to be alone. You're a part of me now. I want to share it with you."

She looks touched, but then she cocks her head to the side. "Are you sure?"

I laugh. "This decision isn't very hard to make compared to the ones in the Chronicles. Of course I'm sure."

Ora follows me out the front door. Esme is stirring vanilla frosting in a bowl. When I tell her where we're going, she immediately asks if we want her to go with us. She thinks everywhere is dangerous now. I assure her we'll be fine and return back soon, but I can feel her wary eyes on our backs as we leave.

I guide Ora to the forest, where I haven't been in weeks. The trees are as beautiful as ever, sunshine glinting off the scalloped leaves. The stream sparkles, glissading past our feet. Ora joins me on my boulder.

"This place is great," she breathes. "So alive. Peaceful, even."

I look around, feeling a surge of pride. "Mother named it the Moonlit Wood."

Ora beams. "What a pretty title."

We sit there, watching the writhing water, the wavering branches on trees.

"I think this is going to be the hardest Chronicle yet," Ora suddenly says quietly. "With the other two, we were in the same places as the artefacts."

"Maybe it was meant to be."

"Or a coincidence. I don't know if it'll play out like that again."

I sniff, breathing in the wonderful fragrance of the woodland. Finally, I reply, "We'll see. But… can't we talk about anything else? Can't we get our minds off this for a second?"

Ora regards me curiously, and her eyebrows knit together. "How could we ever do that? We get the job done, no matter how exhausted we feel. We've been sent on a quest, and we're going to finish it. Everything is on the line. Your brother's life."

I laugh, taken aback. "I know that! You think I'm not aware of the consequences if we don't pull through? You think I don't worry all the time?"

"We need to be top-notch, then! There's no time for faffing about and doing yoga in the wood."

"I can't believe you're telling me this right now."

"Well, I want this all to be over, too. I want to settle. Look, we keep our eyes on the prize, and we plan and plot until we've completed the Heart of Stone. Stay concentrated. We don't have time for dispatching ourselves."

"I know that," I repeat. "I want this more than you."

Ora shrugs. "Maybe. But I work hard."

"I don't?"

"I didn't say that."

"You basically did," I scoff. "What's your problem right now? Why are you acting like this?"

Ora swallows. "Things happened at the orphanage, An. Things that I will never say."

My voice softens. "That's in the past now."

"That was my *life* for twelve years. I've been living in your world of riches and paradise for a short amount of time. I've been given a new life, a better one, and this is the first obstacle I have to overcome. I'm going to overcome it. I just don't want to fail. Because if I do, I won't be able to live with myself. Ever."

"Me, neither." I stare at her, breathing slowly. I can feel the tears coming, but I ferociously push them back. "If I were to lose Dax, I don't know what I'd do. My world would evaporate. Things would… fade."

"Yeah," Ora says, and she seems embarrassed. "I'm sorry."

I don't know what to say so I put my hand in hers and sigh.

I'm not sure how long we stay in the Moonlit Wood, but I do know that Esme has to come and find us. I look up to see a canopy of darkness mottled with stars painted above us.

"What time is it?" Ora asks, startled.

"Too late." Esme's voice comes out coldly. "Do you know how worried I was? You told me you'd be back soon, and I thought something may have happened."

"Nothing happened, except some reflecting on our journeys," I promise her. "We simply lost track of—"

"It doesn't matter now. Come and eat, and then you can go to sleep right after. Tomorrow is a big day."

"Yes. We know," Ora mutters bitterly, as we get up and trail after Esme into the house. The air smells delicious, of spices and cinnamon The table is laid out with stew, baguettes, chicken legs, and noodles. I notice the oven is on, lit up and sizzling.

"Esme! How much did you make?" Ora exclaims gratefully.

"Well, it's your last day before the third Chronicle. I thought I'd better make it special."

It might be my last day in this house. I shove the thought away as I dig in, noshing down as much food as I can handle. The meals that we've had the past days haven't been very appetising; I think back to the raw, stale sandwiches Sebastian always brought to our tent. Speaking of which, we also haven't had very good sleeps. So, after cupcakes, custard tarts, and clafoutis, Ora and I head to our room, settle into our beds with full stomachs, and doze off easily.

The next morning, I wake up early. As soon as Esme comes in, Ora and I are ready. We eat the provided breakfast. Luckily, Esme must have figured that we'd still be stuffed from yesterday's dinner because I finish it all easily.

"We need to go," I say after I've guzzled everything down. Then I notice her facial expression. "Don't tell me you want us to wait another day."

"Not exactly," says Esme nervously.

"What's wrong then?"

"Yes. Um. The door to the athenaeum seems to be stuck."

"Stuck? How?"

"It… won't open."

Panic flares inside me as I jump out of my bed after Ora, and we rush to the closed entry. Together, we press our hands against the wood, but Esme's right — it won't budge.

"You can't waste your power like that when you'll need it in the Fairy Tale Land," warns Esme, but we ignore her and push harder. Minutes pass, and we have to step back from exhaustion. We haven't changed a thing.

"Has this ever happened before?" I pant. "Has it ever gotten stuck?"

"Yes, but this is no accident," Esme grunts. "Someone did this."

"Who has access to the athenaeum, besides us and Mother?"

Esme shakes her head. "I don't know. This is hopeless. A person somehow got hold of the place and locked it."

"Dax is incapable, isn't he? Is it possible that the characters in the remaining Chronicle are controlling him?"

"Maybe… no." Esme huffs with frustration. "Harlow fastened it from the inside long ago when you were born, Anya, and he gave us a special pen to come in. But Veronica has it now, and God help her, she's in jail."

I grunt.

"Wait." Ora suddenly perks up, her eyes rounded as if she's just had an idea. "What did this *pen* look like, exactly?"

"It's a beautiful silver one with a blue butterfly carved into it."

Ora's eyes round even more. "That's not possible."

"What?"

She scurries away to our bedroom. I watch her, curious. I can hear the sounds of drawers rattling, papers being madly removed.

Ora takes a long time lingering in the room, and when I've had enough and am about to go and see what's going on, she at last comes out. In her hand is a beautiful silver pen with a blue butterfly carved into it.

Esme stares at it, shocked.

"She gave it to me the day of the adoption," says Ora. "It provided me some comfort."

"But she knew what danger it possessed."

"Maybe she forgot?" I shrug, but the words sound silly out loud.

"No, she must've given it to you for a reason." Esme grits her teeth in concentration. "That thing is more threatening than you can imagine. Why would she give that to you? To a mere child?"

"I'm not sure," Ora says hastily, "but we'd better get moving."

I watch in awe as she taps the pen against the door, and it flies open with ease. How did Harlow create this? We all step through, and Esme opens the wall. I fall, but I'm used to it by now. I land on my feet, much to my delight, and Ora does the same.

We head upstairs to the third floor, and I check Dax's uneven pulse. Then we make our way to the shelves.

"I have to say, I'm a bit relieved this is the last time we'll be doing this," I admit, but as soon as I do, I know there's something wrong with the words. I *enjoy* the responsibility. I thirst for the power. I hunger for the potential that Harlow so firmly placed in me. I want the danger, the adventure; the sureness that I'm finally doing something right.

"Yes," murmurs Esme, clearly still in deep thought. "You'll be careful, hm? The Fairy Tale Land is a giant place."

"We'll be careful." Ora winks. "As long as you figure out who's messing with our Secret Athenaeum. As long as you get Veronica home safely."

"You mustn't worry about those things." Esme tuts. "Focus on yourselves and your task."

"We'll try, Esme," I sigh.

"Be safe, children." She gives us each a quick hug and reaches for the Chronicle, placing it gently into my trembling hands.

"Ready?" Ora asks me.

"Ready."

We open the pages, but as I feel my body disintegrate, I know that what lies ahead of us is something we could never think to prepare for.

THE FAIRY TALE LAND

A twisted fable of rotten lies, unpredictable romance, and a crown of stardust and strength…

20
Ora

A HONK BUZZES IN MY EAR.

I roll over, expecting my bottom to be stuck in a crate or a dollop of snow, but instead, I find a warm mattress. My eyes fly open, fully alert. I look around, breathing hard, to find myself in a tiny room with thin wooden walls. A creaky door swings open and shut. I leap out of bed, but as soon as I do, I am thrown off balance. I roll to the ground with a groan.

Get up. See what's going on.

I ignore the bruises that have moulded themselves into my knees, and carefully get to my feet. The floor is somehow moving, I realise. Where am I? I warily make my way through the door. I find myself lost in crowds of people screaming and swearing. They're all taller than me, so I can't see what's going on. People stamp on my feet, run into me without noticing, but I don't care. All I care about is finding Anya.

Another buzz sounds, this time louder. People scatter, and, finally, there's a bit of space for me. I tiptoe across the sliding platform beneath me, but there are still too many men and women clouding my sight.

"Excuse me!" I shout. "Anyone!"

A young lady crouches before me. "Have you lost your mother?"

"My sister," I say frantically. "Tell me, where am I?"

"Hmph. Poor kid," she sighs. "We're on our way from Karmen Island. Your home."

"You don't understand," I plead. "I need to find my sister."

"Well, when we load off the *Jolly Roger*, you'll hopefully see her. My father's still bleeding from his gun wound, so I must go attend to him."

"How was your father shot?"

"The question is, how were you *not*? It's not like the Razor Tribe, to spare children. Lucky 'un, you are."

She scampers away, leaving me more confused than ever. The *Jolly Roger* is Captain Hook's ship; I know that from the stories. Am I on that right now? Where am I headed? Towards or away from the artefact? And the big question… is Anya on here with me right now? The vessel rocks back and forth as we ride through the waters. My skin prickles with goosebumps. Suddenly, the floor stops moving, and there is a big thump.

A blaring voice of a man screams, "Arrived at Bluebay!"

Cheers break out. I'm back to not being able to see anything but the woolly grey jackets of men. My ears hurt from the loudness of everything. I am desperate to find Anya.

"Group one, if you have the blue sticker, get off here," the same voice announces. "Good luck in your endeavours."

Alarmed, I look down at my hand to see a pale-blue tag attached to it. I freeze, unsure what to do, and then someone tugs on my shirt. The same woman who told me about my whereabouts stands behind me. "Come, child. This is your stop."

"But… my sister."

"Captain Hook would've put you together if you had the same last name," she promises me.

But we don't.

But we arrived by appearing into thin air.

What am I supposed to tell her, though? What if Anya is getting off right now, and I just can't see her? I reluctantly follow the lady down marble steps, and at last I can see. We are on a shore, and there are people dotted all over.

A man — who I recognise as Captain Hook from the stories — is waving his hand through the air. "Farewell! Good luck!" He sounds surprisingly kind.

"Have a nice time, dear," says the woman, stalking off to the trees behind the shore with an old, bleeding man stumbling after her.

Suddenly, I catch a glimpse of someone on the ship. Anya, curled up on her knees, rocking back and forth. She looks terrified. I scream out her name, but it gets swallowed up by the mobs of men and women, crying and shouting and clapping. She doesn't see me. She doesn't hear me. Her lips are moving as if reciting a prayer. Her hands are clasped together as if trying to bring me to her. I make my way back to the ship's gangway, but it closes up, much to my dismay. I watch in horror as the *Jolly Roger* gives a honk and sails away, moving fast.

"*No!*" My voice is weak in my own ears. My legs give way, and I fall to the sand as the vessel moves farther and farther away.

"Girl, don't ya have someone waitin' for ya? Didn't ya travel here for a reason?" a man's wheezy voice asks me.

I don't even turn. I just ignore him until he's gone, until everyone has drained from the shore and left me alone, sobbing and hopeless. If I do find the artefact, how will I be able to teleport away without Anya? A small pain in my arm brings me back to reality. My eyes flap open, and I have to squint to look at what animal stands in front of me. A…a unicorn? It nips me again expectantly.

"Please stop that," I say hollowly. It knocks its head against me, nuzzling into my skirt. "Well, okay, you're a bit cute." I laugh dryly as it gives a delighted hiccup. Maybe I can sit here, maybe think of a plan. Relax for the slightest moment. Take a nap, perhaps…

"Oh, Swizzle! There you are!"

I spin around to see a young boy stalking towards me, a bit older than me. He has dark skin, deep hazel eyes, and ruffled brown hair. He wears a dazzling crooked grin, and I realise he's looking at me.

"Has Swizzle bothered you, young lady?"

There's something dashing, almost attractive, about his smooth voice. I think he's the most beautiful human being I've ever seen.

"Not at all." I sigh miserably, picking up the squirming thing — which has incredibly soft fur — and handing him to the boy. "Have a good day."

"Wait a second." He regards me intently. "What are you doing here all alone? It's clear you've been crying."

Embarrassed, I quickly wipe my wet cheeks. "It's the seawater," I insist. "It sprayed all over me when I arrived here."

"Hm."

"It's true! The ship rolled away rather clumsily. The seawater did a great deal of splashing to many people."

He laughs.

"What?" I demand.

"Nothing, nothing at all! Ships are *so* clumsy these days. Though, it still doesn't explain why you're here. You've come from Karmen Island?"

"Yes. My sister is riding away on Captain Hook's ship right now. We've been split up."

"Is she going to Raven? Arcterix? Tamatar? Which one's she headed to? Why would Captain Hook part sisters? He usually doesn't do that."

"I... don't know," I say lamely, feeling hope vanish inside me. "Where exactly are we?"

"Bluebay County." He knits his eyebrows together. "You hit your head on the *Jolly Roger* or something?"

"Probably. Can you take me to my sister? Let's go travelling across borders... and..." The words are stupid, make-believe. Out of the blue wild.

"That's not a good idea." His voice is grave, but then he perks up a bit when he says, "Where are you off to now? You have the blue sticker, so you're supposed to be here."

I shrug, letting sand slip through my fingers. "I don't quite know what to do, honestly. I don't know where to go."

"My sister and I take in refugees," he offers. "For a small amount of time, until you gather your own money, make your own life. We have no one staying with us right now, and, well... Swizzle seems to have taken a liking to you."

Is that an invitation to go with him? If I don't, will I spend the rest of my time sitting on this shore, waiting for Anya? Is this my only chance of getting to know the place? Maybe I'm in the land where the Stardust Crown lies. "How generous of you to ask. Maybe I *will* come with you," I finally say. Then I add, "For a small amount of time, of course."

"Of course. Come with me. Would you like to take Swizzle? This sweet guy won't bite."

I take the soft animal in my arms, and he melts against my chest, purring like a cat. "Swizzle is a... cute name. How'd you come up with it?"

"My sister and I love candy. Swizzle sticks are some favourites."

"You and your sister… you live with an adult? Or is your sister much older?"

"Quite the opposite. She's younger. We live together, so it's fine. Don't go looking so shocked now. I'm fifteen, and eight-year-olds live on their own in Bluebay. I've never been to Karmen, so perhaps it's different there, but it's completely natural here."

"Hm. Yes, Karmen was very *different*." It's good that this boy hasn't been there, because I'll be feeding him plenty of lies from my imagination.

"You look shaken. After all you've been through, I'd expect nothing less." He looks concerned, his face contorted with sorrow. "Karmen is such a war zone, especially now with the invading of the Razor Tribe."

"Yes." I clear my throat noisily. "If we could talk about anything else, please, I'd appreciate it."

"Of course." He turns from me, leading out into a small woodland. We walk through, and just behind is a village of small houses. *Not palaces? Isn't this supposed to be the Fairy Tale Land?*

"What's your name, then?" he asks, navigating us through the residences.

"Um." I know I can't say Ora, but I don't feel like making up a whole new name, so I give a little shrug.

"You must have a name."

"Like you said, I bumped my head."

"Not too hard that you forgot everything, I hope."

"Just hard enough, perhaps?"

"Gretel's good with the healing. Don't worry."

I nearly crash into a lamp post. "Did you say Gretel?" I choke out.

"Yes. She's my sister."

"Oh. Right, of course." I stumble after him, thoughts clouding my mind. I remember Esme explaining how they were prince and princess, and their father… King Wheresmeine. But Hansel told me he and his sister don't live with an adult. How can that be? Before I can ask any questions, we turn a corner to find a brilliant house.

"It's made of candy!" I gasp.

Hansel chuckles. "Not *real* candy, of course, but it's what's expected from us. We got a great designer to come in and do all this magic."

"Wow. That's certainly impressive." I cover my mouth when he opens the candy cane door. The inside of the place is how I would always imagine it — the walls embroidered in bright lollipops, cosy mint sofas, trampoline-like flooring with pictures of sweets carved all through it. A staircase of Smarties instead of marble.

"Welcome." Hansel flashes an unbearably handsome smile. "I hope you'll make yourself at home. Gretel, a refugee has joined us!"

Down the stairs comes a beautiful girl, about my age or younger, with long brown curls spiralling down her back studded with golden rose jewels. "Well, *Hansel*, don't just call her a refugee. Would you like me to call you Candy Boy?"

"Don't try," he says, his lips tugging upward. "She says she doesn't remember her name. Hit her head on the ship."

She regards me with pity. "I'll see if I can change that. I've been practising, you know. Bringing back memories, even healing."

"I'm quite aware. Have you done your homework?" interjects Hansel.

"You might well know you should be more concerned about *yourself*. I do everything on time," says Gretel haughtily, but when she looks at me, there's a mischievous little smirk on her face.

"Well, you have school tomorrow, so you'd better not be lying," he warns, catching onto her playful expression. "We'll enrol her, too, of course."

I realise with a jolt he's talking about me. "Oh, that's not necessary."

"Of course it is," Gretel says quickly. "Queen Yzma made it clear all refugees shall join Bluebay Academy immediately. You'll know me, too, so it won't be very scary."

Yzma? The villain from *The Emperor's New Groove*? I recall how warped the stories are in this Chronicle. But that's not the problem. The problem is that I can't waste any time going to school. "It's fine," I insist desperately. "I want to get to know the county."

"And you will," Gretel assures me. "But this is something that must happen. Strict orders.”

“You live under Yzma’s protection,” I say slowly, “but what about your father? Does he rule?”

Hansel stiffens. He and Gretel exchange uneasy glances, and finally he says, “We don’t usually talk about him.”

A realization washes over me. What if Wheresmeine is dead? Who would have possession of the crown then?

“Every king and queen rule different areas in the Fairy Tale Land,” Hansel continues. “We chose to live in Bluebay with Her Highness, Yzma. She’s a good person.”

“But… your father? Why don’t you live with him?”

“We chose to live in Bluebay,” he repeats tensely. “This is a touchy topic, so if you wouldn’t mind…”

I want to beg for Wheresmeine’s location, but I simply blow a puff of air and choose to discuss it later, when I’m more concentrated and rested. Instead, I sit down in a chair and stroke Swizzle, who dozes off easily.

“I hate secrets,” I mutter. “You should probably know that about me.”

Gretel sighs and plops down next to me. “It’s in the past. The past, mingled with pain and hurt and lies. It’s better to leave it all behind. Trust me, we shouldn’t take a trip down memory lane.”

I grunt in response, not sure how to argue with that. I can’t tell her that I only have five days before my time’s up, and that I need to know where her father is situated so that I can steal his most prized possession and destroy her world. I look up at her innocent face; her cheery, forgiving eyes.

An illusion. That’s all she is.

“Are you… okay?” she asks me kindly, and I can sense there’s real care there.

“Yes. Of course.” I try to ignore the knot of guilt forming in the pit of my stomach. “I’m fine.”

“I know you’ve been through a lot, to say the least.” Again, the pity.

“I’m going to take a nip to the bathroom.”

“Down the hallway and make a right!”

I follow the directions to a toilet. When I look at the mirror my hair is a tangled mess of knots from the heavy winds, and my blouse is torn at the hem. I groan and take a brush from the counter. It's too tiring to get the coils out, so I put it into a quick braid and attach a few bobby pins before returning downstairs to join Gretel on the sofa.

"Hm, love that Dutch thang going on with your hair," she says right away.

"Thanks," I mumble.

"You have bags under your eyes," points out Gretel. "Are you tired? You must be, from all that travelling across the border."

"I'm exhausted," I agree. "A nap might do me good. May I go to a room?"

"Yes, of course. I should've thought of that earlier, silly me." Gretel gives me a tender look. "I'll do my homework. I mean, er, I'll *revise* it."

Hansel cuts in sternly. "I'll take her," he says. "You, Gretel, *please* get it done, for God's sake."

"Ugh! Who says I haven't, Candy Boy?"

Hansel takes me upstairs where there is a large corridor and five massive doors, each made of a different kind of candy. He leads me to the fourth door — dotted with sour keys — closest to the stairs, and gives me a nod. "Enjoy your nap."

The words make my insides flutter, but I push down the dazed feeling. It's only here because I'm tired. I watch him join Gretel on the first floor, and then I slip into my room. There is a velvety bed in the centre, and there is a whole shelf lined with frames and tiny antiques along the back wall. There are mainly photos of Hansel and Gretel, posing and smiling, slowly getting older in the pictures from left to right. I can tell how close they are.

I pull open each drawer. They're all empty, but one is locked. Thinking fast, I take a bobby pin from my hair and open the drawer to see a small picture of a man, scowling, in dark clothing. His eyes are beady and deep. The glass over the picture is shattered, as if done by a hammer.

Who is this? Wheresmeine, maybe?

I shiver and peel it away so I can see the next picture — a young girl, good looking, with swampy-green eyes and slick locks of brown hair, maybe seven or eight years old. I turn it around and inscribed in the frame is the name "Laurel". Is this possibly related to Wheresmeine's whereabouts? I run my fingers over her face. She looks almost familiar. As I set it back, I realise there is a stack of papers bundled up. Intrigued, I unfold it to see that they're letters. I know I shouldn't be reading them, but I can't help it.

JUNE 5TH, THURSDAY
WHERESMEINE INDUSTRIES

Hansel, Gretel,

I'm here in Raven, and I think you can assume how well it's going. I don't know how much longer I'll be able to handle it. I miss you terribly. I don't want to hold you back, however. I feel like I may be a burden. Just wanted to let you know I'm safe… for now. He hasn't laid a finger on me. He doesn't know I'm writing, and God knows what he'd do if he did. Please write back to let me know if you've crossed the border safely. Did Captain Hook ever agree to the travels? Are you in Bluebay County or Yuzi Bay, or somewhere else across? I wish I was there as well, but alas, things do not always turn out as planned when we're all together! Although I may not be present with you, I want you to settle. Stop letting him use me as a pawn. If you forget, then there will be nothing for you to worry about, and you can start afresh. I'm in your hearts, and I always will be. It's pointless staying in Raven, waking up and being tortured by his silence, because one day I know it will happen. Tell him it can happen. Tell him you don't care, and then stop caring. For all our sakes, please do this. I know you're going to feel like you haven't completed your duty; like you're letting me down. You're not. Build a large mansion made of candy for me, will you? I've always wanted to live in one of those. It seems mighty fun! Whenever you eat a swizzle stick, think of me. You know how I do adore those. Good luck. I have faith in you. I know you can do it.

Love you tremendously,

Laurel

I close the paper abruptly, questions flooding my mind. Who is this "he" who Laurel kept mentioning? How is she connected to Hansel and Gretel… and Wheresmeine? I curiously open the next letter, expecting another long paragraph, but this one is short.

JUNE 13TH, FRIDAY
WHERESMEINE INDUSTRIES
Hansel, Gretel,
I think it's over for good now. You never did listen to me about just letting me go, but he found a way on his own, I suppose.
Thank you.
You're the best, both of you. Stay united. Never forget me; but, more importantly, do start over.
Is the candy mansion coming along well?
I'm going to visit in my dreams.
One day, Hansel and Gretel. One day.
Love you tremendously,
Laurel

I scrunch the papers back up and put them away. What does it mean, "it's over for good now"? Death? As much as I want to solve the riddles, I truly am exhausted. The bed is comfortable, too. I lie down, wondering where my sister is, wondering what on earth she could be doing, wondering about the artefact and if I'll ever find it.

As soon as I wake up from my nap, I frantically check my watch to see that a couple of hours have passed. I pad down the delicious-looking stairs. Hansel and Gretel are on the couch, watching the news, with Swizzle purring on the warmed floor. In Gretel's lap is a notebook, into which she is writing vigorously with a lollipop pen.

"Ah, hello," she says, turning around to see me. "You look better."

I did take the time to brush out my hair, but I'm not sure that would be accounted for as *better*. I can still feel the dirt crammed under the tips of my nails. "It was a good sleep," I say with a shrug.

"Good. Well, we were thinking about giving you a tour of Bluebay?

Show you the school, maybe?”

This could be a chance to explore the place, see if anything relates to Wheresmeine. Maybe on the way, I’ll be able to push them to give me further insight into why they’re living in a separate place than their father, and where exactly he is. Who knows, maybe tomorrow I’ll be reunited with Anya.

Hansel stands up. “I’ll take you. Gretel over here needs to finish up some work.” He visibly glares at her through the corner of his eye.

“You lollyhead!” she says angrily. “You do all the tours.”

“And I’ll be doing yet another.”

He claws through a colourful cupboard and pulls out a thin rain jacket dotted with tiny flowers. He hands it to me in one fluid movement. “It’s cold out there.”

“Oh. All right.” I gratefully take it from him and slip it on. It’s surprisingly warm against my skin.

“Goodbye, Gretel,” Hansel coos, gracefully opening the door.

She scowls in response.

At that, we walk into the crisp air. We trudge through the lightly snow-coated roads in silence. He looks at me every so often and announces the “important” places, like the statue of the county, which is apparently a landmark, and the Appleby Diner, which is well known and a restaurant we will most likely be eating at in my time here. I don’t care about all that, though, and it feels like a waste. However, I must admit that Bluebay Academy is stunning. It is completely glass, so I can see through each room. There is a library bustling with students, even though it’s a Sunday. Still, no matter its uniqueness, I certainly don’t want to attend tomorrow. I didn’t come here to learn. I came here on a quest seeking the Stardust Crown.

“Ready to head back home?” Hansel asks me, touching my arm. It sends an electrifying jolt through me that I decidedly ignore.

“What?”

“Are you ready?”

“Oh! Yes. Ready. Hey, Hansel, um… about your father. Out of interest.”

He shakes his head. “Did you listen to Gretel? Please, Karmen, it’s off-limits. The past. Is in. The past. Haven't you ever watched *Frozen*? Elsa's pretty keen on that message."

"This isn't a joke! Where is he?"

"Why does it matter to you?"

"It just does!"

He arches an eyebrow. "One question. That's all."

I consider the many things I could ask and finally settle on, "What city does he rule?"

"Raven."

"Raven," I repeat softly under my breath. That's what the mysterious Laurel mentioned in her letter. That's where she was trapped, and maybe still is trapped. "I want to go there. I think that's where my sister is." I actually have no idea where she is, but if Wheresmeine is there, so is the artefact. Hopefully, Anya will find a way to make her way there, too.

"There's a time difference and everything. When it's day here, it's night there. I can't take you there. No one can." His voice is grim.

"Why not?" I demand irritably. "How about that Captain Hook?"

"He's busy," says Hansel. "He doesn't have time to ride a random single overseas."

"Random single. How kind."

"It's true, though," he points out. "He doesn't know you, and he has many groups to travel."

"Fine." I don't know what else to say. Hansel won't take me, and neither will Hook. *I* don't know my way around. I miserably follow Hansel away from the school. As soon as we step into the house, I am greeted with a rush of warmth and a wonderful sugary fragrance.

"We're home!" announces Hansel.

Gretel, who seems to be in the exact same position as when we left, only turns her head to give him a hard glare. "Hello, Karmen." This time she doesn't even acknowledge her brother. Their friendly feud is hysterical, because anyone could tell how much they adore each other.

"I've prepared dinner," says Hansel. "Would you run along and get it from the fridge? Karmen, would you help her set the table? After that, she'll do her 'healing therapy' on you. I'm going to take a quick shower. It was incredibly wet out there today."

I guess I'm being referred to as Karmen now, but that's fine as long as I'm not stealing anyone's identity — besides the title of a refugee. I happily flounce to the kitchen alongside Gretel. She smiles widely at me as she drags a covered metallic bowl onto the table.

"What's that?" I ask.

"Hm." She arches an eyebrow, and I realise she doesn't know. "I guess you'll have to wait and see."

"Then let's do this quickly." We pull out three jellybean-imprinted plates and fuchsia cutlery, setting it all on the table. We take our seats and wait for Hansel to join us.

"Took you long enough!" snorts Gretel when he comes down the stairs, even though it was quite a short shower. "Hansel, what have you prepared for us?"

He slides the cover off the bowl, revealing... fried chicken. Very normal. What did I expect? A savoury cherry pie for a meal? I'm kind of relieved it's only this, not something that may make me want to puke my guts out after dinner.

I politely dig in. It's delicious. Cooked perfectly. A lovely sauce to accompany the skin. I always like having sides, but this is much better than a stale sandwich.

"My recipe." Hansel winks.

"Yeah, yeah, wait until the next course," says Gretel.

Gretel's made a dessert — something called jelly-jolly-pud. This is what I would expect from her. Calling her a sweet tooth is an understatement.

"I bet you didn't have this on your island," she says, "but you really must try it. This is *my* recipe. My very own invention."

It looks like a pudding, but when Hansel cuts into it, it's like a cake. It's all types of colours, dots of candy dappled in.

I stare at it, then reluctantly try a bite. It's the best thing I've ever had. Sweetness erupts in my mouth. All different flavours and textures at once run down my throat. "This is fabulous," I gasp, stuffing more down.

"Yes, thank you very much; I'm quite the baker," Gretel giggles. "For your sake, I'm only letting you have one more slice."

"Mmm." I spoon more between my lips.

"Right. Well, I'm heading to bed," says Hansel, scratching his head.

I look at him in alarm. He's already going to bed? The first day has already been wasted!

"One more question?" I plead. "About—"

"My God, Karmen. Let it go. There's a bathroom upstairs, in case you're wondering. If you want to shower."

Is he suggesting I stink? It's probably true. He spins on his heel and leaves.

"He's a grouch sometimes," Gretel apologises. "Let's go to your bedroom for that healing I've been practising."

I curiously follow her, trying to find a way to convince her to do anything else. But she lays me down and begins. Her fingers are placed on my scalp, and a shivery feeling runs through my veins. It's applied harder, and I can feel my own body trembling.

Memories flood in, and I'm in the orphanage. My parents setting me down on a kerb, saying goodbye and leaving me there. Their faces are blurs.

That desire to be wanted, to fit in, just as a baby. Days on end of hunger and thirst. The presence of loneliness; only the distant chirps of birds to give me comfort. Cold. Hot. Snow. Leaves. Clammy hands seizing me, grabbing me; taking me somewhere warm. Putting me in a bed. Telling me it would be okay. Me believing them. Growing up, realising they were wrong. My favourite professor passing away. Gertrude completely taking over. The whips. The pain. The blood. So many attempts at running away. Failing. Every. Single. Time. Meeting Anya. Being happy for the first time. Now what have I done? I've lost her, too.

Useless.

You leave tomorrow, and you never come back.

Someone wants you. You.

I never thought it would be this cool… this thrilling *to have a sister.*

I'm so happy you're alive. I'm so, so happy you're alive. I don't know what I'd do without you, Ora.

And then I see her shaking on the ship, completely alone…

I saw her on the *Jolly Roger*, and I let the vessel leave. How could I have done that?

"*Stop!*" I realise the scream has come from my own mouth. "Stop. Please." I open my eyes, the dampness of the room pouring into my vision.

Gretel pulls her hands away in shock. "I'm sorry. Did I do something wrong?"

"No."

"Do you remember your name?"

"No."

"Oh. Okay." She sighs and repeats, "I'm sorry."

"It's not your fault. My past's tricky."

She swallows. "Goodnight, Karmen."

"Goodnight."

And as soon as she leaves, I crumple into sobs.

21
Anya

THE SHIP DRAWS TO A HALT.

Water has splashed all over me, and I'm soaked through completely. Blood is pooled on the ground, spilled from thousands of wounds. I don't know where this is travelling, but the skies have turned from black and grey to yellow and pink. I'm exhausted. The urge to jump off the vessel has been impossibly hard to overcome, and only one person has given me information. Her name is Christina. She is sixteen years old, and she comes from Karmen, where her parents died from a nuclear bomb planted by something called the Razor Tribe. She asked me my name, and I told her to call me An. It's not a lie that way. Mother calls me that. *Called.*

We've been sitting together in agony for hours. Apparently, we're going to a place called Raven. I have no idea where Ora is, and I'm afraid she's not here with me.

"At last!" Christina says. "We've arrived. Come on, An."

"I still don't understand what we'll be doing here," I sulk. "I need to find my sister."

"We're here to escape a place of war. Raven has taken us in. We'll be given some kind of new life."

Christina seizes my arm and drags me off the wooden plank to the shore. Everything is a blur. I let her guide me through. The atmosphere is green and mossy, but I'm too tired to properly look around. A booming voice cuts through the air, and my eyes flap open to see everything clearly.

I am in a garden. Christina is by my side, holding my hand, and we're surrounded by maybe twenty other people, all in the range of teenagers. There is a man in a straw hat, a scarred face beneath.

"Welcome to Raven!" he croaks. "The king has chosen you to work for him. You have been rescued from your very treacherous island to work in a land of paradise. You will have the opportunities to be upgraded if you work well. I am Ajax, the king's counsellor. Let us see, tut. Twenty-five of you. Split yourselves into five groups. I can switch you up as I'd like."

"You're with me, lazyhead," Christina whispers in my ear, taking me to a bed of violet floss flowers.

Several people join us — two boys and a girl. I don't know what exactly we're doing, but my mind is too fuzzy to think properly.

"No, no, tut, tut, tut," says Ajax. "Hmph. You, there. The pretty one."

At first, I think he's talking to me, but I follow his gaze to Christina. She looks confused, so he jabs a finger at her. "Join *that* group. And you, join that." He mixes everyone around until I'm with two girls and two boys. Christina is with a flawless girl who has unblemished brown skin and a braid embedded with flowers.

"Yes. This is good. This group" — he gestures to Christina and her partner — "you are *o'pricha.*"

I'm not quite sure what that is, but they both gasp, and their faces go white. Christina is stunned.

"Yes, you are quite blessed," murmurs Ajax. "Be grateful. The king will be in contact with you in short time. Then you'll be in the mighty castle. First, though, makeovers after long trips."

I don't even have time to question Christina before she's rushed away into a little house behind the garden.

"You are" — Ajax waggles his hand at my group — "*deka'ya.* Oh, don't stand there looking so disappointed. Would you rather be dead at Karmen? I didn't think so. The Maple Gardens are not too far from the Leiderhosen Castle. You will see the *o'pricha* there at times, and you must make sure to always be at their service, no matter what. They are at a higher position than you, remember. I'll number you and call you like that. One, two, three, four, five…"

He points to me at four. A part of me wants to leap on him and punch him, because this is exactly what someone must have done to Charlene, but I manage to contain myself and stay still as he waves us off like dogs. If Charlene and Bertrand could contain themselves for years, I can do it for five days.

"So long. I must deal with the others now. Since Raven is a new place to you, I've gone to the trouble of ordering you a *deshka*."

I nearly ask what that is, but I find out soon enough when a rusty-looking vehicle drives up. "Hello," spits the driver miserably, popping her fluffed head out of the shattered window. "Come on in, worthless gardeners."

I nearly demand what she means by that, but I don't want to make too big a scene, so I pile in with my fellows, who I know as one, two, three, and five. The inside of the *deshka* is shabby and grubby, the seats frayed, the floor littered with garbage. It's small, too, so we have to squish in with no seatbelts.

The girl beside me, number three or whatever, is looking out of the window sadly. She has beautiful blonde hair piled into a bun, and she's wearing a bold white lace dress, which is torn at the edges after the boat ride. She seems nice, so I lean in and ask, "What exactly is *deka'ya*?"

She spins around on me, her face furious. So, maybe not so nice, then. "Are you dumb or something? We use the same terms in Karmen. Do you not know Camish?"

"Well…" I clear my throat lamely. "I…My mother died," I fumble on the spot, fiddling my fingers in my lap. "My head's swimming in grief, and I can't think straight."

He regards me kindly. "Sorry to hear that."

"It happens to us all," snaps the girl. "You're no exception. I lost my siblings and both parents, but I went on in life instead of simply forgetting everything I knew. I mean, I didn't just get rid of all my knowledge and the language I spoke because my head was 'swimming in grief'."

He glowers. "Natasha, come on."

"*You* come on. This is nonsense."

"You two know each other?" I cut in.

"Yes. Everyone knows everyone on the island, except, apparently, *you*. There's only one school on our island, and Diesel over here is one grade ahead." Natasha arches an eyebrow expectantly.

"I was home-schooled," I retort. "I didn't go out too much, especially after my mother's death."

"Poor, poor you." Natasha rolls her eyes.

"Oh, come off it." Diesel smiles at me. *Deka'ya* is a word for servant."

Servant. And here I was thinking that I might have been put in yet another palace. I've really been downgraded, then. "Huh." I can't hide my bitterness. "So what do we do?"

"Well, gardening is a big thing here in Raven, so lots of that."

"That doesn't sound too bad."

"The cooking, the cleaning," he continues. "And then we're usually assigned someone to give special attention to. The *o'pricha* are those people. They train to be royals with the king. Ajax claims he knows the right people when he sees them, and I suppose he just recruited some new people. It's rare for refugees to become *o'pricha.* It's never really happened before, but those girls were pretty, and I think that plays a large factor in Ajax's selection. He's a silly man."

"And all the others? In those groups?"

"They'll be assigned some crap jobs, too. We'll see them around, undoubtedly." Diesel groans and shakes his head. "This is the life we'll be stuck in."

Tell me about it. I've been stuck in it once, and now again? I'm sick of kings and queens, to be honest. They're all terrible.

"Who says we have to do this? Why can't we go and have our own lives?" I ask, though the words sound childish rolling off my tongue.

Natasha laughs coldly. "And do what? It's not like we're billionaires. We'd have no jobs, no money… this is the only thing we can do for ourselves. This is how Raven treats their newcomers. Wheresmeine is trash."

"Nat!" scoffs Diesel.

"Did you say Wheresmeine?" I perk up in confusion.

Before she can answer, the *deshka* rattles to a stop. "Out of here, lowly rats," snarls the driver.

"We'll see about that," hisses Natasha. "I am an *o'pricha* at heart, if not more. One day, you will bow to me. One day, you will beg for your life."

"I've heard that one before, you scallywag."

"Scallywag? Did I hear *scallywag*?"

"Come on, Nat." Diesel pulls on her arm, and she steps out furiously after making a vulgar gesture to prove her point.

I crawl into the fresh air after her, glad to be out of the rotten-egg-smelling car. A fantastic garden, even bigger than the other one, awaits us. It's remarkable, to say the least. The *deshka* rumbles and rides away down a narrow dirt road. If I squint hard, I can look in that direction and see a dark palace up ahead.

"We'll have to take many walks down that path," Diesel tells me, following my gaze. "The Leiderhosen Castle is supposed to be very… spooky."

"So, the king's name is Wheresmeine," I murmur.

"Yes."

"He has a crown?"

"Every leading royal does."

"That's… interesting." So maybe I was right after all. Maybe I have landed in the place where the Stardust Crown lies. But Ora hasn't. Only God knows where Ora is.

"Hey. You okay?" Diesel frowns. "You look troubled."

"Thoughtful is all."

"Hm, is someone sulking further?" Natasha interrupts. "What's your name, anyway?"

"Um. It's An."

"Well, *An*, you'll have to learn to keep your feelings bottled up around here. Especially now that you're *deka'ya*. You do your job, sleep in the kitchen, and repeat. You'll learn to be quiet and embrace the darkness eventually."

"The darkness? The kitchen?"

"*Yes*. The king's not known to be thoughtful, so I doubt he'd prepare beds. Too busy snoozing and ordering people about."

"Nat! He's our king now," hisses Diesel warningly. "If we get caught gossiping like this, you know what punishment we'll suffer…"

"Well, Goody Two-shoes, make sure you don't end up in the principal's office. Don't fall in with the wrong crowd," snorts Nat.

"Oh, please." He frowns. "Anyway, An, any more questions? Ooh, see what I did there? *Any*way, *An*, *An*y. I'm clever like that."

Natasha rolls her eyes. "You're hysterical is what."

"Yes, Nat. Hysterical *and* clever."

"Nat," I murmur. "May I call you that?"

She scowls. "Absolutely not."

I suddenly spot a limousine-type car making its way down the craggy pathway towards us. The convertible stretches on through the mud, its metal black and orange, the windows glass but opaque. The tires screech to a stop.

"Someone to come and order us about," sighs Nat. "Splendid."

Sure enough, a door swings open, and a regal-looking man in a suit gracefully sweeps out. He has a deep English accent when he speaks.

"You are" — he scrunches his nose in disgust, as if we give off a horrid stench — "the newest *deka'ya*. Welcome to the Maple Gardens. You'll spend lots of time here. You wake up, make breakfast, walk here, garden until noon, and head back to the Leiderhosen Castle. You prepare a luncheon and a fine dinner. The other *deka'ya* will be there to help, but you'll surely start getting used to it. We've no time for very much gardening today as you've come quite late. We'll have to work with that, but never are you late again, under any circumstances. Wheresmeine will make sure of it."

He takes one step closer in the direction of Nat. "Aren't *you* a pretty one." He strokes his index finger over her face. Her body stiffens, and when he brushes his nail over her lip, she reels back with revulsion.

"Leave her alone," Diesel barks.

I want to chip in, too, but the man talks before I can. "Here at Raven, you'll find that we're like a triangle. What I mean by this is that there is a top and a bottom; a hierarchy. *You* are the bottom, so you listen to me. I am high and important. You are a peasant boy." His tone is serene but cold as ice.

Diesel clenches his jaw, but he doesn't say anything.

"Right, then, there's a good mouse. Everyone, go to the bushes and pick a fancy assortment of vegetables for tonight's dinner. The king is in a good mood. Run along, miscreants. You, however." He laces his fingers in Nat's. "What's your name?"

"Natasha," she mumbles, fuming.

"Natasha. Lovely. We'll be seeing each other around soon. Oh, and sweetheart, the name's Bass." He lets go of her hand, turns on his heel, and climbs back into his car, before speeding down the gravel and making sure to spray a fair share of mud in our direction.

Nat shrieks, wiping away the pebbles from her dress.

"Bass of a bastard is what he is," growls Diesel, glowering after him.

Nat looks uncomfortable for a second, but then her face returns to its snobbish normal, and she looks around. "What are you all staring at? You heard the man. Get to it!"

The boy and girl scurry away, but Diesel and I look at Nat expectantly. "You coming, too?"

"Yes, I suppose," she grunts.

There is a stack of baskets, so we each take one and start to dig. I spot a carrot in the dirt and grip it tightly, yanking with all my might. When it finally comes loose, I tear it from the ground. A scream of frustration escapes my lips as it splits in half and comes flying out. With a groan, I turn around to see everyone staring at me in disbelief.

Then Nat begins to clap, her face lit with amusement. "Well, well, well, the little sulker can't pick a carrot," she chuckles, spinning one of her own in the air. "You must've been spoiled by your rich papa back in Karmen when you were home-schooled. You're not like us."

She's right — I'm not. I live in London in a marvellous house with two marvellous guardians. I attend a posh, luxurious school. I don't understand the word *suffer*. I've never in my life gardened or cooked, let alone done many chores. I've never come close to being a servant, or grappled with money. Each day, there have been meals in front of me and a roof over my head.

The closest I've come to loss is losing my father when I was a baby, but I got to see him again — these people in front of me have watched their parents die in their arms from gun violence, bombings, terrorist attacks. I'm not like them at all.

Illusions. That's all they are.

But this happens in the real world, too. It happens everywhere, and I take no notice, like it's nothing.

It's not nothing.

If Ora were here, she'd know what to do. She'd tell me what to say.

"Now, now, Nat, she'll get the hang of it," says Diesel disapprovingly. "Go and help her."

"Me? Why not you?" she spits. "You'll do it just as well."

"Maybe, but you're the one who pointed it out, so." He arches an eyebrow. "Go on. Get it over with."

"Ugh." She slouches towards me, placing her fingers over mine and helping me pull it from the soil with ease.

I feel like a young child with everyone watching me.

"There you are. Place that in your basket now and keep going on like that." There's something mocking in Nat's voice. She gets to her feet nimbly and shoots a hard glare at Diesel. "All right, I did it. Happy?"

He looks at her with satisfaction. "I'm *ecstatic*."

She rolls her eyes, but a smile tugs at her lips. "Whatever, Diesel." She crouches down and continues drawing tomatoes from the earth.

It seems like hours pass as we pick the vegetables. My hands are sore, moulded with blisters, by the time Bass comes rolling back in his car. He lazily hops out. "You'll have to learn to keep track," he snarls. "You're almost late, so get to it. It's not too far a walk."

"Well, where are you headed?" I blurt.

"The castle," he says, irritated. "But I won't be driving with a load of *deka'ya*. Except maybe Natasha."

"No, no," she intervenes quickly. "I'm feeling quite like a walk, but we'll see you at Leiderhosen soon. Take your baskets, fellows, and hurry along."

"Playing hard to get, are we?" purrs Bass. "Fine. I like that." He gets back into his vehicle and takes off.

We follow it back in the direction of the castle. Nat keeps a steady fast rate down the narrowing route, Diesel by her side. I try to keep up, but my feet are starting to ache tremendously. The journey is far.

"God, Nat, please slow," I pant.

"God, sulker, toughen up," she retorts, speeding her pace. "And to you, I am *Natasha*. For the last time!"

I have no choice but to follow — though I *will* continue persisting in calling her Nat.

The two other *deka'ya*, Amara and Oscar, trail closely behind her. They are both scrawny and small, but clearly quite strong. They got their job done with no complaining, and now, looking at their baskets, I can see how much they collected.

The scenery is dazzling, so I try to let that distract me from my throbbing toes.

It doesn't work.

I trudge on in my pack, until at last we reach the castle. There are guards at the door like in Floe City, but there are no Rime Cards. They must be able to tell by our looks, because they mutter, *"Deka'ya, deka'ya,"* and slide the gates open for us.

"Hmph," sniffs Nat haughtily, holding her nose in the air.

The inside of the whole place is nothing like Frost. This is dark and inky, like there are shadows climbing up the walls. It is massive, but there is barely anything to look at. A word to describe it may even be *bland*.

"Kitchen is in the basement," says a voice from behind us.

We spin around to see Bass, smiling at us mischievously. I can see Nat's cheeks heating, even though there is scarce light.

"Hello, there. Hope you had a nice walk. Especially you, dear Natasha?" he inquires, cocking an eyebrow as if interested to know.

"It was fine," Nat snaps. "In fact, it was *great*. Much better than sitting in the back of your limousine."

He chuckles softly. "Well, I'm glad you enjoyed it. But just for further interest, I don't drive in a limo. It's a *caché*."

Nat goes pale.

"Has that change the game?"

"No. How'd you get your filthy hands on one of those things?" she retorts, regathering herself.

"I told you. I'm at the top of the triangle." He winks. "Maybe one day I can take you for a ride in it. Oh, and one more thing. You've got to change into your work uniforms." He throws a black bundle at us and disappears into an elevator. We all know that we have to take it, too, but we let it shut and move before we press the button.

"What's a *caché*?" asks Amara, picking up a uniform, and I'm happy I don't have to be the one to ask for once.

"Maybe you haven't heard of it. Some refer to it as the 'dream car'," explains Nat, as the elevator opens. We all pile inside, and she hits the "B" circle. "It can transform into different things. Like an airplane, or a bus, or even a mechanical bird. Anything you'd dream of. Very luxurious. Very expensive. Very rare. It pains me to see what idiots they belong to."

We all slip into our suits, putting them overtop our clothes. Unlike the ones at Floe, these are ebony. The itchy feel makes me want to throw them off my body, but I resist. Barely.

The doors glide open smoothly, and we find ourselves in the kitchen. It bustles with people, and a plump woman spots us.

"You're late!" she barks. "I'm Head Chef Louisa, but it's Chef Frau to you. You do what I say, starting *now*. Put those baskets on the counter immediately and start on the stew. You do know how to make the legume stew, I presume?"

"I—" Diesel begins. "No, not entirely."

"Goddammit!" she curses under her breath, making me flinch. *"Alavi! Come here! Immediately!"*

A young man races to Chef Frau's side. His eyes are terrified. The look reminds me of Bertrand... but he's dead. Just like Charlene. Just like everyone in that world.

Illusions.

I push the thoughts from my mind and focus on Frau and Alavi.

"Yes, Chef?" he asks. His voice sounds as if it has been stripped of its warm clothes and left out in the biting cold. He sounds positively bare. Afraid, almost.

"Teach them the makings of our signature legume stew." Frau rolls her eyes and turns to us. "I hope you realise how stupid that sounds. That you can't make a simple *stew*."

"Well, I do know how to make many stews," says Nat daintily. "I'm just not sure how to make this exact legume stew. If it's a signature dish,

I don't want to mess up on an ingredient."

"Well, little missy…" Chef sighs, "I have some respect for that, I suppose. But it doesn't mean I like you. Now, go on, all of you, and Alavi will help you."

We are rushed to a counter, where there is a pan of boiling hot water. Alavi's fingers work quickly at chopping up onions and carrots and so on. He drops them into a bowl and mixes them about, adding some garlic and red sauce. He runs his spoon through and pours it into a golden bowl that I can only assume is real gold. "It's ready, Chef!"

Frau comes by, tries a bit, adds a pinch of salt, and nods. "Good job, Alavi. You can whip up *stew*. Now go make yourself useful and prepare the cauliflower wings."

He nods and hurries away.

"Do it yourself now," Frau snaps at us. "I need fifteen bowls, you hear me? And after that, you do something else. The work never ends until the people above us are happy and fed."

We nod, all a bit frightened, and Nat starts slicing up zucchini. She takes charge, which is a good thing. "Amara, pepper. Put a ton."

Everyone listens, glad that someone knows what they're doing. I let Nat order me around without complaint, even when she trips me when I have a goblet of garlic in my hands. I get a hard spank from Frau, but when she asks how it happened, I take full responsibility, because first of all, Nat's been through a lot in her life, and I know that. Even if she's only an illusion. Second of all, Frau has already taken somewhat of a liking to Nat, so I'm not sure she'd believe me anyway.

The night wears on. Nat and I are ordered to take up the stews for starters, and Diesel, Amara, and Oscar will come soon after with Panzanella.

"Go quickly now. The king *despises* lateness," Frau says hastily.

Amara perks up. "Will we truly see Wheresmeine?"

"Yes, you silly child, but you'd better not make any eye contact. Keep your head down, set it on the table, pour the drinks, and hurry away. That is *all*. Do you think you can manage that?"

We all nod.

"Good, good. I just thought I'd better ask since you seem to be quite rusty on lots of easy things," she says, her tone flat and frosty. "Go, now! What the hell are you waiting for? Three and four, go to the fifteenth floor, and then return for more work. *Now!*"

We rush into the elevator, leaving our three fellows with the angry Madame Frau. My hands are stuck out straight in front of me, balancing trays of heavy bowls of heavy broth. Nat has it harder, because she's also carrying bottles of whiskey and wine.

"Don't they drink anything else than alcohol?" I say, trying to break the frigid silence unfurling between us.

"They're those kind of people, I guess. I hate to be under their weak protection, though it truly is nothing. They'd let us die in a jiffy if it came to it, I'm sure," Nat snorts.

"Yeah, what about Bass?"

"Bass," she says coldly, "is a bastard. Like Diesel said." Then she glares at me. "What are you doing talking to me, anyway? Haven't I made it clear that I want anything but a friendship? Haven't I made it clear that I don't want anything to do with *you?*"

Before I can respond to her snarky remark, the steel doors open. We find our way through a fancy hall, to a dining room embellished with six gold chandeliers. The table stretches far, lit with candles. I keep my eyes glued to the floor, and beside me, Nat does the same. We set down stew in front of each person.

The king sits at the head. His face is hard to make out, but I know that there is no crown. If he is truly Wheresmeine, where is the artefact I need?

I bury my disappointment and start pouring merlot. I only look up when I hear a small shriek from Nat. She is looming over Bass, and there is red liquid all over his white blouse.

"How clumsy am I?" she exclaims, dabbing at it with napkins. "Ever so sorry, sir…"

"Bass," he says through clenched teeth. "We've met, young Natasha."

"I don't seem to recall it." She cocks her head and looks apologetic, or attempts to. "Anyway, I've been here far too long as it is. I am so sorry once again, Sir Bass."

"*Quite* all right."

With empty trays, Nat and I scurry back into the elevator. The remaining *deka'ya* of our small group stream out. Diesel looks highly professional. He gives a single nod and walks away with Amara and Oscar at his feet.

When we are enclosed between the lift's walls, I demand, "Did you do that on purpose, out of pure hatred? He may be a wretch, but he's of high position, Nat. He rules you. He practically owns you."

She turns to me, her eyes dancing with rage and flame. "No man will ever own me. And of course, I didn't do it on purpose. I apologised a countless amount of times, if you didn't notice. Also, *An*. Don't. Call. Me. Nat."

I shake my head, but don't push the topic any further. When we are back in the kitchen, a new line of *deka'ya* are already waiting to leave. They run past us like we're nothing.

"Servants three and four!" barks Madame Frau. "You took an awfully long time."

We don't dare mention the mishap. Instead, we stare her in the eye awkwardly, waiting for our next job.

Frau lets out a bitter grunt. "Dessert. Chocolate fudge cake, the king's favourite. The recipe's on the table over there, so you'd better not mess up. If it's wrong…"

"It won't be," says Diesel.

"You're right. It won't. Because while you make that one, I'll be making twenty."

"Um. Yes, Chef," he replies swiftly.

Nat picks up the slip of paper in her hands and starts loading heaps of brown and white sugar into a glass dish. I don't know what to do, so I lamely crack in egg whites and knead the paste with my knuckles while Nat does the rest. I think she's happy to.

Diesel joins in at some point, while Amara and Oscar prepare their own batter. There are twenty-five cakes in the oven after a long hour passes. Frau lied. We end up making far more than one cake each, and she certainly made less than twenty. Some servants run them up to the eating hall, and then all the *deka'ya* are crowded in the kitchen, slumped over from fatigue and exhaustion, spooning tiny dollops of stew into our mouths.

"Good work today," announces Madame Frau, taking a bite of leftover cake. "You're all dismissed."

Everyone bustles over to a white door — that I hadn't seen before — and push it open. It reveals rows and rows of small beds. A simple room, really, filled with filthy cots and blankets.

"Do we get beds?" Nat says loudly.

A young woman turns to us. She looks like she's in her early twenties, fair but tired. "Newcomers take the floor," she explains ruefully. "As you can see, this place is pretty crammed. It may take a couple of weeks to get some new beds installed."

"A couple of weeks?" Nat explodes. "That's crazy! This place is giant. Doesn't the king have the decency to prepare another room? Or rather, get his servants to? Not like he does anything on his own!"

Everyone goes quiet.

Frau swallows furiously and gets up from her bed. "Who said that?"

"I did." It takes me a second to realise the words have come from my own lips, but I speak up confidently. "I said it."

She makes her way over to me. Her hand is across my face before I can register what she's doing. I can feel the pain consuming me. My face goes numb, red and raw. I do not protest. She does it six times, the force harder and angrier with each strike.

"We do not talk about our king disrespectfully like that," Frau finally says, holding her head high. "He is our leader. You agree with his choices. *That* is not an option." Then she crawls back under her sheets.

I watch her, and then I lay my head on the carpeted floor, feeling my burning cheeks, thinking of anything, anything that could get me out of this place and back to Ora.

Someone throws a blanket over me. I open my eyes and see Nat looking at me. Her eyes ask the question. *What on Earth did you just do?*

Stillness stretches between us like an elastic band. "Don't thank me," I murmur at last.

"Why?" Her voice is demanding.

I lay my head down and ignore this. I can't answer.

I can't tell her that it's because I'm going to have to kill her at the end of this.

22
Ora

SUNLIGHT STREAMS THROUGH A SMALL CRACK IN THE WINDOW.

"Wake up!" A girl rattles my shoulders.

"Gretel," I moan, "what time is it?"

"It's six."

"AM? Why?"

"It's a long way to school. Six is the time to get up."

A realisation, floods through me. "I don't feel well. Can I stay home?"

She giggles. "No! It's okay if you're nervous. I remember my first day. I was petrified."

"No, I—"

"But you know what really helped? My brother's Nerd pancakes! Get it? Nerd, the candy. Nerd, because it's school. Right?"

"Um, that's really great, but—"

"Awesome, so there's no uniform. You can go in some regular clothes. I realise you haven't packed from Karmen, so you're welcome to borrow any of mine. Meet us downstairs in thirty? That'll be enough time."

Before I can argue, she bounces away cheerfully. I don't know if there's a way to get out of this, but I do know that I can't afford to get kicked out of this place. Hansel and Gretel have the answers I need. I might have to waste five hours at the academy.

I grouchily force myself out of the comfortable mattress to see that Gretel has laid out some outfits for me to choose from. I take a pair of leggings, a denim jacket, and a striped white-red shirt. All the other costumes are either too bright, tacky, or flashy for me. I'm looking to be discreet, not draw attention to myself.

In my comfy clothes, I trail down the stairs. A candy scent floods through the air. I've only been here a day, but that's long enough to know how homey this is, even with its abnormalities.

"Morning, Karmen!" I hear Hansel's voice. "In here!"

I follow his sound to the kitchen. Sure enough, there is a tall stack of pancakes, studded with rainbow dots. "Let me guess," I say. "Nerd pancakes?"

Gretel, sitting at the table, turns to me with a grin. "You'll love them."

"Well, you told me that about the jelly-jolly-pud, so who am I to turn this down?" I jab a fork into a round disc and pop it in my mouth keenly. There are lots of flavours, but the Nerds are hard and too sweet. I can barely taste the mixture. It takes everything within me not to gag and spit it out.

"Well? You like?" Gretel asks eagerly.

"Oh, yes," I lie with exaggerated enthusiasm.

Hansel must catch on, because he intervenes, "Gretel's a sweet tooth — maybe too much of one. Sometimes what she likes can be…"

"Hansi, what are you trying to say?" She arches an eyebrow.

"Nothing, nothing." He winks at me as she digs into another pancake. I watch as he goes through the fridge and pulls out an energy bar, which is exactly what I need right now. I bite into it gratefully as he says, "So, Karmen, Gretel told me her 'healing therapy' didn't work."

I nearly choke on my food. "Nope," I mumble, shifting awkwardly in my seat.

"That's too bad." He must sense how uncomfortable I feel, because he changes the subject. "Ready for school?" he asks kindly.

"Well, I guess I have to be," I chuckle nervously.

"Trust me, the academy is great."

"Yeah." For some reason, I doubt that I'm going to have the time of my life. "Well, shall we get going?"

"Yes!" Gretel leaps from her seat, retrieves her backpack, and then hands me one. "We keep spares for the refugees. You'll probably need it."

"Okay." I sling the empty pouch over my shoulder and follow her out the door. Hansel walks beside me. The wind blows against my cheeks, prickling my skin. "I'm a bit nervous for ninth grade," I say, trying to make conversation. "Hansel, what grade are you in?"

"Grade ten," he says. "It's *great* fun."

"Oh, come off it, you," Gretel scoffs, rolling her eyes. "You're the smartest one there, and you do the least amount of work."

He cocks an eyebrow but doesn't argue.

When we arrive, I still can't help gaping a bit. It's stunning, all clear and transparent. Hansel and Gretel must be used to it, because they don't give the glass building a second glance. There are children scampering about —young, middle grades, big high schoolers taller and broader than Hansel.

"Ready?" he asks me.

I don't really get time to answer before someone ploughs into my back.

"Ohmigod, ow!" comes a voice from behind me.

I spin around to see a girl with caramel skin and locks of brown curls. Her gown is yellow, ruffled and extravagant. She looks furious, but all the anger somehow floods away in the snap of a finger.

"Grets!" she exclaims, throwing her arms around her.

"Hi!" Gretel squeaks.

"Who is this?" She gestures to me disdainfully.

"Another refugee," explains Gretel. "Karmen."

"Karmen?" she snorts. "Like, after the island?"

"She can't remember her name, so that's what we call her."

"Clever girl. Well, *Karmen*, you just banged into me."

I arch an eyebrow. "Actually, you banged into *me*." The words escape my mouth before I can stop them.

"She didn't mean it," Gretel says. "Karmen, this is Bella, Princess Belle's daughter. She's my best friend."

"Yes." Bella beams in agreement. She pulls open the door, carelessly running it over my shoe. "What classes does she take, Grets?"

She asks the question as if I'm not here. Frankly, I wish I wasn't.

"Same as us," Gretel replies. "Yzma made sure. Hansel contacted her last night, and bless her soul, she enrolled Karmen straightaway."

"Hm, bless her," Bella murmurs, but I can see her glaring at me coldly from the corner of my eye. "Come now, let's not be late for sorcery. Oh! Hansi, hello! I didn't even notice you." Her voice has turned somewhat flirty, and she's twisting a strand of hair with her finger.

He smiles, charming as always. "Hello to you, too. How's that biology project coming along?"

Bella pouts. "I might need more help."

"At lunch I have robotics club, but tomorrow."

"Okay, sounds great. You're the best."

Hansel winks. "I try my best. Goodbye. Goodbye, Karmen."

Hansel dashes away, and I notice Bella is steadily glowering at me. I don't want to get on even *more* of her bad side — if that's possible.

"Bella, could you be any less subtle?" sings Gretel. "You are *obsessed*."

"Is it so obvious?" She looks concerned.

"Tone it down a bit, perhaps," says Gretel. "Don't look so desperate. Show him the cool side of you. I'll talk to him, too."

Bella smiles at her gratefully. "One day, it'll happen. I know it will."

"So do I." Gretel winks.

I shuffle after them up a blue set of stairs. It's better being invisible than being the centre of attention, tortured by Bella. I know that much already.

In my name-labelled locker, there are three sets of books wrapped in plastic, each one tagged with a subject. I take the sorcery ones and follow Gretel and Bella to a classroom. They sit in the front row, but I go to the back. Gretel throws a reassuring glance in my direction, but I stay put, and people start pouring in. Four girls swarm around Gretel and Bella. It's like an enclosed circle, so all I can see are their backs and the sounds of giggling and whispers.

A teacher comes in at last, and everyone takes their seats. "Hello, everyone!" he says. "We have a new student today. Her name is… well. What is your name?"

I clear my throat. "Karmen."

Some snicker in response to that. The teacher looks intrigued. "What an interesting name. My name is Mr Maji. Everyone, Karmen is from, er, Karmen. She's a refugee, new to Bluebay, so I expect you'll all treat her with *respect*."

"Yes, Mr Maji," everyone mumbles in response, but I can sense some mockery there.

"Good, good. Elaina, if you please, the cauldrons."

A sharp, pretty girl, shoots to her feet; the one sitting beside Gretel. "Yes, Mr Maji," she says clearly, and gracefully makes her way over to a massive collection of drawers. She pulls each open to reveal bounties of huge black pots. Elaina, one by one, distributes them. A part of me wants to help, because she alone is heaving them into her arms and setting them down gently, but I don't want to attract any more attention.

When mine is on my desk, I try picking it up to feel the weight. It is ridiculously heavy. The steel is cold and smooth as a pebble. Elaina takes her seat, and a boy named Charming Junior — I mean, seriously, what kind of a name is that? — hands out giant metal spoons.

"Good, good," repeats Mr Maji. "Thank you, Elaina and C.J. Now, everyone, open up to page 116. Today we will be mastering how to create the Firenix Potion."

"Firenix," C.J. whispers to me. "You're lucky you get to come for the most interesting thing."

Curious, I flip open my book, half expecting to fall right in. I find page 116:

The Potion of <u>Firenix</u>
(The art of fire clay)
Materials:
1. Cauldron and mixer/mixing tool
2. Lava
3. Candles and wax
4. The petals of a heat-ray flower
5. A droplet of sunshine
6. Flame gel

Sculpt it! Stretch it! Tear it! Firenix, once cool, is a pretty cool thing!
****Warning: Remember to wear FP smocks***

"Yes? Is everyone excited?" whoops the enthusiastic teacher.

"Yes, Mr Maji," everyone responds in unison.

"Good, good. Come now, everyone, and collect your fireproof smocks and your crate of materials. There is one for each partnership."

Partnership?

"I'll make them today," says Mr Maji, tapping his foot on the ground. "Who would like to go with Karmen, our new girl, today?"

"I will," volunteers Gretel contentedly, much to Bella's dismay.

"Hm? Who said that?" He slips his glasses over his eyes and looks at Gretel's group. "You? Did you say that?"

"No, I—"

"Good, good. Bella, please go join Karmen."

"But—"

"*Now.*"

She sulkily slouches over to the empty seat beside me, her lips curved downward into a displeased scowl. Mr Maji takes no notice and pairs up the rest of the students. Gretel ends up with Rosa, one of her friends.

I fetch the ingredients and smocks. The desk is big enough to fit the whole wooden basket, but I set it on the floor because it would take up too much space. The FP smocks are white and made of something similar to rubber. The gloves attached feel solid and barely bendable, which is an unusual composition choice for gloves.

"All right, follow my lead, since you're obviously new to this," says Bella bitterly.

I hold my tongue, and Bella picks up a glass bottle containing a sloshy red solution. Lava. That must be. "How in the hell did you get this?" she demands to Mr Maji, reading my mind.

"I have my ways." He winks. "The world is full of *magic.*"

She rolls her eyes and pours the whole lot into the cauldron. It hisses and sizzles, and she stirs it around a bit, which only makes everything louder. "Here," Bella tells me, shoving an irregularly large matchbox at my face. "Light it, drop it in the flame, and let the wax drip a bit."

It sounds easy enough, and I've certainly lit a candle before at the orphanage. I run the stick over the dappled row of tiny bumps until the tip erupts into brightness. Satisfied with myself, I hold it over the cauldron. The fire grows bigger and bigger, creeping down the stick, and just when I think it's going to burn my fingers, it slides off. Like Bella instructed, I let some wax dribble over the edge, too.

"There," I say. "Maybe I'm not as useless as you thought."

"No. You definitely still are." With that, Bella picks up a stunning baby-pink flower. She peels away the petals delicately and drops each one into the mixture.

All I can think of are the letters I discovered yesterday. Still so many unanswered questions, and I'm sculpting fire instead of trying to figure them out… and *Anya*. I'm going to school instead of finding her. Is there any way to get out of this?

I take a turn running the spoon through. The flower explodes into tiny pieces and dissolves.

"Hey," I snap, as I see Bella picking up a closed opaque container. "My turn."

"No, sweetheart. This stuff is dangerous."

"I did the candles."

"Yes. Candles are *candles*. This is sunlight. If you mess up…"

"I won't."

"For some reason, I don't trust you." She narrows her eyes.

Frustrated, I snatch the small box from her hands and open the lid. Light blinds me.

"Idiot!" I hear Bella's voice. "You need the protective sunglasses!"

I can't see anything, so I try to feel for the cap. My hand slaps over the desk, and I feel the glove sinking into the potion. It starts to sting, like the material is wearing off.

With a scream, I pull away, but the cauldron comes with me. I hear it slam into the ground with a thump, and my body tumbles to the floor.

Pain shoots through me. There are shouts ringing out around me. At last, my vision floods back, but as soon as it does, I wish it hadn't. I am sprawled on the floor. The desk has toppled over completely, and everyone is staring at me. Including Mr Maji.

I stagger to a sitting position. Then, "Karmen, you're kind of on fire."

I don't even know who says it, but I completely freak out. I realise it's my arm, which I wipe at frantically, practically squealing until it's disappeared.

Mr Maji sighs. "This is bad. Now the *floors* are so very ruined, with all those burning substances, and look at you, too. I think you'd better go to the nurse and get cleaned up. Yes, why don't you go do that as we sort this whole charade out."

I clumsily clamber to my feet, ignoring the stings in my arms and legs. I've been injured worse than this before.

"Bella, please go with her as you are her partner," says Mr Maji sternly.

"Oh, it's quite all right," I interrupt. "I know my way around." That's a lie, but I'll do anything else than walk around with her.

"If you say so," he says.

I am out the door in seconds, limp and in agony, and a part of me wants to go straight out of the school and to Hansel and Gretel's house. Maybe I could. Maybe I'll say I wasn't feeling well, and I forgot to sign out with the principal. Yes, that'll do.

I'm stumbling down the stairs when someone bumps into me. I hit the floor this time because I'm weaker, and the push is stronger. I angrily get up, preparing to yell at Bella, but instead I see Hansel, looking very apologetic. He helps me to my feet, and I feel myself blushing with embarrassment.

"So sorry," he says. "Are you all right?"

"I'm fine."

"But those *burns*. Are they Firenix? Oh, God, Karmen, what have you done? How did it happen?"

"There may have been an incident in class," I admit sheepishly. "I'm trying to find the nurse's office."

"Well, you're going the wrong way, so let me help you." He takes my hand and guides me back upstairs.

"Why aren't *you* in class?" I ask.

He grins slyly. "It's awfully boring, you know. A waste of time. I'm not a fan of this whole schooling system. Sometimes I like to take walks... or eat someplace else."

"You mean ditch."

He chuckles. "Well, that's a strong word."

"Where were you off to?"

"A shopping mall, but I would much rather help a young lady in need."

"Oh, please take me there. I hate this academy."

Hansel hesitates and then says, "I'd better not. You're hurt, so keep walking."

"Please?"

"No, Karmen."

He's firm, so I give a grunt and don't argue it any further.

We reach a large office where a stout man sits in a fluffy orange chair in front of a desk. There are shelves and shelves crammed with vials and bottles of liquid, an assortment of vivid colours. "Hellooooo," he trills in an Australian accent. "You, girl, are the one with Firenix burns?"

"Yes, that's me," I say sheepishly.

"And Hansel! To what do I owe the pleasure?"

"Just accompanying the young lady in need."

"Hm, how very thoughtful of you. Young lady in need, Karmen, my name is Nurse Winston Curble, and *you* are in some very deep trouble for ruining Maji's prized floors. But first, we must treat your wounds. Take a seat, sweetheart. You too, Hansel."

We both do as he says, and I take the bigger chair directly in front of Nurse Winston. I'm shaking, so Hansel sets a hand on my knee, which does provide some comfort.

Winston Curble takes a needle, and without warning, jabs it into a burn. I hold in a scream as he rubs a cream over my injury. Then he covers it with a small pad of tissue. He continues doing this to the rest of my wounds until I'm basically bundled in plasters.

"Take these off tomorrow," Winston instructs me. "They'll all be gone then."

"You really are magic, Win," says Hansel, getting to his feet. "Thanks so much."

"That's my job."

As soon as Hansel and I have exited the room, I ask, "Is he your best friend or something? You seem very close."

He laughs handsomely. "Hell no. I just like being friendly to all the teachers."

"You're the class pet in every course, basically."

He shrugs with a grin. "You could put it that way. It's lunch now, so you'd better get going."

I want to ask if I can go home, but I know what the answer will be. Instead, I say, "How about you?"

"I wasn't kidding when I said I had robotics club," Hansel replies with a wink. "See you after school." He disappears down a corridor, leaving me alone.

Luckily, there are flocks of students heading to the cafeteria, so I follow them. The place is crammed, but I can see Gretel sitting with Bella, Elaina, and Rosa. There's a spare seat, so I force myself to go there after I collect a tray of macaroni.

"Can I sit here?" I ask somewhat timorously.

She spins around, and so do her friends. "Hey!" she exclaims. "Are you all right after what happened? Yes, of course, come sit with us!"

I'm about to when Bella blocks it off. "Actually, Grets, Mary's sitting here."

"Surely, she can pull up a chair…" begins Rosa.

"No, actually, she can't." Bella cocks her head at me. "So sorry."

I clench my jaw. "Fine. I'll find somewhere else."

"Wait," Gretel starts.

"It's fine," I assure her, trying to sound warm. "I know where I want to sit anyway." I slip out of the busy cafeteria and find a bathroom cubicle. It's big enough, so I sit on the lid of the toilet and munch away quietly. My hands get all dirty, so I turn on the tap, but it's out of order. *Great.*

I go to the nearby washroom, which has six stalls, but immediately when I enter, I hear grunting. Bella has Hansel pinned up against the wall, and she's kissing him fiercely. I rush out of the bathroom as fast as I can, careful not to be seen. So much for robotics club.

…

217

The day drones on, full of boring classes and Bella's torture. There's mathematics, which I'm not so bad at. Finally, classes end after what seems an eternity. I meet Hansel at the front, and we walk home together. Gretel's gone to Bella's to study.

"So did it get any better?" he inquires.

"No," I admit. "It only got worse, frankly."

"Sorry to hear that."

"Sure you are."

"Oh, come on! You know, I actually relate to you. I feel the exact same way, every single day. And look, that rhymed."

I roll my eyes. "You relate because you're too *smart*, boo-hoo. But everyone adores you, and you know that."

"Maybe so, but I don't return the fan love."

I allow myself a laugh as we weave through snow-coated grass. We reach the candy house, and my goosebumps disappear. Swizzle greets us happily. Hansel starts on his homework, but I've got none, so I go back to my room and reread the letters from Laurel. Nothing becomes clearer. If anything, more questions arise, and I get even more confused. There's a knock on my door — probably Gretel, back from Bella's house. I frantically put away the papers and open the door.

Surprisingly, it's Hansel.

"What's up?" I say.

His lips move but I can barely focus on what he's saying, I'm too busy shrugging off the nerves that have risen in me.

He clears his throat. "So?"

"Hm?" I say.

"I said, are you okay with going to the Appleby Diner now?"

"Sure," I reply with relief. "Will Gretel meet us there?"

"She's already on her way."

"Great. Let's go." I follow him down the stairs and into the fresh air. I like walking everywhere, getting exercise, enjoying the view. But I'd rather be discovering answers.

It's started to snow harder, little flakes gliding down from the sky. I catch some on my tongue, and Hansel laughs. "Do you not get much in Karmen?"

"Um, no." *Or London. Where I'm really from. Because I've been lying to you.*

We arrive at the diner then. The waitress seems to know Hansel, because she leads him to a booth and gives him a pot of tea.

"Where's Gretel?" I ask, as he pours me a cup.

"She should be getting here any moment now," he says.

The waitress, Wendy, comes by, and Hansel orders shrimp linguine. I order their signature halibut and green salad.

"Sounds good," says Wendy, jotting it down. Then she gives a warm smile to Hansel. "You know, *you* look good today."

"Why, thank you, Wendy."

She flushes and scurries away.

"She's crushing on you," I tell him.

"What?"

"You're oblivious."

"Oh, and you're one to know."

"What's that supposed to mean?"

"You haven't a single memory. You don't even remember your name. Don't tell me who's crushing on me."

"Wow," I say, arching an eyebrow. "You're getting pretty defensive about this."

"Yeah, well, I can make my own choices."

"I never said you couldn't!"

There is a buzz from his pocket. He checks his phone and sighs. "Gretel stopped on the way at her favourite pizza place with Bella. She wants to sleep over. Bella will bring her to school tomorrow."

"Okay."

"Okay."

"Hansel. Is something wrong?"

He swallows. "Sorry."

"Hansel."

"I have my eyes on another girl is all."

"Bella."

"Bella?"

"I saw you two, today, in the bathroom."

Hansel presses his lips together. "It was a mistake."

"There seemed to be some chemistry there."

"No, that's just my natural charm." He winks. "I know. This isn't funny. I don't know how long you were there, but I pulled away quickly."

"Oh. Well, I wasn't there too long," I admit.

"Hm. The girl who I have a crush on is from Karmen, actually."

"Oh," I say dumbly, heart pounding.

And he scooches over beside me and kisses me.

You know what the worst part is?

I kiss back.

23
Anya

I'M UP AT 5AM.

I know well enough that if I do anything further to upset Frau, I'm done for, and so is my face. I can still feel her clammy fingers imprinted on my skin. Nat, Diesel, Amara, and Oscar are all woken by her. The rest of the *deka'ya* are awake before us.

"You five," says Frau, waggling her finger at us, "go to the Maple Gardens and collect some fruit. I'll need syrup from the trees, too. Understood? The more important people will start making pastries. You've got to be quick about it. You have a couple of hours, so you'll have to do with that."

Everyone floods out of the white room, leaving my companions and me alone. We quickly change out of our flimsy suits and into the jade frocks laid out for us. We take the elevator upstairs and make our way down the narrow pathway in silence. The sun is moving over the horizon, setting a yellow-pink glow through the sky. We all take a bit of time to study the beauty.

Then Amara says, "I really miss Karmen Island." It's abrupt, but everyone stops moving for a second, and I can almost hear the pounding hearts.

Nat's face twists in remembrance and pain, but then she clears her throat loudly. "We all do," she says, her tone too sharp.

A single tear runs down Amara's cheek, and Oscar pats her head half-heartedly, though he looks crushed himself.

All of them have suffered. Faced loss. Deaths. Not me, at least not as harshly as them.

We reach the Maple Gardens, and Diesel starts plucking peaches right away. Oscar and Amara begin on the strawberries and raspberries.

Now looking at the garden, it's huge. Nat doesn't give me time to gape. She tugs on my hand urgently.

"You heard Frau. Let's get this done. We're on maple trees." She collects her tools, drilling a hole in the bark of a silver maple and jamming in a spile. I hold the bucket as sap begins to fall.

"There's barely any in here," I point out, recalling knowledge from TV shows I used to watch with Dax. "Shouldn't we leave the bucket here for a few days?"

"The royals are impatient," she says, "so we have to go tap more trees now. Every day. That is why two hours is not *short*."

It's also a waste of time. I'm in the same place as Wheresmeine, and I haven't seen the Stardust Crown once. I haven't made a move yet. I don't even know where Ora is. For all I know, she could be in a dungeon.

Nat and I go around collecting sap, shivering in the cool air. Oscar and Amara have rows of baskets by the end of it, and Diesel is practically wobbling, he has so many crates of apples and peaches. Nat and I have a full canister of sap, which is impressive considering the circumstances. The walk back to the castle is much slower since we're all balancing food. I am the one to carry our bucket, as Nat shouts orders like, "Straighten your back!" or "That's going to drop, and if it does, you go back and do it again!" or "If that stuff goes to the ground, so do you!"

It's an intense journey.

We reach the kitchen in good time, although, of course, Frau doesn't commend us. She simply says, "Get to it! You three, on the pie! You two, on the syrup."

Nat and I head over to the stoves, boiling the sap in multiple pans. The pie looks much more fun to make. Today we don't have to bring up the food. Frau heard about Nat's incident, which she got a good whipping for, and decided that the five new servants would not be serving for at least a month. Which is fine with me, except I don't get to see Wheresmeine. What if he's wearing his crown tonight? There's nothing I can do about that now. I need to find Ora. It's already day two. I haven't located her *or* the artefact.

This is a complete disaster, and I'm starting to doubt that I'll be able to complete my mission. If I don't by the fifth day, will I be able to go home empty-handed? Will I be able to face the disappointment? What if Ora teleports and I don't, or the other way around? What will we do then?

When everyone upstairs has eaten, we get the remnants, which aren't quite bad; some pancakes — no syrup left — cold omelettes, bowls of oatmeal with brown sugar, scraps of pie, and some strips of turkey bacon each. A feast, I'd say, compared to the dinner we had last night, and I end up with a full stomach.

"Now, don't just laze around, you cows," barks Frau, and we all scramble to our feet. "The newest two *o'pricha* need two maids to help them tidy for the big gala coming up tonight. We'll put two new *deka'ya* up and see how you do. If you do well, only good can come from that. If you do badly… well, don't. Tomorrow, we'll put out two new maids and see how *they* do. Like that, you understand? The other three will help prepare luncheons."

Cooking sounds much better than being what Charlene was, so I keep my head to the floor. Unfortunately, I'm called out with Diesel, though he looks very pleased about it. Then I remember I may get to see Chris, and at least she's someone I know.

"Chef," whines Alavi, "what about the well-trained *deka'ya*?"

"Well, maybe there's someone in the crowd who's better, you sulky pig," snarls Frau. "I do *not* appreciate complaining. You should know this by now. An and Dike, go. An, you're on the third floor with Miss Nitya, bedroom nine, and Dike, you're on the seventh floor with Christina, bedroom three."

Diesel doesn't bother arguing with Frau. He hurries to the elevator, me at his side. I try to bury my disappointment that I don't get to be with Chris. "Ready?" he asks me.

"I guess. I don't really know what to do," I admit.

"Get them changed. Brush their hair. Put on their jewellery. It's not too hard." He looks uncertain, though.

I reach the third floor and cautiously step out, giving a nervous wave to Diesel. There is a corridor of ten doors, and I walk down to what I hope is the ninth. I give a wary knock. There is a groan, and then the door swings open.

The stunning girl that I remember next to Chris now stands in front of me in a robe. "You're An?" she demands.

"Um. Yes."

"Well, come in. You're late. Help me! Now!"

She sits down in a chair in front of a massive mirror. Even though she's wearing plain white, she's still flawless. She's not too much older than me, maybe Chris's age. Ora taught me hairstyles, thank goodness, but first, changing.

"Excuse me, Miss Nitya, but what will you be wearing?" I peep.

"Well, you choose!" she shrieks irritably. "The wardrobe is *there*."

I try not to roll my eyes as I follow her gaze. All the dresses are beautiful. I choose the most gala-like one, red and gold with a jewelled bodice.

"Well," says Nitya sharply, "at least you have some fashion sense." She slips into the shimmery gown and I pull her hair into a Dutch-braided bun like Ora did for me in the Realm of Monsters. Looking at Nitya makes me think of Ora. I shrug the thought away and put a diamond pendant on her neck, which is extremely heavy.

"Hm," says Nitya, touching her bare skin. "I do look quite splendid, don't I?"

"Yes, you do." The voice comes from behind us.

We spin around to see Chris, all dazzled up herself. I didn't even hear the door open.

"Christina!" I exclaim, making my way to her and lightly embracing her. She gently pushes me away.

"An," she whispers, "we can't do this now. We're… different."

Nitya gets to her feet, and Chris moves past me to her.

"What is the servant doing touching you?" There's something chilly in her voice.

Chris looks at me. "We met briefly on the ship."

"Well." Nitya smiles slyly. "She's really in no position to be doing that, is she?"

I watch in horror as Nitya wraps her arms around Chris and kisses her lightly. Nitya pulls away and throws a cold glance at me.

"What are you still doing here? Go!"

"Chris—" I begin, but she silences me with a look.

"Please," she says, looking down at me like I truly am just a measly servant to her. "We're different. And right now, my girlfriend and I need some privacy."

Feeling crushed, I slink away, out of the room and back downstairs. What does she mean, we're different? Of course we are, but only because of Ajax; only because of our positions.

Diesel is already waiting. "You were fast," I tell him, trying not to sound upset.

"Yeah, I have experience," he replies sadly, somewhat helplessly. "I used to do styles on my mother each morning… though it's a little weird doing up a teenager."

Frau butts in, "Okay, no trips down memory lane. You may get started on the food prepping on the wagyu meatballs."

"Yes, Chef," Diesel says firmly, his feelings suddenly drained.

We both hurry over to a counter, shaping the ground beef into spheres, placing them delicately onto trays, and popping them in the oven.

When all the food is ready, the *deka'ya* — who aren't serving — settle into crouching positions to nibble on cucumber-tuna sandwiches and other bits and pieces of food. The elevator's doors slowly stretch open, and everyone rises. Chris steps out, much to my surprise.

Frau sweeps into a curtsy. "Miss Christina," she breathes. "How may we be of your assistance?"

"I need…" — she contemptuously jabs a finger at me — "*her.*"

I feel a pang in my gut. Why me?

"Of course, this one," tuts Frau. "Always getting into trouble, she is."

"Actually" — Chris clears her throat — "she did a rather marvellous job on Miss Nitya. But I have other matters to discuss with the young lady. Privately." The sharpness her voice holds is unbearably different to when I first met her.

"Right, of course," stammers Frau. "You may go through that door if you'd like. I apologise for the room's… grubbiness."

Chris nods and gracefully walks through. Curious, I follow after her, closing the entrance behind me.

Chris looks around. "Hm. Grubby is an understatement."

"Why are you being like this?" I burst.

Her face screws up in guilt. "It's how it has to be. I can't... hug a servant in public."

"Is that all you think I am?" I ask.

"No! That's not what I meant. Please, this is just how I have to act, or I'll be thrown out. I have to act like I fit in."

"So it's all an act?"

"Well. Yes."

"Even Nitya?"

Chris smiles at that. "No, Nitya's real. I know she can seem a little threatening at first, but she's actually pretty cool. Anyway, An, I wanted to apologise. And say hi."

"Well. Hi."

She sighs. "An, I truly am sorry."

I shrug. "Shouldn't you be at the gala?"

"I hate galas."

I laugh, though it's forced. "You're *o'pricha*. You don't need to apologise to me. That's how the triangle works."

"I don't apply to the triangle."

"Well, it sounds like you want to."

Chris swallows. "I still want to be friends."

"Yeah." But I know that's impossible. High positions don't speak down to low ones. We're slaves, and even if it's an illusion here, this happens in the real world. This violation of equal rights... it all exists somewhere. Maybe it's better we haven't gotten close, because I'll hopefully be leaving soon.

Chris gives me another smile. "I should get back to the gala, or people will start wondering. See you around."

"Yeah. See you."

She slips out first, and me after, because that's how it's supposed to be or something.

"Well?" asks Nat expectantly. "What did she say?"

"Nothing much." I arch an eyebrow. "She just wanted to thank me personally for doing up her girlfriend so well."

"Girlfriend?" Frau repeats, and Nat and I both turn to her expectantly. She regathers herself and says, "Well. Congratulations are in order, I suppose. You can go do Miss Nitya again tomorrow."

Alavi, stirring stew, slumps over, but he doesn't say anything.

I try not to show disappointment. I know better than to argue with Frau by now. This is supposed to be an honour, and maybe it will give me another chance to see Chris again. But what will I say to her? I can't embrace her; I can barely even have a conversation with her without being called out as disrespectful.

I return to eating a sandwich, which is soggy now and has some parts torn away. "Who ate it?" I ask, munching on a crumb and looking around.

Nat sighs. "They're good sandwiches," she says with an innocent expression. "Don't leave one unsupervised next time is the only advice I can give you."

"Nat!" I roll my eyes and snatch a cookie from her plate because there's no bread left.

"Natasha," she corrects, grabbing it back with a non-joking fierceness.

"Nat." Back to me.

"Natasha." Back to her.

"Nat." Back to me.

Then she breaks the thing from my grasp and throws the cookie at my face.

"*Girls!*" scolds Frau, gathering the remnants and dumping them in the compost bag. "Fighting over food, how silly are you?" I expect a slap, but instead she says, "For your punishment, you will be the only ones to go to the gardens and collect the vegetables, while your friends stay here and... relax. That's double the work for you! I'll find a task to put them up to, but it certainly won't be walking two kilometres to the maple and back."

"That's hardly fair," grumbles Nat. "*She* took my cookie in the first place."

"Oh, come on. You stole my sandwich." The words sound so silly aloud.

Frau stands there, red in the cheeks, her hands clenched into fists.

"This is not about a stupid cookie," she fumes, glowering at us. "This is about your constant squabbling! I don't know if you were enemies back on Karmen Island, but here, you work together. So sort it out. When you come back, there should be peace. Or else."

Nat doesn't question the consequences. I think we both know they will be harsh. She simply glares at me until we have to set off to the gardens.

How efficient this will be, I do wonder.

We walk in utter silence, like there is a divide of anger separating us. When Dax used to be mad at me, he would put up a cereal box on the table so that we couldn't see each other. That's what this reminds me of, because I feel completely invisible.

Finally, I turn to her, my legs throbbing. "Natasha," I say calmly, "Frau *will* punish us further if we don't make up."

"Yes, well, we can act 'made up' when we're around her."

"That's basically impossible when it comes to you."

"What's that supposed to mean?"

I grunt in frustration. "Look, I don't know *why* you hold such a grudge on me. What do we even have to make up for? Clearly, there's something."

She's quiet for a moment. Then she says, "Just that you don't seem like one of us. You don't seem to fit in. It's like you're not scarred the way we are. Maybe I'm jealous."

"Jealous of me?" I say in disbelief.

"I know. Weird, right?"

"Nat, what happened to you?" I breathe.

For a second, I think she's going to yell at me about calling her Nat. Instead, she talks serenely, her eyes going foggy. "The Razor Tribe happened. I don't know how. There were so many of them. All armed; all wearing these black masks that will always haunt me. Hard, coal eyes. Holding out their guns. My whole family was in there." She chokes on a sob. "They asked for money, but we barely had any. We were poor, and we couldn't give away our last pieces. The taxes were getting higher, and we couldn't afford to lose any more. So Papa lied, and when they found out…when they found the chest of money…they shot. Randomly. With three children and two adults in the house, they shot. There was so much blood. So many screams. Sirens. The smell of gunpowder was everywhere, and all I could hear was the gunshots. Over and over, even when they had stopped. When I was put in a stretcher, rolled into an ambulance; operated on, that's all I could hear. Over. And over. And over. Pounding in my ears. When I was told they had all died, that none of them had made it, that I was completely alone, that's all I could hear. Over. And over. And over. Diesel saved me. He's like a brother to me. His family adopted me and everything. But then bombs fell. And Diesel and I escaped." She wipes away tears.

I watch her, seeing the pain play out in her eyes. She's right. I'm not scarred like she is. Not like this. "I'm so sorry," I whisper, giving her a doting hug. "I'm so, so sorry."

"I don't know why I'm jealous." She shrugs with a sniff. "We come from the same place, the same war zone. But I feel something different, and I don't like different. I don't like change, and I'm getting so much of it. Diesel is the only thing I know, but we seem to be getting more distant lately because of all the work. We're servants. The bottom of the food chain."

I nod as we reach the gardens. I know she's right, and I feel guilty that I'll get to leave this life to be safe. That I'll kill all these people. They seem so real.

No.

They are illusions.

"An?"

I turn to Nat, who is holding out a basket for me. I take it gratefully and start picking vegetables. It takes longer than I would have thought, but at least it's peaceful, a concept I haven't been very familiar with lately.

Peace, such a faraway term. It may be peaceful for now, but I know there's more coming my way. I can feel it in my bones.

It's terrifying.

Nat comes over and helps with the tomatoes. I think she's had much more experience than me. I've had the good life having someone make food for me every day, but I know there were probably days in Karmen that Nat couldn't eat.

She pulls the vegetables from the soil, and I plop them into baskets. Like that. It's much more efficient than doing it alone.

We stay in the gardens until late at night; until a slice of moon has appeared in the sky freckled with stars. The walk back is peaceful, too. We can hear the birds chirping from branches up high and the buzzing from crickets dancing around our feet.

"This walk sucks," Nat decides, interrupting the relaxing noise.

"You mean how long it is?"

"That, too."

I snort loudly. "My shoes suck, too."

"One day, I'm going to steal Bass's bastard car, and we'll ride around the gardens and plough down all the maple trees, because we tapped every single one this morning, and we didn't even get to eat a drop of syrup."

"Sounds like a plan."

When we arrive back at the Leiderhosen Castle, we head straight to the kitchen carrying our overflowing crates in our blistered hands.

"Well, would you look at that!" exclaims Frau. "You did it, and all in good time, too. Did you make up?"

"Somewhat," says Nat.

"Well, stop standing there dumbly and make yourselves useful!" Frau snarls, her tone back to its malicious usual. "*Now!*"

We help Alavi and Diesel make a quiche, which is actually quite fun. As emotional as Alavi is, he's a good chef — even if Frau constantly says otherwise. Just as the food has gone into the oven, the elevator slides open. For a second, I think it may be Chris again, but instead it's Bass.

"What the hell are you doing here?" blurts Diesel.

Frau's face goes white. "I apologise, Sir Bass, for his rude behaviour. So sorry, sir. I'm trying to teach him manners, but… oh my, am I rambling on? So sorry, sir. May we be of your assistance on this fine evening?"

Bass smiles. "Yes, actually. And I forgive you for your misteaching, though you must promise to tidy him up."

"Yes, Sir Bass. Of course, Sir Bass." Frau looks petrified, which is unusual.

"Natasha, dear, hello." He leans in and pecks her on the cheek.

"What do you want?" she snaps, brushing him away.

"I want *you*," he declares. "Now. I have your permission, little chef?"

"Yes, sir. Go, Natasha — you heard him," says Frau.

"No," Nat says. "I have to make food."

"It's all right, girl. I'll take care of you. I merely want to show you something very quickly." Bass takes Nat's arm and strides with her into the elevator.

She's stiff and pale as a ghost as the doors close.

"Chef Frau!" Diesel practically shouts, when they're gone. "How could you let her go? He didn't even tell her where he was taking her!"

"I respect Sir Bass," snaps Frau. "He will not hurt her, and he told me they would be back soon. So excuse me very much! It's not your job to tell *me* what to do."

"I need to go after her."

"You will do no such thing!" And Frau strikes him with her rolling pin, eight times. Eight.

I rush to his side as Frau continues with her chores. "Are you all right?" I ask.

"Yes." Diesel gets to his knees, wiping his nose. "But is Nat?"

"Nat's strong," I assure him. "She can fend for herself."

But she doesn't return for the whole of dinner. Even as the *deka'ya* nibble on leftovers, she does not come back. Then Frau announces it's time for bed.

"But Nat!" Diesel argues. "Nat's not here yet!"

"She will come soon," says Frau with a scowl. "Now, you know I don't appreciate repeating myself. Get. Into. Bed."

Diesel and I exchange glances. We can do that, but we know we won't be able to sleep. We creep in after Frau and lie next to each other on the floor, wide awake, for what seems hours. When we hear the elevator open, we rush out of the bedroom, not caring about Frau's consequences.

Nat is alone, and even in the dark lighting, I can see she's been crying. Her face is red. She doesn't look injured, but she looks scarred. Even more scarred than before. Bass is nowhere to be seen.

"What happened?" Diesel demands, though I think we both have an idea.

"Nat?" I say gently, as tears start to run down her cheeks.

"I don't want to talk about it. Ever." She is firm, but it looks like she's slowly breaking down, her insides cracking into millions of pieces.

"Nat, we're here," Diesel says, embracing her warmly.

She buries her face into his shoulder and collapses to the floor.

"Nat, we're here." He keeps repeating the words like if he says it enough times, it's going to start mattering.

Then I realise.

Nat, the strongest girl here, is broken.

For good this time.

24
Ora

I WAKE UP THINKING IT MAY ALL HAVE BEEN A DREAM.

Maybe I never kissed him. Maybe I wasn't so silly to let myself start to fall in love with an illusion who I will have to destroy. Maybe I wasn't so idiotic to let my feelings get caught in this whole charade. But as my sheets soak in sunlight, all I can think of is him. It's real. My feelings are real, even if he isn't. It's the stupidest thing I've ever done, letting my heart into this; but how could I have stopped it? How can I push down this affection towards him?

Everything is at stake here. I can't get to Anya, and I can't get to the artefact. I'm fooling around, kissing boys, while she may be struggling for her life. Esme is depending on me. My new family. I can't let them down like this. I have no ideas of what to do.

Unless…

Hansel and I are closer now. What if he tells me answers? But will I be using him if I do that? Does that even matter anymore? I've hurt many people for this quest, and now I might need to hurt him, too. Even if… even if what? Nothing. Even if *nothing*.

I get myself out of bed and go to Gretel's room, picking out a neon pink dress. It's all I can find, and anyway, what if a tiny part of me wants to impress Hansel? What if I want to show off to Bella just a pinch after her barbarity towards me yesterday?

I head downstairs. A magnificent smell is in the air, and I follow it to the kitchen. I expect to see Hansel making food, but instead, there is a stack of Olaf waffles on the table with a note beside it:

> *Karmen,*
>
> *So sorry, but I had to leave early for soccer try-outs this morning. Tried waking you up, but you sleep like a corpse, so I*

I ponder over the message. Not *dear* Karmen? Not *love* Hans? Not a single word about last night at the diner? I slap the paper onto the table, angry at myself for acting like such a brat. What, do I think he's going to be obsessed with me? Now it's like it never happened. Isn't this what I wanted? This is good. It's perfect.

I eat the waffles, which taste marvellous, and then I start walking to the school. I don't need Hansel's map, as generous as it is for him to have offered. I memorise routes very easily; it's a gift, I suppose.

I reach Bluebay Academy in no time, going up to my locker and grabbing my books. Gretel and Bella are chatting nearby. I try to pass them unseen, but the colour of my outfit isn't subtle.

"Karmen!" exclaims Gretel, throwing her arms around me.

"Oh, hey," I reply, forcing a grin. "How are you?"

"Fine, thank you very much," says Bella, even though I wasn't talking to her. "Gretel and I had an amaze sleepover."

"Aw, well that's great." I laugh with as much sincerity as I can muster, making Bella's face screw up in frustration. "Anyway, I have other things to attend to. Goodbye. Goodbye, Grets!"

"Bye!" Gretel calls after me, not catching onto her best friend and my inside feud.

I can feel Bella's glare on my back, but for some reason, that only makes me feel more triumphant. I get to my first class early, which is, luckily, math. This is basically one of the only classes *not* connected to fairy tales and magic. The teacher, Miss Rainbow, is also one of the only teachers who doesn't despise me — unlike Mr Maji. Every one of the staff has heard about my little incident.

Children start to flood in. I've been bold and taken the front row. Bella stops at my desk.

"Hello again," I say as cheerfully as I can. "Is there something you need?"

"Yes, actually. My *seat*."

"Oh, come on. The seats aren't reserved, are they?"

"This is mine. It's claimed. It's been like this forever," she says. "So move over."

Gretel cuts into the conversation. "Karmen, why are you in Bella's seat?"

"Yeah, Karmen, why?" repeats Bella proudly.

"Just sit beside Bella," says Gretel. "We can all be together that way."

I swallow my pride. "All right. But I think I'll sit at the back. It was nice there." I collect my books clumsily and start walking away.

"Thank you very much," Bella growls, giving my foot a stamp and nearly tripping me.

Miss Rainbow enters then. "Hello, class!"

"Hello, Miss Rainbow," everyone replies.

"Please open up to page forty-one…"

"God, more algebra? I hate algebra!" C.J. huffs.

So classes go on like that. I find myself doodling about Hansel, which is not like me. At all. I tear out the pages and rip them up at the end of each subject.

When lunch comes, my confidence drains out. I definitely don't want to face the humiliation of asking to sit with Bella's table again, so I begin to navigate through the cafeteria when someone grabs my hand suddenly.

I spin around. "Hansel?"

"Want to come sit with me?"

"Do I?"

He chuckles. "Come on."

I'm led right into the centre table, which I kind of expect to be crammed with people, but instead has no one.

"Where are all your friends?" I ask him.

"Told them to clear out today," he says. "I want to sit with just you."

I feel my cheeks heat up. "Yesterday's events were…"

"Amazing."

I can't tell him it was a mistake. I have to, but I can't, so all I say is, "Yes. Then why did you run away this morning?"

"I had soccer try-outs!"

"Yeah, yeah."

"Yeah, yeah. Do you think I'm lying?"

I can feel myself smiling.

"Okay. Let me convince you, then." He scoots over so that his hip is touching mine. Then he leans in so his breath is on my cheek, and he kisses me, this time more passionately than last night.

But it's wrong. This is so wrong.

I pull away. "Everyone's watching," I say, because it's true.

Bella is glowering at me from across the room, and Gretel looks utterly confused.

"Okay, well…" Hansel grins. "At home, then."

Yes. No. "We'll see."

He looks surprised, almost hurt, but when he opens his mouth to respond, the bell intervenes, and lunch is over.

Hansel waves off his uncertainty, pecks me on the forehead, and goes to class, which is unexpected because a part of me thought he may ditch. Maybe he's sticking around for me. Maybe.

I pour out with everyone else, but now people actually talk to me. It's mainly questions about me and Hansel, so I tell them it's complicated and leave it at that.

The day is slow, but when it ends, there Hansel is, waiting at the entrance. Gretel joins us after saying goodbye to her friends.

The walk is silent at first, but finally, Gretel explodes. "So what the lolly-gods was that at lunch? Are you two dating now?"

"I mean—" Hans starts.

"Not really," I interrupt. "What about it?"

Gretel surprisingly giggles. "Just that it's super adorable! I could see you guys together from the beginning."

I arch an eyebrow. "I thought you were all for Hella?"

"Bella and Hansel?" Gretel snorts. "Nah, I just kind of had to go along with it because she's my best friend. But *them*? They could never work out. Plus, Karel sounds better."

We get home, and Swizzle greets us. "Today, I'm doing homework with this little guy," decides Gretel.

"Fine. We'll be upstairs." Hansel takes me straight to his room. "Is everything okay? You're acting…on edge."

"I'm perfect."

"Okay." He starts kissing me, and I allow myself to enjoy it, even though I know how wrong this is.

I run my hands through his hair, tipping my head back for him to kiss my neck.

"I didn't know feelings could develop this fast," he breathes. "This is only our third day, but I trust you with my life."

Guilt threads through me.

"I don't know how it's been such a short amount of time, and I already really, really like you."

I should tell him it's stupid, that this is unwise. But I say, "I really, really like you, too." It's so crazy, us saying these things. It's ridiculous. I'm such an idiot.

His hands skim over my thighs.

And then something inside me snaps. The reality comes flooding back. I push him off me.

Hansel stumbles back in surprise. "What? Did I do something wrong? Are you crying?"

"I don't… we can't…" Tears bubble in my eyes.

"Karmen?"

"I can't…"

"Karmen, talk to me. We can sort it out."

I rub my temples, angry at myself for toying with his emotions, real or not. "Hans…" I shake my head. "My name is Ora."

He drops his hand. "That's impossible."

"I'm telling the truth."

"From the prophecy."

My voice cracks. "Yes."

"The prophecy was right? You're coming to collect his crown. That's why you wanted to know about my father."

I crumple to the ground, sobbing. "I'm sorry. I don't even know how… this makes no sense… I have to do this for my sister and my family. And I don't even know how I could let myself develop feelings for you when I have to do what I have to do… I'm awful. This is awful. Kick me out. Do something. Anything, Hans. I don't *want* to hurt you, but I have to. And I don't know how I'll be able to leave you now that I've fallen for you." This is a disaster.

I am a disaster.

He crouches beside me and embraces me in a hug, wrapping his arms around my waist. "I don't know why I still trust you, Ora."

The words surprise me, and I want him to take them back right away. How can he still be so kind to me when we've just acknowledged I have to kill him and his sister and everyone he cares about?

"Don't. Don't trust me," I say.

"But I do. And this whole world is a mess. Maybe if you crush it, we'll all go to a better place. Maybe we can have new beginnings."

"How can you say that? How can you want me to obliterate all your people?"

"Because there's something wrong about not only this county, but about the whole Fairy Tale Land. Something's off. I know it. I think it's a curse, Ora. I think you can put us out of it by completing the Heart of Stone."

I look up to see that he is looking at me intently. "Hansel," I say in a fragile voice, "you live in a Chronicle. You don't really exist."

"I think we do. Look. This all exists, doesn't it?" Hansel sighs. "There's some curse, I'm telling you. And you can save us."

"No, Hansel."

"Yes. Think about it."

I consider everything he's saying. I don't want to argue if there's still a chance at getting the artefact. "You really believe it?"

"Yes. I really do. My sister and I came up with the theory when we were younger, and many people have thought of it… but *look*. It's real. Now it all makes sense."

"But you might be wrong. If I get the artefact and put it in the Heart of Stone, you might all be gone. Forever. You understand that? You understand you may die?"

"There's a curse." He sounds almost mad when he says it. "I understand *that*. You may not believe it, but I do. I know it."

"Kick me out. Send me somewhere else. I can't do this to you."

"No, Ora. I want hope, and now I finally have it."

"It's false hope!"

"You'll be the hero to everyone in Fairy Tale Land."

"I wish I could tell you you're right."

Hansel's lips curve into a steady smile. "I'll prove *you* wrong. Tomorrow. We leave at dawn for Raven. We're getting you that crown."

25
Anya

AFTER LAST NIGHT'S HAPPENINGS, I COULDN'T SLEEP.

I listened helplessly to Nat sobbing into Diesel's arms. I think everyone else must have heard, too, but they didn't know how to help, so they didn't say anything.

Now it's morning, and I feel useless. It is my third day here, and I don't have a clue as to where the artefact may be. All four of my companions are up. Diesel, Amara, Oscar, and I are waiting near the elevator as Frau apologises to Nat for letting her go so willingly. What Bass did may have been terrible — how he touched her — but we're servants. There's nothing we can do, and *that* is revolting.

The walk to the gardens is not peaceful in any way. The birds still chirp, and the crickets still buzz, but everyone knows what happened last night. To Nat. One of our very own. By an untouchable like Bass. We all know that he will never face the consequences of his disgusting actions. We all know that because he is of high position, he won't be punished.

We pick the fruit and tap the trees, and we head back like every other morning. Except it's not like every other morning. It's different, and we all know it.

Frau embraces Nat in a tight hug when we get back. "Would you like to take work off today?" she asks.

"No," replies Nat. "Anything to keep my mind off what happened yesterday."

"Would you like to go prepare one of the new *o'pricha* for the dinner party tonight? It's a very big event, so it's a very big opportunity."

Nat shrugs. "Sure, I guess."

"There's a good girl. And, An, I did promise you that you could go also, so off the two of you go," says Frau, watching us go into the elevator.

When we reach the third floor, I'm determined not to get off.

Nat gestures. "This is your stop."

"Actually… do you think you could do Nitya today? Please? It's only that Chris and I are friends."

She snorts. "Is Nitya a complete brat?"

"Well," I say, pausing to consider my wording, "I think you'll definitely get along with her."

Nat rolls her eyes. "Charming."

"Please, Nat?"

She scoffs but steps off.

"Thank you! Have fun!" I call after her gratefully, as she turns on her heel, and the doors close. The elevator brings me to the ninth floor, and I knock on the third door down, only to realise it's the second. Bass pops his head through before I can hurry on.

"Hello," he purrs. "Here for second dibs?"

I clench my jaw, wanting to spit in his face. "Leave me alone." I glower at him.

Bass strokes his chin. "Every party has a pooper. Come in, won't you?"

"No." I walk down a door and bang ferociously.

Chris luckily opens up and lets me in. She looks over to see Bass, still in the corridor.

"Young lady Christina," he says with a smile. "Hello, there."

"God, Bass, stay on your own property," shouts Chris, slamming the door shut. Then she looks at me. "What an idiot."

I nod as she sits down on a ruffled chair.

Chris sighs furiously. "I hate this place. I hate it all. If I could get out of here, An, I swear to God…"

"I know." I start braiding her hair. "I wasn't fair when you came yesterday. I know this is the only choice you have."

"No, you don't need to apologise," Chris grunts.

"We've got to do something."

"I agree. Sounds like you have something in mind."

"My friends and I need money."

"Go on."

"I've heard of the Stardust Crown. It would sell for millions. It would put the king into a rage, and maybe it would give us a chance to escape. Travel somewhere better. He'd lose all his servants and—"

"And he'd hire new ones," interjects Chris. "This is a crazy plan."

"Well, we need a crazy miracle. You get the better life up here. Below you, people suffer. So *I'm* going to get the crown."

Chris scoffs and shakes her head. "An, listen to me. If you somehow got your hands on that thing, no one would buy it off you. And if they did, the king would kill you. With the snap of a finger. How would you get out, anyway? Captain Hook needs money for living. He won't just take you there."

Doesn't matter. Once I get my hands on that thing, I teleport and leave you all behind. I teleport and you all die. This is a false plan, tricking you into doing a favour for me.

I clear my throat, trying to ignore the guilt knotting up in the pit of my stomach. "If we somehow hailed Captain Hook, we could give *him* the crown to take us somewhere. Then he'd get his pay, and in return, he'd take us somewhere safe and keep quiet. The king would never be able to kill us because we'd be gone."

"It's too risky. I don't even know if Captain Hook would take the crown. If anyone from Raven found him with it…"

"You don't think he's so stupid, do you? He'd carve out the jewels and sell those. He'd smash the rest." I swallow and go on. "Trust me, Chris. More people will only get hurt if we continue living like this. Do you know where the crown is?"

"An."

"Do you know where the crown is?" I repeat, firmer this time.

Chris closes her eyes and nods. "Tonight's a big dinner for everyone, but I suppose we can attempt to find it tomorrow."

"Yes," I say, trying not to sound too relieved. "That'll do."

"Get the silver dress, would you?" Chris slips out of her clothes, and I zip up the beautiful gown on her.

"So what's the proposal? Refresh me," I say.

"Tomorrow, at midnight, I'll be at the kitchen with the key to the

Shed. Meet me at the elevator, and we'll execute the plan."

"The Shed?"

"You'll see."

"Right. Well, until then." I leave the room and go downstairs to the basement.

Nat joins us a whole ten minutes after.

"Where were you?" exclaims Diesel, as if worried.

"Oh, relax." Nat smiles a tiny smile. "An, you were so right. Nitya and I had an instant connection."

"On what, courtly gossip?" I snort.

"Precisely," Nat says naturally.

I roll my eyes, but I'm happy she's finally becoming a little more out there; a little more like herself. "Classic Nat," I mutter with a grin.

She ignores me and turns to Frau. "Chef, what shall we do next?"

"We're trying a new recipe. Pea soup. Doesn't that sound fantastic?"

"Yes, Chef."

"*Alavi! Teach them!*"

"Yes, Chef!"

So time goes on.

And all I can do is wait, hoping that nothing goes wrong before tomorrow night.

26
Ora

I DON'T EVEN KNOW WHAT TIME HANSEL WAKES ME UP.

All I know is that it is insanely early, somewhere before 4am.

"Up, up, up!" he says into my ear.

"Why at this time?" I groan, checking the clock to read three thirty. "Holy lollyhead, it's the middle of the night!"

Hansel laughs.

"What?"

"Nothing. Only that you said 'lollyhead'. Gretel's rubbing off on you."

"I'm just *tired*." I push my hand onto his forehead, and he laughs again. My fingers linger, brushing over his cheeks. I try to master the lines of his face, praying that this isn't the last time I see him.

He takes my palms in his and kisses them. "We'll be fine," he promises, as if reading my mind. "Both of us."

I change into the warm clothes laid out for me. We go downstairs, where Gretel is waiting with Swizzle in her lap.

"Gretel?" I demand. "What are you doing here?"

"He told me everything, duh," she chortles. "Let's go break the curse."

"You told her?" I turn to Hansel. "Is that a good idea?"

"I'm literally right here, and I can hear you, even if you're whispering," Gretel warns, popping a candy in her mouth.

"I promise you she's a good asset," Hansel assures me. "There's no one in the world that I trust more than my little sister. She's my best friend."

"Okay. If you're sure." I raise my voice. "Is someone going to tell me why I was woken up at this hour? I'm an early riser, sure, but before five is a no-no.”

He laughs. “Sorry, but this is how it had to be.”

“Because… drum roll, please…” Gretel thrums her fingers against the table excitedly. “We’re stealing a ship!”

“Lower your voice,” hisses Hansel. “The neighbours may hear.”

“Neighbours?” Gretel snorts. “We have, like, zero neighbours. We’re pretty much in the middle of nowhere. I mean, you know that, right?”

We both ignore her. I nearly lose my balance and fall off the stairs. “What do you mean, we’re stealing a ship?”

“We contacted Captain Hook, but he’s busy already,” Hansel explains gently. “I know you have a limited time, and this is already the fourth day. We can’t wait another week, so…”

“So we’re stealing a ship,” I finish in disbelief. “What, we’re just going to go to the water, hop on a boat, and sail away? Hope we don’t get caught?”

Hansel purses his lips together. “We know a guy.”

“That’s never a good start to a sentence,” I groan.

“He’s a thief, one of our father’s old friends,” he continues. “Charlie steals ships, and he’ll fetch us and bring us where we want to go.”

“Not for free, though,” I grumble.

“Well, no,” Hansel sighs. “We’re using all our coin and trading Charlie the house. But once the curse is broken, it won’t matter.”

“You’ll be dead,” I squeak.

“Stop saying that. We’ll be brought somewhere better, and one day, I’ll be reunited with you,” he promises, briefly brushing his lips against mine. “It’s worth it, and we’ve already paid him.”

“What if I die trying to get the crown? What happens to you then?”

“That won’t happen. I have faith.” Hansel gives me so charming a smile that my heart seems to break in two. “Let’s go. Charlie’s probably waiting.”

I take one last look at the candy house; one last look at what could have been. Gretel picks up Swizzle, and we head out to the glistening sea where I first arrived.

This is where I met Hansel.

There is a small ship waiting — bad condition, peeling wood and paint, shattered windows — certainly not worth all the money Hansel and Gretel possess. Or *possessed*.

"This is a rip-off," I tell them.

"What does it matter, anyway?" says Gretel, stroking her unicorn. "You'll break the curse, and everything will perish."

Things could go wrong. How can I tell them that without coaxing them gently away? Without getting what I came here for?

I reluctantly follow them onto the boat. The floors are battered, and we could fall overboard if the craft rocked even a pinch.

A man awaits us. His face is scarred and jagged, and there's an eyepatch over his right eye. When he smiles, his teeth are crooked and blackened. "Hansi! Gretel! What a delight to see you again," he exclaims.

"Yes, what a delight," agrees Hansel, though his teeth are gritted. "We need to go to Raven."

"Right, then Raven it is. Siddown, kids," says Charlie. "I'm going to start steering. We'll get there at some point in the morning tomorrow, perhaps in the afternoon if it's very choppy."

"Tomorrow?" I gape, when Charlie has gone to the wheel and cannot hear us. "That's a *really* long time."

"Yes, well I did tell you it's far away," Hansel says.

"That means…" I shake my head.

"What?"

I breathe sharply in and out. "That means Anya spent a day on this ship going from Bluebay to wherever she went, most likely. Which means…"

"No," he interrupts. "Captain Hook's ship is fuelled with magic. She got there that evening. Which *means* she's probably asleep awaiting her fourth day. Don't worry."

"We're getting the crown, but not Anya. Where is she? She could be anywhere!" I'm desperate in my own ears, but I can't stop. "What if she's not okay?"

"Whoa, there. After the crown, the next stop is your friend, wherever she may be."

That's miserably vague, and after I get the crown, I'll barely have any time.

We find nearby seats, so we sit down, and I lay my head in Hansel's lap, falling asleep almost instantaneously.

When I wake up, Hansel's eyes are closed, and so are Gretel's. We're all in the same position as before I dozed off, but now we're moving. The water is leaping below, splashing against the sides of our boat. The sound reminds me of the conch shell Colton bought me for my birthday once. I remember putting it up against my ear and smiling to myself at the beauty that only I could hear. My secret. There's a difference now.

It's real.

Everything.

A part of me mourns my past self, who always had her walls up and didn't trust anybody; who didn't know what it truly felt like to lose someone, or love someone. Letting yourself be vulnerable is scary, especially if the people you care about could die at any second.

I guess I've been squeezing Hansel's hand too tightly, because he jerks awake with a frown. When he sees me, though, his face lights up. "How was the nap, K… Ora?"

"Surprisingly good, with everything going on," I admit. "How long has it been?"

"Not very long," he chuckles. "But we'll get there eventually. Boy, when I see my father…" He clenches his fists, and I uncurl them gently.

"You never told me what happened," I say. "I should know before we get there, don't you think?"

He struggles for words, but finally nods. "Yeah." He shakes Gretel and tells her that it's time for the truth.

She nods, too, but the movement seems grave.

"Before you do explain, though, I should probably tell you something." I heave a sigh. "When I was in the guest bedroom, I was going through the drawers, and I found some letters. I shouldn't have read them, but I did. They were sent from Wheresmeine Industries, so I thought it may be helpful. It was nosy, I know. She was in Raven? She kept talking about this man torturing her… and then in the second one, she said she would die. Laurel, her name was."

Hansel's whole body, tenses. His hand goes cold in mine. Gretel winces like I've impaled her. She hugs Swizzle tightly to her chest.

Hansel looks at Gretel, then back to me. "You explain."

Gretel grits her teeth, trembling. "Laurel was… our little sister."

"Your sister?" I repeat. "But it's always been you two, Hansel and Gretel…"

"Maybe that's what you were told," she says with a mirthless laugh. "But it's not true. Laurel was one of us, and she was amazing. We three lived in Raven with our mother and father. We were happy, too. But then our mother died, and darkness fell upon the whole city. It was a murder. No one knew who did it, but we suspected our father. When we confronted him, he went into a rage. He had countless blackmails to force us not to release the truth. He was dangerous, and he still is. So what did the three of us do? We left the palace.

"We tried crossing the border, but Wheresmeine caught us. He took Laurel, the weakest, and brought her back. We tried to save her, but it was pointless. Hansel and I came to Bluebay and started new lives. Our father killed our sister. She's dead. And he will never be punished for it. Now it's time to end him so he doesn't get the chance to do that to anyone else. We're done with fear."

I process the whole story. It's so hard to imagine another Leiderhosen among us. What monster would kill his own wife and child?

"Wow," I finally say. "I'm so sorry. That must've been devastating."

"We regret not going back to save her every day," mutters Hansel. "There are so many things we should've done. That *I* should've done. I'm the eldest, and I walked away."

"This wasn't your fault, for the last time, Hans," says Gretel. "It was Wheresmeine."

"Mother would be disappointed in me."

"She *wouldn't*. You beat yourself up too much."

Hansel shrugs.

Gretel sighs. "You're the best big brother I could ask for."

There's a long silence.

"I think I'm going to go back to bed," Gretel says, and she's snoring in seconds.

I bury my face back into Hansel's neck. "I'm so scared," I murmur.

"Everything will work out."

But he hesitates.

There's definitely some uncertainty there.

27
Anya

THE NEXT DAY CONSISTS OF ONE THING. WAITING.

Waiting is definitely not my strong suit. It's the fourth day already, but tonight I am getting the artefact. And when I do? Will I simply abandon Ora, wherever she may be? I push the thought away, though I know I shouldn't. This is happening soon, and when I collect the crown, I won't be able to just stand there. Wheresmeine will be trying to get his prize back. His guards will be hunting me down. Chris will wonder what I'm doing.

I'll be standing there. Wondering if I should save Dax or Ora. It has to be Dax, I know. I can't stay here for the rest of my life, and even if I wanted to, once I have the Stardust Crown in my hands, everyone will be after me, seeking my blood on their hands for who knows how much money. I get the artefact. I teleport home. I put it into the Heart of Stone. I get my brother back, but I lose my sister. That's the plan, and I know that's how it has to be. I've tried endlessly to connect telepathically with Ora, but she must be too far away.

Hours drone on. I garden, cook, and cook some more. I don't get to do up Nitya or Chris today because there are no big events. Though I suppose I should be grateful for that, because then, Chris wouldn't be able to guide me to the Shed, wherever that is.

Nat is still a bit traumatised, and sometimes I find her curled in the corner of the kitchen, hunched over and weeping. She doesn't like people seeing her weak, so she dries her cheeks and tells me that it's the onions and that she's incredibly sensitive to them.

I don't dare argue. The majority of the time, I'll pull her up to her feet, and we'll go have a snack or stir some noodles; but occasionally — rarely — I'll sit with her, and she'll cry into my shoulder, telling me that the onions are very, very strong that day.

Bass hasn't been spotted since the accident. If he stepped foot in here, I swear Diesel would throw a fist.

Frau seems to be warmer after the incident with Bass and Nat. She still yells a whole lot, but there's not as much physical violence involved.

The day bores me. Time seems to be passing more slowly than ever. Eternally slow.

Frau has to tell me to keep shaping meatballs, because every now and then I stop altogether, completely zoned out, thinking about everything that could go wrong; about everything that could be *going* wrong.

"An!"

I snap back to reality to see Frau glaring at me and the drooping ball of mince in my hand. "Oops!" I say for what seems the millionth time. "My mind's just really off work today. Sorry, Chef."

"An," she groans, "why don't you go… mash some potatoes? Hopefully you won't mess that up, too?"

"Right. Sorry, Chef, I'll get right to it."

Dusk comes, and I dig through the earth extra passionately, uncaring about my raw, grated skin. All I care about is my mission.

I don't even let myself bother about the walk. In fact, a part of me even enjoys it. Though it's not as peaceful as yesterday, I still enjoy the liveliness of it all.

Frau lets us serve dinner today, which is supposed to be some kind of honour. I keep my head down, but Wheresmeine makes me shiver, even without eye contact. I thump the food down hard and rush away, with Nat by my side.

In the elevator, she says, "Just seeing him gives me the creeps."

I realise she's talking about Bass. I put my hand on hers as she trembles. She reddens, her mind clearly going back to the day that Bass did what he did.

I slap her across the face.

Her eyes fly open, and she stares at me furiously. "What the hell was that for?"

"I had to snap you out of your memories."

"Great. Thanks."

"Look, I'm sorry, but—"

"I wish it would all be over. Then I would stop waking up just to find out that none of my family is still with me. And now, after what happened…"

"Nat, don't talk like that. It's a bad day for you."

"It's been like this since the Razor Tribe invaded my home. This is average. Sometimes it gets worse."

The elevator opens, and we step out. Nat runs straight to the bedroom, and I don't follow her.

Frau looks up from her work with a sigh. "That poor girl's terrified."

I shake my head. "You shouldn't be sending her up to those dinners. Bass brings out the worst in her."

"I agree," says Frau sadly. "I told her that, but she said she needed to face him."

"She's not strong enough."

"No. She's not. Now eat up."

After munching on some bagels, Diesel and I prepare a plate of dinner for Nat. She's lying on the bedroom floor, her face blank. She sits up when we enter, but refuses to eat.

"Come on," whispers Diesel. "It's good for you."

"Nothing's good for me at this point. Nothing helps the issue."

So we all sit there in silence, regarding each other; regarding the full plate of dinner. We sit until Frau and the rest of the *deka'ya* pour in.

"Bedtime," she clucks. "Natasha, dear, do you want to come into the hallway and have another chat?"

Another?

Well, I guess that explains Frau's friendliness. She's been acting as Nat's therapist. I'm not judging, though, not after everything she's been through.

"No," grumbles Nat, closing her eyes. "I want to sleep."

"Right. Of course," Frau says softly, her eyes understanding and filled with sorrow. "Goodnight, everyone."

"Night, Chef," everyone echoes.

I say it especially cheerily because, hopefully, this is the last time I will have to address Frau. Though a part of me may miss this — sleeping on the ground, wondering what happens next. Or maybe I hate it. I think it's a bit of both, oddly.

I slouch against the cool floor, not bothering to put a blanket down. I'm steaming.

The elevator clicks open, and my insides light up with joy. This may really work. Tonight, I may see my brother. Being sure to stay quiet, I creep past pillows and heads and beds, making my way out the door and warily closing it behind me.

Chris awaits me in the murky kitchen. I can see her troubled expression.

"What's wrong?" I whisper. "You're not backing out, are you?"

"No, no," Chris says quickly, keeping her voice low. "It's just that this is… sort of scary, I guess."

I swallow my guilt, gathering all the confidence I can muster. "We'll be fine. Because if we don't do this, so many *other* things could go wrong."

"Yeah," she murmurs, though her face is screwed up and red. "Yeah, this is good. This is fine. We'll be heroes. We'll save all the servants who deserve better lives."

"Exactly. Now, please, Chef Frau will come out and whip us both if we stay any longer," I say with a small chuckle.

We silently sneak into the elevator.

"An?"

Terrified, I turn around to see Nat and Diesel looking at me curiously. "Please go back to sleep," I beg. "Please."

"No way," breathes Nat. "What are you doing leaving in the middle of the night with an *o'pricha*?"

"God, Nat, you wouldn't understand," I implore. "This is private. This is…"

"Just tell them," says Chris as if she's given up.

"Okay," I say in bewilderment, clearly outnumbered. "We're collecting the Stardust Crown so that we can give it to Captain Hook, and he'll ship us somewhere better. He'll break out the jewels for payment and—"

"Hold on," interrupts Nat, raising a hand to silence me. "That's utterly ridiculous, An. Wheresmeine will send out his guards looking for us."

"Captain Hook won't say a word. No one will know he even shipped us anywhere. And we get a chance at peace. It's worth the risk," I insist. "If you're not interested, don't tell."

"Who said I'm not interested?" snorts Nat. "I'm *interested*. Got nothing better to do — especially because, you know, I'm pregnant."

My mouth drops open. "That's too early. You can't already know."

"Oh, yes I can," says Nat. "It only takes a day after the you-know-what to know about pregnancy."

Of course. Magic. The strangest things happen here. "So what, you took a pregnancy test?"

"What the *hell* is a pregnancy test?" Nat asks. "I was told in my dreams, as it always happens."

I don't even inquire who she was told by. I seem clueless enough, so I just nod my head in awe.

Diesel's fists clench. "I'll kill that Bass. I'll tear him to pieces, I swear."

"Yeah, well, I don't know what to do. I'm only sixteen, and I'm a servant, too. You know what? I want to get my mind off it. Let's go. Diesel?"

He doesn't even hesitate. "I'm in. All in."

"Good. We need to leave now," hurries Chris, reopening the elevator.

We all step in and shut it quickly.

"So, tell me, where exactly is the Shed?" I ask Chris.

"You'll see, though it is a bit of a ways from here," she admits. "It's definitely… interesting."

"Sounds intriguing," says Nat, a challenging edge to her voice. "How come you know where it is, and we don't?"

Chris opens her mouth and then closes it, shaking her head all the while. "It's unfair," she mutters. "You should know, too."

The elevator rides to the fifteenth floor, and Chris beckons us to the door we go through each day to the gardens. "It's a long walk," she warns us. "Farther than the maple… about eight or nine kilometres, I think."

Diesel and I silently groan, but Nat gives a full-out whine.

"No way I'm walking nine kilometres. I have an idea that *won't* require breaking our toes. Come on," she beckons.

Our curiosity roused, we follow her around the back of the castle, into the parking lot that I didn't know existed. It's quite fantastic — really very elegant and large, with actual paintings hung on the walls.

"No, Nat," I hiss when I realize what's happening. "This is ridiculous."

She ignores me, and, with a smile, stops at the marvellous car that Bass drove by in. The *caché*, as I recall.

"This is theft," says Chris in a low voice. "Is this solely for the purpose of vengeance? Because payback isn't going to—"

"It's not payback," Nat snaps. "This is redemption, and it works in our favour. He's the only one with a *caché,* and we need it. It's a mere coincidence, I'd say. Maybe God wants vengeance on this monster, too."

"How do you plan to get in?" demands Chris, obviously irritated.

"Like this." Nat punches her fist through the glass window, and it shatters. With a sly grin, she pulls herself into the vehicle and opens all the doors, wiping away the blood beginning to formulate on her knuckles.

I climb into the back with Diesel. Chris sits at the driver's seat, and Nat sits beside her.

"So how does this work?" Chris asks nervously.

"One second."

"I'm driving, so you'd better explain this all to me."

"Oh, we're all driving, sweetheart." Nat opens a tiny drawer and pulls out a tiny whiteboard with a tiny marker.

"This is really impressive," I snort. "What are we doing, school shopping?"

Nat rolls her eyes and writes neatly on the board: four cheetahs.

I gasp as the car breaks apart. Everything whirls around, and when my vision floods back to me, I'm on the back of a… cheetah? The fur isn't soft, though. It's incredibly hard, like metal. And it isn't moving or breathing in any way.

"What the hell?" I say, looking around. At my side, Chris, Nat, and Diesel are *also* on cheetahs.

Nat shrugs. "Well, it is a magic car."

"When you said it could transform into anything, I thought you meant vehicle-wise."

"It *is* a vehicle. These things are robots that go at the *speed* of cheetahs. A trick on the eye." Nat turns to Chris. "Guide the way, princess."

"I don't know how to ride this animal!"

"It's not really an animal," Nat retorts. "I seriously just said that."

"I—"

"Okay, hon, all you have to do is announce the address."

"I don't know the address," says Chris lamely. "The only thing I do know is that it's called the Shed."

"Great, how very useful," groans Nat. "You'll have to have memorised the way."

"I have."

"At least there's that, then. Press the tiny green button and steer the car by its 'ears'. We'll go after you."

I look closely at the pattern of the mechanical cheetah, now realising that the dots in front of me are actually buttons. It's unnoticeable unless you really inspect it.

Chris warily clicks down and the cheetah starts moving — quick. Sickeningly quick. A scream escapes her lips, but Nat activates her car as well. Then Diesel. Then me. I can barely see anything because I'm going so fast, and the darkness doesn't help. I follow Diesel's exotic blue shirt, holding a firm grip on the pointy ears. They're slippery, but I hang tight for dear life. If I fall... well, that would be bad, to say the least.

My heart is hammering in my chest, and everything is spinning. My stomach is swimming, and if I weren't moving so insanely rapidly, I'd puke.

Luckily, time moves insanely rapidly, too. When Diesel halts in front of me, I stop my cheetah with great relief. After some dizziness has disappeared, I peel my body off and look around. Though the night sky is heavy, I can recognise that we're at the place where we all first met up. Where Chris and Nitya were named *o'pricha*, and I was named *deka'ya*. I remember the small hut where Ajax stood and announced it.

"Wait," I say. "*That* is the Shed? That small, measly, battered—"

"Yes," interrupts Chris, "and I know it isn't what you'd expect; but it creates less suspicion than something more… grand."

"An, even *I* am bamboozled, and usually I'm ahead of you in, like, everything," says Nat with a sigh. "Christina, there's no guards or anything?"

"It's locked," says Chris.

"It's locked, but—"

"Enough chitchat, Natasha," she interrupts. "Let's go in. It'll be morning quite soon."

Nat rolls her eyes and turns her back, focusing on the cheetahs, who mould together back into Bass's car.

Chris jams her key into the Shed door, and it swings open easily. We all hurry in and shut it behind us. It is small, very rusty; completely empty. Except for, at the very back, something that catches my eye. The Stardust Crown. Shimmering, purely made of gold and jewels, engraved with stones. It's beautiful.

"There's another gala tomorrow night," explains Chris, picking it up delicately. "He always wears his crown to galas."

"I still don't understand why it's in the middle of nowhere, unprotected," points out Nat unhelpfully.

"Yeah…" Chris's voice trails away, her eyes staring down at the ground.

"What?"

"Nothing."

"All right," I say dubiously. "Pass me the crown."

"I… I… can't do that."

"What do you mean, you can't? Pass it to me!" There's urgency in my voice.

"The young lady said no," says a voice from behind us.

We spin around to see Wheresmeine, his coal eyes blacker than ever. He's wearing a toothy smile, and it grows bigger when Chris hands him the crown. "Bravo," he purrs.

She smiles weakly.

Nat turns to Chris. "This is a trap!" she cries out furiously. "You brought us right to him!"

"That she did," he agrees. "This is what you would call a *set-up*." He chuckles to himself, and Diesel glares at him angrily.

"Chris, how could you?" I murmur.

"I'm sorry," she whispers back.

"She's not the traitor here, and you know it," Wheresmeine snarls. "*Anya.*"

"How did you…?" I gape.

"I know everything around here, you foolish child," he says, his eyes lit up with satisfaction. "You think I'm so stupid not to recognise you? You're not from Karmen Island. When Chris told me of your plans, I knew my suspicions were confirmed. And here we are."

Nat looks genuinely hurt. "You lied," she whispers. "An for Anya. Home-schooled. I shouldn't have believed it. I shouldn't have believed you'd actually be here for me. All you were doing was buttering me up to help you get the crown. This is an artefact for you. You were using us."

"Yes, yes, she's a backstabber," interrupts Wheresmeine. "I don't care about your pettiness. All I wish is for you to perish. And my wish will come true, as they always do."

"I'm sorry," says Chris one last time. "Let's go, Your Majesty."

He roars with laughter. "Ho! Christina, you're not one of us. You don't fit in. You just apologised to the enemy, for Lord's sake. I can sense the longing. You wanted to go. If I hadn't shown up, you would've left with them."

"That's not true," she pleads.

"Oh, yes, it is." He laughs again. "You'll all die now, fools."

Chris goes pale.

"I've no mercy." He flicks his wrists, and he's gone.

I rush to the door of the Shed, but it's locked from the outside.

When Chris brings out her key, it fades into the air. "Damn it," she mutters. "Damn Wheresmeine."

"Damn *you*!" shouts Diesel. "Serves you right to go through this with us after what you planned to do!”

“I had to do it,” she says. “I was under his ruling. I had no choice. And honestly, why are you getting mad at *me*? An, or shall I say *Anya*, is the real snake here! What, are we just all fake characters to you? Our world may be a Chronicle, but we’re still alive.”

I suck in a breath. “Forget that now. We need to get out of here.”

“For what?” shrieks Chris.

It’s then that I realise Nat hasn’t been talking at all, which is very unusual. I follow her gaze to a purple-blue fire sneaking through the small crack underneath the door.

“What is that?” I breathe as it creeps towards us.

She trembles. “Ink fire.”

Ink fire. I remember Esme explaining this. Something that destroys everything in its path.

And it is the only thing that can destroy my teleporter, which means I might be in some serious trouble.

28
Ora

I WAKE UP LYING AGAINST HANSEL, HIS BREATH WARM DOWN MY NECK.

I focus on the lapping waves and the chirping birds, forcing myself not to think about anything else.

"Ora, you're awake," whispers Hansel, giving me a gentle peck. "We're pulling into Raven soon. Wasn't so long a trip after all, right?"

"I wouldn't be so sure," I scoff with a delicate smile. "But I'm grateful to you for finding Charlie so quickly. Even if it meant…"

"Stealing a boat?" Hansel laughs.

"Yeah. That." I pause, then say, "It's my final day here in this world, you know."

Hansel's eyes deepen, and he takes my hands. "We'll find our way back to each other. The curse will break. Fate has its charm."

"I hope you're right," I say, burying my face in his shoulder for a second and allowing myself to feel safe.

Meanwhile, Gretel has just woken up. "Morning, lovebirds!"

"It's not so much morning anymore," snorts Hansel. "Nearly there."

"Thank the lolly-gods! I was getting impatient," she says. "You know me and patience. We're not friends. And if we were on here another day, I'd blow something up."

"I *do* know you," he admits, grinning. "Look ahead. The castle should come into sight soon."

I squint. Sure enough, I can see the grounds. But they're illuminated with something colourful.

"Do you see that?" says Gretel, picking up on it. "What is it?"

The ship draws closer until we've arrived at shore. Behind, we can see the town billowing in flames, but they're not normal.

I know it's ink fire, as soon as I see it.

"Oh lolly-gods," Gretel breathes.

"The artefact," I cry. "It's somewhere here!"

Charlie joins us, looking alarmed. "You want me to take you back to Bluebay County?"

"No, Charlie," says Hansel right away. "This is our stop."

Charlie withdraws a staircase, and we carefully trail down it one by one.

"Don't die!" the shipman calls, before sailing away.

"Gretel, listen to me," warns Hansel. "You have to stay here."

"No way!"

"This isn't something you can argue with. This is the only place that's safe for now. Keep a lookout."

"For what?"

"Anything!"

"I'm coming with you, Hansi—"

"It's not up to you." His voice is grave. "Stay here, Gretel. I'll take care of myself. Come on, Ora."

I spare one last glance at Gretel's concern-plastered face, before hurrying away with Hansel. Everything is lit up. I can barely see a thing.

"How did this happen?" he whispers.

"We're going to find out." I drag him by the arm. There are bodies sprawled everywhere, but I can see in the distance a girl crouched over, sobbing. "Hans, over there!"

We run through the fire trying to battle the heat, and stop short at the girl. As soon as I see the jet-black hair, I feel a blossom of hope arise inside me. She looks up, her face tear-stained.

"Ora?" she whispers. "Ora! I was trying to get it, but it was all a set-up… and Chris betrayed us… and Wheresmeine left ink fire and ran to safety. I opened the door with an eyeglass screwdriver I had in my pocket… but then… everyone started to fall…"

"Anya…" I feel tears well in my eyes. "So much has happened. What's that in your hand?"

She holds up broken pieces of gold, and I gasp. "This is the Stardust Crown. This fire destroyed a door to a room I was locked in, and when I came out, the king was weak from the burns. I had to fight him for the crown, but I have it."

"I'm so happy to see you, and we have much to talk about, but I need to know where your teleporter is."

"In my pocket. Or rather, it was. But it's melted now." Her face is distressed, and my heart drops.

I shake my head in bewilderment. "There must be some way…"

She gets to her feet. "Tell me."

I hand her my dissolving crystal. "Take it."

She regards me with horror. "You're kidding."

"You have to listen to me. There's some kind of curse here, and if you complete the Heart of Stone, it may be lifted, and everyone will survive—"

"You can't believe that. You can't have *hope* in that."

I hesitate, then say, "It wouldn't matter if I did, Anya. You have to go. Save Dax."

"Every Chronicle, you stay longer than I do," Anya cries. "Not again."

"It's how it has to be. I'll do muscle magic."

"You're always right, Ora, but this time you're wrong. There has to be another way. You'll die."

"There's no other way!" I'm practically screaming. *"Go!"*

Anya's eyes are round in fright as she takes my teleporter. "One day, Ora."

And she's gone.

29
Anya

NO. THIS IS ALL WRONG.

That's all I can think when I see the athenaeum walls. Then I'm in Mother's arms, and she's crying, and I'm crying. I don't want to question how she's here. She doesn't question me, either. Esme takes the bits of crown from me, and with a swish of her hand, it glues itself back together. Relief tumbles through me with the knowledge that it still works.

"Congratulations," she says, beaming. "Where's Ora?"

I am silent.

"Oh," she murmurs, her face crumpling.

"She's still alive," I inform Esme, though a part of me is dubious.

"Oh." Esme stares at the shattered artefact.

"She claims she's doing muscle magic. Do we…do we wait?"

"Dax doesn't have that time. He'll be gone in seconds."

I nod, struggling against tears.

Esme swallows. "I don't know what else we can do, Anya. I don't know…"

I push down my guilt. All she did was help, and now we're going to let her die. "Put it in," I sigh. "Please."

Esme, fingers shaking, does what I say. The crown slides into a liquid and erupts into light. We all squint, and when our visions have returned, the Heart is completely stoned over. I crane my neck to see that all three Ash Chronicles have disappeared. With Ora.

"She's gone," I bawl into Mother, who looks heartbroken. I'm praying that Ora's muscle magic will work; that she'll appear in thin air. She doesn't.

"He's awake," Esme whispers. "Dax is awake!"

Excitement arises inside me as soon as I see his lovely face and his blinking eyes. He's alive.

"Dax," I cry. I press my face to his, but as soon as I do, something feels off.

After a few seconds, he shoves me off.

"What's wrong, sweetie?" asks Mother. "You're home!"

He sucks in a strangled breath. "Who are you?"